BLACK HEART

# FOUR

FROM *USA TODAY* BESTSELLING AUTHORS

## SARA CATE
## RACHEL LEIGH

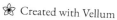

*This book is dedicated to our BTB.*
*Just this once, we'll call her by name.*
*Thank you, Amanda. We love you.*

# *Trigger Warning*

*Four is a Dark Reverse Harem Romance that contains explicit sexual content, graphic language, and situations that some readers may find uncomfortable, such as dub con, murder, torture, and abuse. The Black family men are rough, controlling, and a little bit crazy, but don't worry...she puts them in their place. Enjoy!*

*One*

His shaking hands slide up my skirt, cupping my ass against the kitchen island as he hoists me up onto the countertop.

"We have to be fast," he whispers against my neck. "Your dad will be back at any second, and if he catches me with my hands up your dress, he's going to kill me."

He's not wrong. My dad will literally kill him. So, fast is fine by me. I like these quick romps with the guards anyway, and this guy is one of my father's new recruits.

I gasp against his ear as his fingers reach the inside of my panties, sliding through the moisture pooling there. I feel him growl into the warmth of my neck as he finds me wet. My dad should really know better than to hire these good-looking guys. And since he's put me on this new strict, no-leaving-the-house order, I get bored—so fucking bored. And boredom leads to this: quick fucks in the kitchen while the rest of the guards check the perimeter.

"Your father has given me strict orders to not let you leave," he says, his voice flat. "But he never said anything about making you come."

*Ha. Nice one.* I let out a quiet moan as he shoves a finger in. I'd pant his name if I could remember it. Instead, I settle on breathing demands in his ear. "Faster, harder, more."

He does a decent job of it, and after a few minutes, I manage a nice little climax. Nothing earth-shattering, but it takes the edge off. Just after he pulls his fingers out from under my dress, he lifts them to his lips, and I guess if I was more attracted to him, I would find that sexy, but as it is, he's just hot enough. He's younger than the rest, maybe in his late twenties, and he has a cocky attitude. It'll probably be the attitude that lands him without a job, but I don't care. He's been flirting with me for a while now, so I knew, sooner or later, he'd make a move. It wasn't enough he got a job working security for Damon Pavetta, the oldest crime boss in the city. He has to try and fuck his daughter, too.

"You're a bad little girl, aren't you?" he asks, leaning in.

Somewhere across the house, we hear a noise, and I use it as an excuse to push him away. It's not that I mind letting him fuck me here, but his holier than thou attitude is starting to get on my nerves. Of course, he doesn't really care that I want my space because he leans back toward me again.

"I think we have a few more minutes," he says with a smile. At least he has nice, white teeth. As his hands move toward his zipper, I glance at the closed office door. My father is behind it with a few other men I don't know, and they've been in there all day.

Normally, it's not this strict. I usually have the freedom to go places, even if it's with security, but for the past week, my dad hasn't even allowed me to go out to the pool until his men scout the yard. Something is going on, but of course, he doesn't tell me about it.

"If my dad catches you, you know you're dead, right?"

"With my dick in this pussy, I'd die a happy man."

Glancing down, I see he already has it out, and it's not-surprisingly underwhelming. God, why do guys with the biggest attitudes always have the smallest dicks? As it is, this one is barely worth my time, but since it would seem I have nothing but time on my hands, I roll my eyes and let him settle between my legs.

I'm waiting to feel him there when a window breaks across the room. I flinch as something warm and red sprays across my face, too stunned to react.

The guard between my legs is suddenly a heap on the floor and the room breaks out in chaos. There are gunshots behind the door to my father's office, and I drop to the floor, crawling on my hands and knees toward the corner of the kitchen, behind the island.

I let out a scream as men, more of my father's guards, enter the room, looking for me only to find the security guard with his dick out, dead on the floor.

"Help me!" I scream, waving to them from the floor.

Just as one of them notices me, there's another muted pop and his brains spray across the wall. Screaming, I cover my face as he lands with a thud. Soon after, the others drop, one by one, until I'm alone among a pile of dead security guards.

When the door to my father's office bursts open, I cower, my breath coming out in heavy gasps, but I try to keep it silent while I hide. No one emerges for a moment, and I silently pray.

*Please, Daddy, don't be dead. Please, Daddy, don't let me die here.*

Someone staggers out, and I let out a yelp as I spot my father's face. There's blood covering his shirt and on his hands, but he sees me immediately, relief coloring his features.

"They're coming, Iris. Quick, come here!"

I don't have time to ask who's coming or what is happening, because I hear commotion somewhere near the front door and run for my dad, knowing somewhere out that window is a sniper with deadly aim. Keeping low, I move with him past the open office door where I spot three more men dead on the floor.

"You're bleeding," I cry, but he doesn't answer as he pushes me down the hallway.

"Are you hurt?" he asks, and I quickly shake my head.

"You have to get out of here, Iris." We move in a rush toward the back of the house, and his hand is firm on the flesh of my arm.

"What's happening?" I cry.

My dad has dealt in shady business my whole life, so a little gunfire and blood doesn't really affect me much, but something about this has me scared. And maybe it's because my dad, for the first time in my life, looks terrified.

Suddenly, there's a voice calling from behind us. "Oh, Mr. Pavetta," someone sings in a haunting tone, and chills run up my spine.

"Who is that?" I cry. My father and I reach the door to the garage, and he peeks his head through the gap, before opening it and dragging me toward his car. I notice the limp in his walk and look back to see a trail of blood coming from the house.

"Daddy, what is going on?"

Without answering, he opens the car and shoves me into the driver's seat. With the push of a button, the car purrs to life. Before he looks back, the garage door starts to open.

"Listen to me, Iris," my father says, leaning down with his face close to mine. His gray hair is frazzled and sweat drips over his temple and down to my lap. "Drive away as fast as you can. Don't look back."

I keep waiting for him to get in the car with me, but he doesn't. Instead, he shoves something into my hand. "Find Silas Black."

"Who?" I gasp, looking down at the crisp white piece of

paper scribbled with just a name and an address. My voice shakes, the adrenaline scrambling my mind.

Someone appears in the doorway to the garage. I peer over my father's shoulder to stare wide-eyed at a man I've never seen before. He's young, probably in his thirties, and there is something about his face that terrifies me. With a thick brow and a broad nose, he holds a face full of evil in his eyes alone. Everything about his expression is menacing, and it makes me want to curl up in my dad's arms.

"Oh, there she is. There's my pearl. Hello, Iris," the man says, looking directly at me, and I shiver. I don't understand how he knows my name.

"Who is that?" I ask, but my dad is too busy trying to get my attention.

"Don't look back, do you hear me? Just drive."

There's a gunshot, and I scream. My dad winces and falls to his knees.

"Daddy!"

"If you just hand her over, Mr. Pavetta, I promise absolutely no harm will come to her. She'll be treated like the precious pearl she is for the rest of her life."

I glance around my father to see the man approaching. My dad staggers back to his feet and grabs my face, forcing me to look into his eyes. "Silas Black."

Then, he pulls away, shutting the car door and yelling through the glass, "Drive!"

Another loud shot rings out, and blood splatters across the windshield. I'm frozen in place, staring up at my father's cold, dead eyes. They stay on my face as he falls across the hood, and I can't seem to look away, my blood turning to ice in my veins.

My heart is hammering in my chest as I spot my father's murderer with his evil eyes and menacing smile, stalking closer, in a rush to get to me. On instinct and with a sob lodged in my throat, I hit the gas. Tears pour from my eyes as

Dad's body falls quickly off the car and I'm out of the garage in seconds. More shots ring out, but my father knew well enough to put me in the car with bulletproof glass.

My ears are still ringing as I reach the road, speeding through the street without stopping. Struggling to breathe with the image of my father's eyes seared into my brain, I keep my foot on the gas. I don't even know where I'm going.

It could be minutes or it could be hours, but when I'm finally out of the city and in the country, the fog in my brain starts to clear. I can't go home, and somewhere deep down, I know the man who killed my father and all of his men is after me. With no one to turn to and nowhere to go, I look down at the card still clutched between my fingers and the steering wheel.

I wipe my tears and start to formulate a plan. My father is dead, and I'm alone. All I have is blood on my face and a name on a card in my hand.

*Silas Black.*

## Two

GLANCING back and forth from the road to the rearview mirror, I attempt to calm my heart that's violently beating in my chest. *No one is following me*, I remind myself, over and over again. I'm reassured when I continue to drive down the desolate road, outside the city limits. With no other car in sight, I muster up the courage to pull over on the side of the road. Reaching into the pocket of my dress, I pull out my phone. My hands tremble as I type the address into the GPS.

*Twenty-Two minutes.*

I'm not sure why my dad was so hell-bent on me finding this man. It's not like he can bring my dad back. No one can. He's gone, and now, I have no one.

Pulling back onto the road, my mind replays everything. It all happened so fast, and none of it makes any sense.

As if time is standing still and I'm still stuck in that harrowing moment, my phone alerts me that I've arrived at my destination. I take in my surroundings. A black wrought-iron gate sits between my car and the narrow driveway that extends so far down, I can't see what's at the end of it. Cameras surround me on both sides of the car as I roll down my window to press the button on the box in hopes that whoever is on the receiving end can offer me some sort of hope and guidance in this situation. But, before I have a chance, a voice comes through the speaker.

"Can I help you, ma'am?" he asks in a masculine and gruff tone.

"I think so." My voice cracks. "My name is Iris Pavetta. My father sent me." I wait for some sort of response from the man, but it never comes. Instead, the gates begin opening.

Slowly creeping down the driveway, my heart rate speeds up again. Unsure of what I'm driving into, I put my trust in Dad, knowing he would never send me into harm's way. Sure, my dad was a criminal and he did a lot of terrible things, but he always did what was best for me. It was the one certainty in my life.

Cyprus trees that extend at least eight feet in height line both sides, until I reach the cobblestone path that circles the front of the house. Two men wearing all black, with their hands folded behind their backs, stand guard out front. I pull directly in front of the house, take a deep breath and step out of the car. A warm breeze hits the side of my face and an eerie feeling washes over me. Security is nothing new to me. I've lived my life under a watchful eye—surrounded by armed guards and remote houses. This is different, though. I'm stepping out into the unknown in a body that doesn't even feel like mine anymore.

"I'm looking for Silas Black," I tell the two men who are watching me intently.

Without a word, one of them pushes the door open as his eyes stay glued to mine. They both step aside to make way for me. Looking back and forth between the two of them, I walk into the house while the door closes behind me. The sound of it latching startles me, until a man's pleas ring in my ears, and I freeze. What have I just walked into?

"Hello," I say in a hushed voice. When no one responds, I try a bit louder, "Hello."

Stepping hesitantly into the house, furnished with a modern-day all-white decor, my footsteps echo in the open room. The cries continue so I peek around the corner that leads into the kitchen.

My hand slaps over my mouth when I see a young man staring back at me. His black disheveled hair is flipped to the side and tattoos cascade from his neck downward. Emotion-less dark blue eyes stare into mine. But that's not what has my stomach in knots. It's the man strapped to a chair in front of him with blood pooling at his feet.

"What the fuck happened to you?" he says to me, like we're old friends, but I have no idea who this guy is.

My fingers graze over the dried blood on my face and I look down at my dress stained with deep red bursts of color. "Are you Silas Black?"

"Maybe," he says, skeptically. "Who are you?" His gaze returns to the man in front of him. Flipping a blade open, he runs it down the length of the man's arm, leaving a trail of fresh blood. I cringe at the sight. The man in the chair screams.

"I'm Iris Pavetta. My father sent me." I can't seem to keep my hands from shaking, so I keep them clasped tightly in front of me.

"As in Damon Pavetta?"

I nod, although he wouldn't know it. His focus is solely on the man he's torturing. "There was an ambush. My father was killed."

Completely ignoring me, he leans closer to the man in the

chair. His lips almost touch the man's ear lobe and his jaw clenches. "You ready to give me that fucking name?"

When the man doesn't speak, he steels his back and a sinister smirk spreads across his face—so menacing it sends chills down my spine. Grabbing a hold of the man's hand, he doesn't hesitate when he bends a finger all the way back to his wrist. When the man's muffled cries come through the cloth that's shoved in his mouth, bile rises in my throat. "I want you to think of that name. I'll be back."

His focus shifts to me. "So, your father was killed? What the hell does that have to do with Silas Black?" He flips the blade back in and hooks the knife clip to his pocket. Blood drips down his pant leg, but he's either oblivious or doesn't care.

"I'm not really sure." My shoulders shrug. "My father's last words were to come here and find Silas, so here I am. I have nowhere else to go."

"The only reason I let you in this house is because of your last name. I've heard Silas talk about Damon Pavetta. But personally, I don't give a fuck. So if you plan on laying some sob story on me, you can turn around and walk back out that door." He points his finger behind me, and for a moment, I contemplate grabbing it and breaking it the same way he just did to the man behind him.

"Look," I snap, my voice growing angry, "I've had a terrible fucking day and I don't need your shit. I just need to talk to Silas."

He smiles, finally looking me in the eye, as if my yelling at him somehow piqued his interest. For a moment I think if he didn't look like such a psychopath, he'd actually be pretty hot. He can't be any older than me, with that baby face, sharp dimples, and bright blue eyes. As he approaches, I square my shoulders and try to hide the shiver that races up my spine.

Grabbing a rag off the kitchen counter, he wipes his

bloody hands on it, then tosses it at me. "Clean yourself up. You look like shit." I take a step back and let it fall to the ground.

Pinching my eyebrows together, I snarl, "I'm not touching that."

"Suit yourself." He pushes past me and leaves the room. I'm left standing here with a man who is bound and fighting to free himself. He whimpers at me for help, but I don't interfere. It's been etched in my brain to stay out of other people's business. Things can get messy real fast.

Moments later, footsteps come from outside the kitchen. When I turn around, I gasp. A new man approaches, an older man, probably early forties, with sharp, menacing features and eyes so dark they're almost black.

"Iris?" he questions as he comes closer.

The overpowering scent of his cologne and his intimidating presence fill my senses and, for some reason, it offers a calming vibe. I nod in response.

He extends his hand, clean and free of blood, unlike myself and the guy I just met. "I'm Silas Black. It's a pleasure to finally meet you." As I put my hand in his, I can't tear my eyes away. I've never met him before, but somehow, it feels like he knows me.

Dropping my hand to my side, I shuffle through the thousands of questions that run rampant in my mind. Unsure of where to start, I go for the most obvious. "How do you know my father?"

The younger guy appears out of nowhere and stalks past us with intent. When the chair holding the tortured man tips over and his whimpers continue, Silas grimaces.

"In the kitchen again, Gabriel? Can you please use the garage like I already asked you?"

"It's hot as balls out there. Give me a temperature-controlled torture room, and I'll stop using the kitchen."

Silas lets out an exasperated sigh as he nods his head behind him, placing a comforting hand on my lower back, leading us away from the chaos that is about to continue.

"With granite countertops," the evil-looking boy shouts after us. I feel like I'm in the middle of some fucked-up family squabble.

Walking through the corridor, I notice the walls are bare. No family photos, no signs of life. His home is beautiful, but it's so empty and lifeless. We reach the back side of the house and Silas directs me into a room—or office rather. "Have a seat," he tells me while he sits down behind a large cherry oak desk. "Tell me, Iris. Why did your father send you?"

I sit down and my skin immediately sticks to the cold leather of the chair. I swallow down the lump lodged in my throat. "My father was killed only hours ago."

His expression remains callous and indifferent. He clicks his tongue on the roof of his mouth. "Ah, that's too bad."

My blood begins to boil. "Too bad? Are you fucking kidding me, right now? I just witnessed my father and all his men get murdered and you're acting like it was no big deal!"

He doesn't react. "These things happen in his line of business."

I have to clench my fists at my side. "Who the fuck are you? How did you know my father?" I demand. "Why were my father's last words 'Find Silas Black?'"

After tapping his finger to the desk, for what feels like minutes, deep in thought, he finally speaks, "I owed your father a favor. I imagine that is exactly why you're here. To collect."

"That's it? You owed him a favor?" I shriek.

He doesn't answer. Just pulls a piece of paper from his desk and a pen. "Do you have somewhere safe to go?"

I shake my head. "I have no idea where I'm safe anymore."

"Very well. What is it that you'd like?"

My body tenses up from the pressure of being put on the spot. What is he talking about? I have no idea what I want. I want my dad back, but that's not possible. I want to live. For whatever reason, the assailants had their sights set on me.

*If you just hand her over, Mr. Pavetta, I promise absolutely no harm will come to her. She'll be treated like the precious pearl she is for the rest of her life.*

"Whoever killed my father is after me. I need you to protect me until I can protect myself."

Cocking a brow, he looks at me in confusion "That's all you want?"

What more is there? He's waiting, as if he's expecting me to have a specific request. If I'm dead, what good is any other favor to me?

"Yes. That's exactly what I want."

Then it dawns on me. Revenge. That's what I want.

I'll make them pay.

Every single one of them.

## Three

"This will be your room," Silas says, as he leads me down a long hallway. The screaming from the kitchen has stopped, so I can only assume the man is dead or he finally fessed up to whatever name that crazy looking boy was trying to get him to say. And if it wasn't for that little scene of casual torture, this would look like an ordinary mansion. The decor is ornate and expensive looking. There's clearly a staff of cleaners and cooks who keep things in order. It reminds me enough of my own home that I assume Silas Black is another mafia leader I've never heard of. We're not far enough out of the city and out of my father's territory, but who knows. Who else owes people favors like this and tortures victims in their kitchen?

The way he reacted to my dad's murder, like it was nothing, just part of doing business, sent chills up my spine.

"You may stay for one month."

"That's it?" I ask as I look into the room. It's a simple guest room, clean with contemporary decor to fit anyone's tastes.

"I assume your father had off-shore accounts. I'll help you set up what you need to live safely: anonymity, money, security. Might be best to leave the country, so consider where you'd like to go."

Then he just turns and walks away.

"That's it?" I call, but he doesn't respond. Chasing after him, I grab his arm and spin him around. "Hey!"

When he glares down at me, I almost cower. He's so tall with that cold glare and those dark eyes that part of me is intimidated. But after the day I've had and the fact that I literally have nothing to lose, I don't give a shit how scary he is. I want answers, and I want them now.

"Who the fuck are you? Where am I? How did you know my father? And how are you going to help me get revenge on those motherfuckers who killed everyone I know?"

I squeeze the sleeve of his black button-up shirt in my fist, my long nails digging into his skin, but he doesn't react. Instead, his brow curves inward and his eyes narrow, sprouting crow's feet across his golden tanned skin. Then he backs me up, pushing me into my room.

"Let me be clear. I owed your father a favor, one that involved your life, and I keep my word, so I will ensure you remain safe, but I don't owe *you* anything. You will be a guest here for one month. If you get in our way, piss off my sons, ask too many questions, or make yourself a threat, I will consider my debt to your father paid and toss your pretty ass out onto the street. So I suggest you take a shower, clean that filthy fucking blood off your face and watch your goddamn mouth. Are we clear?"

Heat fills every pore of my face as I glare up at him, finding it harder and harder to keep up my stern expression when all I really want to do is break down and sob.

"Yes," I grit through my teeth. Then he turns, leaving me

shaking in the guest room doorway. Looking down at my clothes, I realize I don't have anything else to wear. I literally have my phone and this dress, that's it. Pulling my phone out of my pocket, I look back up at Silas.

"But I don't have any clothes."

Pausing, he glares back at me like I'm a dead bug on the bottom of his shoe. Then, he turns toward the kitchen and shouts, "Gabriel!"

A moment later, the boy with the crystal blue eyes shows up, staring at me with a smile that makes me want to shut myself in my room and lock the door.

"Get our guest something of yours she can wear. Show her the bathroom, and Gabriel..." he says sternly to the boy, "Behave."

My stomach clenches with the sudden urge to throw up.

Gabriel turns back to me with mischief in his eyes. "Yes, sir."

He stalks toward me, running his tongue over the ring in his bottom lip. He still has blood on his shirt. When he reaches the end of the hallway, he motions for me to follow. Looking back toward Silas as he heads toward the kitchen, I can't decide which of them scares me more.

"Come on, Princess," Gabriel calls. "Time to pick out your dress for the ball."

He's teasing me, and I growl at him as I follow behind him. We come to a dark bedroom with a black light glowing from the ceiling. It reeks of smoke and cologne, but it's warm and somehow inviting. The bed is large and unmade with thick blankets and a plush mattress. It makes me want to crawl into it and fall asleep.

While I'm staring at the bed, a soft piece of clothing smacks me in the face. Leaning down, I pick up what feels like black sweatpants and a satin-texture T-shirt. Then I watch as

Gabriel walks toward me with a pair of thin, sporty boxer briefs. "You'll model these for me, right?" He puts his underwear on the pile of clothes in my hands.

"I hope they're clean," I mutter with a scowl.

"Smell them and find out."

"You're disgusting."

He bolts toward me so quickly, I don't have time to react. All I feel is his wet tongue glide across my cheek and up my forehead. I let out a shriek as he licks the dried blood splattered across my face. Then, he hums with a smirk on his face, and if I wasn't so fucking terrified of him, I might try to slap him.

Instead, I turn my back and march away.

"Bathroom is on the right, Princess," he calls after me.

Holding up my middle finger, I let him see it before I lock myself in and rush to the sink to wash his disgusting saliva off my face.


The shower is large, with glass doors and double showerheads. I crank the heat up as high as it will go and stand under the stream, letting it burn my skin while I cry. I have no clue where I am or who I am with. All I know is my father sent me here in a moment of desperation. It's either this or death, and that fact does little to comfort me in any way.

The face of the man who killed my father is at the front of my mind as I shut my eyes. He's not very old, not much older than me, but there was pure evil in his expression. The moments of the day replay, and I try to remember any important details now that my head is clearer than before.

I was in the kitchen with the guard. The others were securing the perimeter. My father was in a meeting.

Then there was a gunshot, but from where? It came in from the window and was so precise that whoever was making those shots was able to take down each guard with a single bullet.

If they wanted me dead, I would be. That much is clear.

I remember him calling me a pearl, and even though I've never seen that man in my life, he seemed almost fond of me, as if he wanted...*me.*

Were they after me? Am I the reason my father is dead?

I scrub my face three times to get all the blood off, and my skin burns when I turn off the water. As I step out of the shower, I hear voices downstairs. Staying as quiet as I can, I press my ear to the door. I hear Silas's voice. But then there's a new one. It's not Gabriel's. This one is deeper, more commanding, but still young.

Dressing quickly, I open the bathroom door as silently as I can, tiptoeing down the hallway to hear their conversation.

Pressing my face around the corner, I spot a new man in black. He's as tall as Silas and his back is to me, so I can't make out his face.

Gabriel is on the couch, lounging with his back against the pillows as he uses a knife to pick between his fingernails.

"Who is she?" the new man asks. I'm not sure why the sound of his voice sends a wave of flutters through my stomach. It's stern and serious, with little to no sentiment in his tone.

"I told you. I owed a favor to Damon Pavetta. She'll only be here for a month. Don't talk to her, touch her, or tell her anything," Silas says from somewhere in the kitchen, out of my line of vision.

The new man turns his head, finally giving me a glimpse of his face. He's young with the same tan skin and dark hair as Silas. There's a broad slope to his nose and a roundness to his chin that makes him look like a Greek statue, only meaner, more severe.

"Pavetta," he mutters, as if my father and my life mean nothing, and I guess to them, they don't.

"How come we never heard about this debt?" Gabriel asks from the couch, looking a great deal less interested than the other guy. Then I remember what Silas said. He mentioned his sons. Are these his sons? I could believe the tall one is, but Gabriel looks nothing like him.

"Because it was a long time ago," Silas answers.

"We don't take sides," the new one replies with his jaw clenched.

"We're not. I'm keeping my word to Pavetta. In a month, she'll be gone."

"We should just kill her and get it over with."

My hand claps silently over my mouth, and my heart begins hammering in my chest.

"Oh, can I do it?" Gabriel begs, jumping up with a sickening smile on his face.

"We're not killing her. Keep your fucking voices down," Silas scolds them.

I watch from the doorway, trying to keep my breathing quiet that it becomes hard to breathe. The new man in black paces, looking distraught.

"What happens when Vincent Maretti comes looking for her? We'll have the whole fucking mafia on our doorstep. We're better off handing her over now and wiping our hands clean of the whole fucking thing."

"How do you know it's Maretti?" Silas asks, and that name echoes in my head. I've heard it before.

"Word is all over town. The whole Pavetta family is gone, and Maretti rules the city."

Silas steps into view, meeting the new man toe-to-toe. With a blank expression on his face, he says, "I told you, Baron. She stays. We honor our word."

"Your word. Not mine," he mutters as he walks away.

Before I know it, this new one, Baron, is walking down the hallway, and I barely have enough time to escape back to my room. Just before I shut the door, he stops. Turning his head, he stares at me through the crack, and I can't help but shudder.

Something tells me this is the one I have to fear the most.

## Four

"VINCENT MARETTI." I mutter under my breath. *Maretti.*
It sounds so familiar, but I can't even begin to remember
where I've heard the name before. Regardless, I'll know soon
enough. Silas said I have a month. That means I have one
month to find out everything I can about this Maretti guy and
everyone else who had a part in my father's death because I
refuse to flee the country and live my life in fear.

No. I'll get my revenge and these goons who watched me
cower and beg for my life, will soon be begging for theirs.

A knock at the door startles me. When I don't respond,
the knocks come louder, followed by a voice. "Ms. Pavetta."
Only it's not one of the guys, it's a woman with a gentle voice
that cracks when she speaks.

Walking at an amble pace to the door, I open it with no
hesitation. "Good evening. Mr. Black has requested your presence in the dining room for dinner," the fragile woman says.
She's probably in her early sixties, with dark hair full of silver
that glistens in the light. I'm more drawn to her eyes—they
hold fear. For whatever reason, this lady seems tense. Her
hands are folded neatly in front of her ar   n, which leads me

to believe she's an employee. And quite possibly someone that can help me to better understand the mysterious men I'm staying with.

"Thank you, Mrs..." I trail off, allowing her to finish.

"Please, call me Carol." She smiles. It's warm and comforting and exactly what I need right now.

I return the gesture. "Thank you, Carol," I repeat. When she turns to walk away, I place a hand on her shoulder to stop her. "Carol, can I ask you a question?"

Without turning around, her head shakes. "I'm sorry, Ms. Pavetta. I've been given strict orders not to fraternize with guests. Enjoy your evening." She begins to walk away again, taking with her any hope I had of having someone on my side. "Carol," I whisper-shout, catching up to her down the hallway. "Could you do me a small favor?"

When she turns around, I can see the hesitation in her eyes. "I'm sorry—"

I cut her off. "Could you please just find me some paper and a pen?"

She continues on her way with no response. Standing in the hallway, I glance down at my clothes. The baggy sweatpants are two sizes too big and the T-shirt may be clean but it still holds a man's scent. I tug the collar up and draw in a deep breath. It smells like cedarwood and sage with a hint of musk. Regardless of what I'm wearing, I'm starving, so I head down the winding staircase in search of the dining room.

My fingers graze over the cold metal banister to the staircase. Each step drawing me closer to the voices downstairs. I can't make out what they are saying, but when I reach the bottom and stumble, it must grab their attention because the chatter stops.

Seconds later, Silas rounds the corner from the sitting room. "Iris, looking much better now that you've cleaned up that mess on your face." He steps aside and waves me in the direction he came. "After you."

I thank him with a nod and join the two other guys inside the dining room. Another room with bare walls, yet there's a beautiful glass chandelier hanging over the twelve-seat oak table and it gives the room all the decoration needed. It's absolutely beautiful.

All eyes shoot to me. Baron takes a sip of his water, glaring at me over the rim of his glass, while Gabriel slouches back in his chair with his arms crossed over his chest. I'm immediately drawn to the tattoo on his arm. A web that captures a skull with tiny spiders crawling out of the eyes and roses surrounding it. It's a very well-designed piece of art, but the image makes my skin crawl. Running my hands over my bare arms, I shiver as the chills cascade down my back.

Silas places a comforting hand on the small of my back, alleviating the uneasy feeling. "Have a seat." He steps past me and pulls out a chair opposite Gabriel and Baron. I can feel their eyes dance over every inch of my body as I sit at their table, in their house, a complete stranger.

A door shutting has my body jolting, until I realize it's just Carol. Grabbing the glass of water in front of me, my hands tremble as I take a sip. Sheer exhaustion has taken over my mind and my body. It feels as if I'm living in a constant state of panic. What if this Maretti guy shows up here? I wasn't safe in my own home—am I truly safe in this one?

I have no doubt if Maretti did show up looking for me, the two younger ones would hand me over in a heartbeat.

Carol places a black spiral notebook in front of me and adds a pen on top with her head hung low. I set the water down and look up at her. "Thank you." She turns and walks away quickly, but Silas snaps his fingers drawing her back.

"A word, Carol." His chair slides back and he's on his feet in a matter of seconds. Stalking toward the poor lady as she stares down at the floor. "What's this?" He points toward me —or the notebook rather.

I jump up in her defense. "It's not her fault. I asked her for it. C'mon, it's just a notebook and a pen. I need to take some notes." Silas snaps to face me so fast my head spins. Both Gabriel and Baron push their chairs back, like they, too, are ready to jump to someone's defense—namely, their father. "Are you all serious right now?" I chuckle. "It's a damn notebook. I need to write everything I remember down before the memories of today fade from my mind."

Silas directs his attention back to Carol. "You may leave. In the future, consult with me before talking to Ms. Pavetta." She gives him a nod and disappears into the kitchen.

Gabriel and Baron sit back down and I mutter under my breath, "Assholes."

"What's that?" Gabriel stretches his neck and tips his ear toward me. "Could you say that a little louder for the assholes on the other side of the table?"

Rolling my eyes, I sit back down and grab the pen, pushing the button on top continuously as my eyes dance from person to person.

When the cook comes out holding a platter in each hand, breaking the awkward tension, I breathe a sigh of relief. He places one of the silver platters in front of me before lifting the lid. Rice pilaf, steamed broccoli, and salmon. It smells good, really damn good. "Thank you." I look up with a smile.

Baron seems to be too busy on his phone to even notice the cook bringing out dinner. Or, he just doesn't care. No one seems to acknowledge the cook's presence except for me.

Looking up from my plate, I notice I'm still under Gabriel's watchful stare as he chews on a toothpick that's gripped between his forefinger and thumb. His eyes harbor anger and his smirk is laced with disdain. For whatever reason, this guy doesn't like me.

Unlucky for him, I've never been one to keep my thoughts to myself. "What the hell is your problem?" I mirror his menacing glare, and it seems to catch him off guard.

He straightens up in his chair, leans forward with his elbows pressed firmly on the table and pulls out the toothpick. "I don't like strangers who mooch off my family."

"Gabriel!" Silas snaps with a stern voice. "Watch yourself, boy."

Suddenly my appetite diminishes. My stomach twists into knots and every bit of trauma from the day hits me all at once. I push my plate away and grab the notebook and pen off the table. Keeping a hateful eye on Gabriel, I say, "Thank you, Mr. Black. But I suddenly feel nauseous from my view at the table." With that, I walk out of the dining room and toward the steps.

These guys have no intention of making things easy on me, but they will soon learn that my backbone doesn't bend, regardless of my current situation.

I'm lying on my stomach on the bed when there's a knock at the door. I immediately assume it's Carol again. "Come in," I holler. When the door opens, I continue to write, without lifting my head to greet her.

Vincent Maretti: Called me his pearl. Why??

Snipers? 3-4 of them. Who are they?

"Thanks again for the paper and pen." When I lift my head, my heart jumps into my throat. "Mr. Black." I close the notebook and scoot to a sitting position. "I'm sorry, I thought you were—"

"Carol? The housekeeper who gave you that?" He nods toward the closed book.

"Yes. I just assumed it was her because she was here earlier."

"I imagine you are hungry after the events of the day." He holds up the topped platter. He walks closer and sets it down on the empty nightstand beside the bed. "Mind if I have a look?" He looks at the notebook again.

Unsure why, I hesitate. He already knows what happened and who was behind the ambush. But what will he think of me if he knows that I have every intention of destroying every man who played a part in my father's death? Will he think I'm crazy? Emotionally irrational?

I slide it toward him, and to my surprise, he takes a seat on the edge of the bed. Something about Silas offers me warmth and sense of calm. It could be because he reminds me a lot of my father. A man of few words, but the way he carries himself says it all. He's fierce, strong-willed, and doesn't help just anyone. If it weren't for the favor he owes my father, I wouldn't be sitting here right now.

"Where do you plan to find the answers to these questions?" He closes the book and slides it back toward me.

My shoulders shrug. "I have no idea. But I won't give up until I do."

I'm not even sure where to start. I doubt anyone in this house will give me any insight on this Vincent guy. If this family is anything like my own, we don't interfere in other people's affairs. Especially when it comes to personal vendettas, which I have no doubt Vincent Maretti had with my father.

The corner of his lip tugs up and a fire lights behind his eyes. "A fighter. I like that."

"If I surrender, I might as well die. But I still have a lot of living to do. My only other choice is to fight like hell. Not just for my family, but for myself."

"Tell me this, once you have your answers, what do you plan to do with them?"

"What do you think I should do?"

His fingers tap against the black notebook. "That's irrelevant. You made up your mind when you asked for this notebook. Don't back down. But most importantly, never let your conscience win."

He stands up and heads back for the door to leave me alone with my thoughts. Just as he pulls the door open, I grab his attention. "Mr. Black?" When he turns around with one hand on the door, I continue, "Will you help me?"

There's a beat of silence before he responds, "How bad do you want revenge?"

"More than anything." I don't even have to think about it. Right now, it's all I want.

"Prove it." With that, he walks out and shuts the door behind him, leaving me to wonder exactly what proving it means.

Opening my notebook again, I jot down three words.

Kill Vincent Maretti

I TOSS and turn in bed all night. The insomnia could be from the day I've had—watching your father being murdered will do that to you—or the more likely culprit to my sleep- lessness is the incessant music playing down the hall. It's muffled from the thick walls, but it has a heavy bass, and it's just loud enough to keep me from fully settling down to sleep. No matter how hard I try to drown it out, it just won't go away.

No. Fuck this. After the day I've had, a little common decency is the least I deserve, and I refuse to let these privileged assholes treat me like some pesky house fly. Silas wanted me to prove that I can stand up for myself. I'll start by teaching his son some manners.

Stomping out of my bedroom, I head down the hall toward the dark room where the music is coming from. Of course, it's Gabriel's room. The baby-faced boy with the scary tattoos and evil eyes.

Steeling my shoulders, I shove the door open and look inside. He's passed out on his bed, face down and snoring loud enough to be heard over the racket. I spot his phone on the table next to his bed, with the music app open, probably Bluetooth connected to the speakers positioned in the walls.

Crossing the space, I grab the phone and hit pause. I really should have known better. The abrupt silence is almost more jarring than the music, and even though I turn and quickly scurry to leave, two hands wrap around my waist before I can make my exit.

The room turns upside down as I'm hoisted off the floor right before I land hard against the mattress, the air getting punched out of my lungs. Gabriel's wild sneer pops up only a couple inches from my face. I let out a shriek just before his hand covers my mouth, silencing me.

"What the fuck are you doing in here?" he whispers, his nose running down the length of my cheek to my chin. His body covers mine, but I still let out a muffled cry and try to squirm out from under his weight. He's pinned flat against me in nothing but his underwear. My fingers dig into the flesh of his chest as I try and shove him away. Even in the darkness, I can see the inky black tattoos that start at his neck and cascade down his well-defined pecs. How far down they go, I can't quite see.

"What is it, Princess? You want to call me an asshole again? My dad's not here to stop me this time." When I feel the rock-hard thickness in his boxers grind against my leg, I start to flail. There's a wild look in his eyes as he keeps his stare trained on my face. When he grinds again, this time against my thigh and not between my legs, I watch as his eyelids become hooded and he bites his lower lip, almost as if the outside of my thigh is the most action he's seen in a long time.

*No way.* This is not happening today. After the shit I've been through, I will bite this fucker's face off before I let him have me like this.

My hands are powerless against his body, but the more I fight, the more his grip slips against my mouth. The sick fuck is actually laughing. I finally manage to get my teeth around the palm of his hand, and I bite down with everything I have. His laugh turns into a scream as he quickly pulls away. Just before I let go, I taste blood on my lips.

"You crazy bitch!" he snaps.

"*I'm* crazy?" I shriek in response. In a rush, I jump from the bed, and with adrenaline still coursing through my body, I swing my arms at his face, which he blocks with his forearms, his menacing laugh echoing through his room.

"I wasn't going to do anything, damn," he says, holding up his hands in surrender. I watch as he inspects his hand before trying to shake off the pain.

"You've been nothing but an asshole to me all day," I snap. I don't know why I'm still standing here. I should just go back to my room, lock the door, and stay as far away from this psycho as I can, but then...there's just something about Gabriel that doesn't scare me as much as he probably wants it to. Maybe it's because he's my age, a kid like me born into a fucked-up family, and we've both just been so hardened by everything we've had to endure. Or maybe it's because I've seen a lot of fucked-up shit, especially today, and some teenage punk with tattoos and a hard-on can't scare me anymore. And then, maybe it's just because he's hot.

I don't leave. Instead, I look around. As I turn my back, I hear the flick of a lighter and the sound of a cigarette crackling as it's lit.

"That's a disgusting habit," I snarl, turning back toward him. He's sitting on the edge of his bed, feet on the floor and knees wide as he leans forward to draw in a drag. Suddenly, that bad habit looks sexy as fuck. The red-hot cherry lights up his face in the darkness, and for the first time, I notice the small black heart tattooed right next to his left eye.

His husky voice in the darkness feels like silk running

down the back of my neck. "In this life, lung cancer is the least of my worries."

Across from his bed are three shelves that take up the long wall. The open window illuminates the room with moonlight, and it's only enough to make out the scattered black and white sketches piled on the shelves. There are a few weapons too. And I take a mental stock of it all, wishing I had photographic memory in case I ever needed anything. They must not be used to guests because everything is just out in the open instead of locked away.

I spot a black pistol to my right and a belt with knives on the shelf to the left. There's a box of bullets on the top shelf. I feel his presence behind me as his hand reaches around to grab the gun. With his eyes on me, he takes it back to the bed and shoves it under his pillow. "Don't get any ideas."

"What do you guys do, anyway?" I ask, leaning back against the shelf. "You're not mafia or I would have heard of you."

He doesn't answer, just takes another puff of his cigarette.

"Drug dealers?"

No response.

"Arms dealers? Cartel?" Still no response.

They're all so cold, so emotionless and serious. Silas spoke for a moment about their business. His words echo in my ears from when he brought me dinner. *Don't let your conscience win.*

My eyes dart up to meet Gabriel's. "Assassins."

There's a subtle tick in his eye and the corner of his mouth lifts just barely, and I know I got it right. Of course, it makes so much sense now. Yesterday, Baron had said they don't take sides, and it would explain why I've never heard of them. My dad never used assassins. If he had business to take care of, he did it himself, a fact he probably wouldn't want me to know, but he was never as good at hiding his secrets as he thought he was.

For some reason, knowing they're hitmen actually settles my worries a bit. It's not like they were hired to kill me, which means they have no reason to. Except for the fact that Gabriel is looking at me like he'd do it for free.

"You bit the shit out of my hand, Princess," he growls.

"Don't call me that."

"Isn't that what *you* are? I bet your daddy kept you locked in a tower too. Now you want us to protect you."

"I can take care of myself," I bark back, even though I know it's not true. I can't do shit right now. I have no money, no connections, except for this one. I definitely need Silas Black to take care of me—I just don't want to admit it.

"Oh yeah, how are you going to take care of yourself when those assholes show up to take you back? And trust me, they will."

"Why do you say that?" There's a shake to my voice, no matter how strong I try to sound.

"Because Vincent Maretti doesn't take no for an answer. You think *I'm* a sick fuck..." He winks at me, and my stomach turns.

"Then, help me." Turning toward him, I suddenly realize how insane I sound asking for more of his help. A few minutes ago, I was almost certain he would rape and kill me if he could, then dispose of my body like it was trash. It wasn't that long ago that he literally asked for the honors of doing exactly that. And now I'm asking for his help. Like we're going to be friends or something.

His left brow lifts as he stares at me over his lit cigarette. "Why the fuck would I help you?"

Apparently I stand there thinking too long about what kind of freaky sexual favors I would be willing to do to learn how to become a killer, because Gabriel snuffs his cigarette out in the ashtray and shakes his head. "I don't want whatever is going through your head right now."

I have half a mind to be offended when he stands up and walks toward me. "Then what *do* you want?" I whisper.

He's only inches from my face, and all I can smell is the smoke on his skin. I'm frozen in place as he looks me over, staring down at me like I'm a helpless animal that he doesn't know yet what to do with. I feel the tips of his finger against my bare arm, and I shudder. There's something about the way he touches me, like I'm a novelty he can't resist.

Suddenly, he grabs my hand and steers me toward the door. "The only thing I want from you, Princess, is for you to get the fuck out of my room." I'm sent flying through the doorway just before it slams behind me.

Reeling in the dark hallway, I stare at his door. For a moment, it seemed like he would actually open up to me, like he would *help* me. So now I just have to figure out what I can do to get him to do just that.

## Six

AFTER A RESTLESS NIGHT of tossing and turning and fighting to drown out the loud music blasting all night long, the sun peeks through the cracked open blinds. Though, that's not what woke me. It's the constant thudding on the bedroom door. Throwing the blanket off me, I jump up. I've learned that I need to find out who is on the other side before welcoming them in. Yesterday I thought it was Carol and it was Silas; this time, it could be Satan himself.

Continued pounding on the door has me more furious than concerned. "I'm coming," I huff with heavy steps as I cross the floor. Without caring about my appearance, I rip the door open. "What the hell is your problem?" It's Gabriel. He's standing there with folded clothes in his hands—my clothes—only, they are clean.

"Get your ass dressed. We're going out." He shoves the clothes to my chest.

"It's like seven o'clock in the morning. Why are we even awake?"

Stuffing his hands in the pockets of his black jeans, his smirk returns. "Because, Princess, we don't sleep all day in this house. We work. Now get your ass dressed and meet me down-stairs in ten minutes." He turns around and walks away like he expects me to listen to his commands like some obedient puppy.

Tossing the clothes into the bedroom, I cross my arms over my chest, "What if I don't wanna go?" I smirk back, though he can't see it with his back to me.

That changes quickly when he turns around and eats up the space between us. Grabbing me by the waist, he lifts me up and carries me into the room. "Then you can fucking leave." He sets me back down on my feet and my body feels like a statue. Unable to move. Unable to speak. "Get dressed and meet me downstairs. Got it?"

This time, I nod. Agreeing to his demand. Just like a fucking obedient puppy. These guys sure do have a way of changing minds quickly. I suppose if my guess is correct and they are assassins, mind-fucking can come in handy.

His blue eyes bore into mine and behind this tough guy facade, I see familiarity. The reflection of my green eyes in his, but more than that, I see pain. A life full of trials and tribula-tions. Hiding, and being hidden. Isolation and darkness. With a desperation to break free.

I know that feeling. The desire to be heard and wake up to face a day that involves more than constant supervision because the life you've been tossed into is dangerous. Their lives here are no different. There are secrets in these walls, and if they could talk, I'm sure they'd tell me to run like hell.

But I don't. Instead, I stay. I'll stand my ground and I'll fight like hell against whatever life throws at me next because my mind only sees one thing right now—revenge. I can almost taste its sweetness. I wonder if Gabriel has ever had an appetite for revenge. My tongue darts over my bottom lip and his eyes drift down to watch. Only mere inches from me, I can hear his breath hitch.

I'm not even sure why he is still standing here or why I am either, but something doesn't let me move. I wonder if he feels it, too. When his eyes slide back up to mine, any morsel of emotion that I thought I saw is gone. The eyes looking back at me now are empty. "Clothes on. Now." He flicks his thumb across my chin then turns around.

Once he's gone, I take a deep breath, unsure how long I was even holding it.

*What the fuck was that?*

Was I seriously just admiring that deranged jackass?

Sweeping away any thoughts that slithered into my mind, I grab my clothes off the floor and go into the adjoined bathroom. I set them down and press my palms to the cold marble vanity and look in the mirror, barely recognizing the girl staring back at me. If I were like most eighteen-year-old girls, I'd be crying right now. These bags under my eyes would be absorbing my tears. Only, I'm not like other girls. My heart aches something fierce, but more than anything, I'm fueled by an indescribable need to make those son-of-a-bitches pay for what they took from me.

Once I'm cleaned up and dressed, I head downstairs where I find Gabriel waiting for me. He's slouched back on the couch in the waiting room with his hands on his knees. His jaw ticks in a fury. "Bout damn time."

"Listen. You woke me up and started barking orders. You're lucky I'm even down here right now. I should be sleeping since your need to blast music through this house at all hours of the night kept me up."

"You heard that, did ya? I played that especially for you. Sort of a welcome to the house melody."

I heave a sigh. "How thoughtful of you. Should I feel special, or do you play satanic melodies for all of your house guests?"

Gabriel pushes himself up off his knees and stands up.

"You should feel special. You're the first guest we've had in years." He walks quickly toward the door, and I follow. Catching up to him, he steps aside then opens it for me.

"Wait a minute, no guests in years? What about girlfriends or family?"

"This is our family." He closes the door and we walk down the stairs toward a car that is waiting for us. A man dressed professionally in a black suit stands beside the open back door.

"And girlfriends?" I question as Gabriel nods at the driver. He slides in first and I stand there wondering if I dare get in this car with him. I have no idea where we are going or what his intentions are. There is something so mysterious about this guy, and I'm not sure if I should be intrigued or fear for my life.

Against my better judgment, I get in. The driver closes the door and I look at Gabriel, awaiting his response. "Well? What about girlfriends? Surely with three men living in this house, you've had them over as guests?"

When he still doesn't respond, I let it go. It's obvious these men like their privacy and refuse to divulge any information about their personal lives. So be it. I'll find out everything I need to know about them soon enough. If I'm trusting these guys to protect me, I need to know exactly why I should. For all I know, they could be the enemy in disguise.

We pull up to a small boutique in the middle of the city. Gabriel remained silent the entire drive, even when I asked him where we were going. Once the driver shifts into park and his door opens then closes, Gabriel extends his open hand out to me while we are still sitting in the back seat. I look down at his hand, wondering what the hell he is doing. "What?"

"Give me your phone," he says point-blankly.

I chuckle. "You're out of your damn mind."

"Give me your phone, now."

"Why in the world would I do that?"

Reaching into the pocket of his black leather jacket, he pulls out a phone and hands it to me. "Your father was killed last night, correct? Someone is after you. These guys mean business and they play dirty. If they want to find you, they will move mountains to do just that. You're probably being tracked as we speak. This is your new phone. Baron put in the only phone numbers you need." I take the phone from him and reluctantly give him mine. "Don't call us unless it's an emergency. We don't do small talk." With that, he opens his door and gets out. Instantly, mine swings open and the driver is waiting for me on the other side.

When I see Gabriel walking toward the boutique with no hesitation behind his steps, I slide out quickly and chase after him. "What are we doing here?" I look up and read the name, 'Bella's Boutique.'"

"They have chick clothes and unless you plan to wear that heinous outfit all day, every day, you need to shop." He hands me a credit card and for the first time in twenty-four hours, I smile.

That's the best thing I've heard all day.

When I go to walk in and Gabriel pushes his back against the building and kicks a leg up, I question if he's coming. "Aren't you coming with me?"

Popping a toothpick in his mouth, he snickers, "Not really my thing."

Shrugging my shoulders, I go inside. I'm actually glad he's not coming. He's sort of a drag and would probably rush me. Shopping is my forte. It's what I do best. I won't admit that to Gabriel, though. He'd never let me live down this princess title he's already given me.

Twenty minutes in, and I've already got a worker walking behind me with her arms full. Tossing dresses, shirts, jeans, bras, and anything else that I can into her arms, I continue until I can no longer see her face over the pile. "I think that'll do," I tell her. I swear she let out a sigh of relief, but I can't be sure.

When I check out and the total tallies up to over three-grand, I don't even bat an eye when I swipe the credit card. Silas said he owed my dad a favor. I'm just making sure he pays up.

Gabriel is now leaning against the front of the store and the look of agitation on his face is amusing. "Damn, woman." He pushes himself up and walks over to the employee standing beside me. "Did you buy the entire fucking store?" Taking the bags from her, he walks over to the open trunk of the car and throws them all in like they aren't worth more than pennies.

My hands press to my hips and I grin. "You gave a girl a credit card and never mentioned a limit. Big mistake."

Once we are back in the car, I feel like I should use this time to find out more about the guy sitting next to me. "So, tell me, Gabriel, what do you do for fun?"

His head is tipped down as he types on his phone. I lean over to get a look at what he's so invested in, but he pulls back. "Nosey much?"

"I am. Talking to anyone special?"

He huffs. "I hurt people for fun and the only person in my life that I consider special is myself."

I'd say it's sad he feels that way, but there isn't really anyone in my life that I'd consider special either. The only person who was is gone. "You never answered my question earlier. Do you all have girlfriends? Is Silas married?"

"You sure do ask a lot of questions."

"I think I'm warranted a few since I have no idea who you guys even are."

"We don't do relationships. No time and no desire. Our lives revolve around business."

The car comes to a stop, but I'm not finished talking. "Gabriel," I say calmly, "have you ever even had a girlfriend?" His silence begins to answer the question for me. When he doesn't get out either, I feel like I need to pry further. "Do you guys ever do anything fun?"

"When you begin your career at the age of six years old, after having everything in your life ripped away from you, you tend to miss out on normalcy."

*Six years old?*

"What happened when you were six?"

My question must have hit a nerve because he's suddenly fleeing from the car in a rage. "Gabriel, wait," I holler as I follow behind him. "Did I say something wrong?"

He turns around and there is a fire in his eyes. "Would you stop asking so many damn questions and leave me the fuck alone?"

"I'm sorry. I was just curious."

"Curiosity gets people killed. Now back the fuck off."

And, he's gone.

He may not have answered my questions, but I got my answers. Gabriel has never had meaningful relationships, because he's never had a chance to build them.

## Seven

THERE IS something really fucking eerie about fawning over a brand-new wardrobe when you know there is a perfectly good one still at your house...that you can never go back to. This is a fresh start, a new life...that I didn't want.

Pulling each item out of the bags and looking them over, I chase that post-shopping endorphin high, but it starts to feel empty after the third bag. Hanging each item in the closet, I turn and let out a short scream as I notice a pair of wolf-like eyes watching me from the hallway.

Baron.

I stand there frozen for one, two, three seconds, waiting for him to say something. He has yet to speak one word to me, but he doesn't have to for me to feel how much he dislikes me. And not in a playful, *I might kill you, I might not*, way like Gabriel. Baron stares at me like I'm already dead.

Without a word, he turns and walks away. "Hey!" I call, chasing him down the hall. I grab his arm and spin him toward me, but he remains silent, a bored expression on his face. "What the fuck is your problem?"

Waiting, I give him an impatient expression. Unlike

Gabriel's soft profile, Baron is all sharp angles and dark features. Instead of super dark irises like Silas, Baron's are more golden-hued, and it's the only warm part of him. At least he looks like Silas, almost a spitting image.

"I know you talk," I say, stepping back, "I heard you talk to your dad."

Clearly bored with me, he turns away again and heads down the hallway toward what I assume is his room. "Fine, fuck you then," I call.

Silas is gone all morning and Gabriel left shortly after we got back from shopping. That leaves only me and Baron, and he's still giving me the cold, awkward silent treatment. I can't download any apps on my new phone, so I'm stuck watching TV and raiding their overstocked pantry. It's only been a day, but I already feel so restless. I can't sit here and do nothing while Vincent Maretti is out there, probably tracking me down at this very moment. I didn't survive all of that just to get fat on some hitman's couch.

When I hear the front door open, I jump up and run toward it to find Silas walking in. The setting sun shines through the window above the door, casting him in a warm glow. And even in all that black, he practically illuminates the space he's in. Like a crackling fire I'm dying to stand next to.

"Can I talk to you please?" I ask, coming off a little too eager. I barely give him a chance to walk in the door.

"It's been a long day, Iris. Give me a moment."

I follow him to his office where I watch as he patiently unbuttons each wrist of his black shirt and folds each up carefully, almost ceremoniously, and if I wasn't suddenly enraptured by his fucking forearms, I might interrupt the process.

"I have been sitting here all day waiting for you to come home. We need to talk, *now*."

He raises an eyebrow at me and pulls a bottle of amber liquid from the glass cabinet behind him. "Sitting around all day? According to my credit card statement, you've been a little busy today."

"You said my dad had money in an off-shore account. How much?"

"These things take time, Iris." He sounds annoyed, but there's a hint of kindness there.

"Well, then how much would you charge me to kill Vincent Maretti?"

The liquor bottle lands with a thunk against the hardwood desk as he glares at me. "Let me guess. Gabriel?" he mutters as a warning.

"I figured it out on my own."

He responds with a displeased groan, so I continue. "I need Maretti dead, and I don't care what it costs. I don't even care if there's enough left over for my fresh start. If he's dead, then I'm free."

"No." He sits in his large office chair like it's his throne and swirls his drink in his hand.

"What? Why?"

"A lot of reasons, Iris. We don't take every job thrown our way. Vincent Maretti is elusive, heavily guarded, and killing him won't make you free. There are at least ten others who would seek revenge. You're better off taking the money and disappearing."

"You saw my notebook. You said prove it. So I'm proving it. I don't want to run and hide and plan a slow revenge. I want to kill him now."

A gentle smirk lifts the corner of his lips as he takes a sip of his drink. "You'll kill Maretti?"

"And his whole fucking family."

He looks taken back. Then, he leans forward. "I said prove it, Iris. Not claim it. Talk is cheap, sweetheart."

"Okay what do you want me to do? How do I prove it? I already stood up to Gabriel, and that was fucking terrifying."

A deep chuckle carries across the room, tickling the back of my neck as he smiles. And I watch as he leans back, staring at me like he's sizing me up. I suddenly feel like I'm applying for a job and I'm waiting to see if he'll hire me.

"What if I asked you to kill a man tomorrow? Could you do it?"

"Who?" I ask.

"You can't ask those questions. You were paid to make a hit. Could you do it? No questions asked."

"No questions asked? But you said you don't take every job. Don't you ask questions?"

"I don't take the jobs that are more risk to my boys than they are worth. I don't care what the hit is guilty of, and I don't dwell on the illusion of guilty or innocent. Now answer my question. Could you do it? Kill a man in cold blood just because I told you to."

My head says yes, without question. But my gut knows my head is full of shit and come time to pull the trigger, that stance may change. "But I don't want to kill some random stranger. I want to kill Vincent Maretti."

"You can't handle it, Iris. You don't have to feel bad about that." He finishes the drink in his glass and grabs the bottle to refill it.

I watch his hands as he puts the stopper back on the bottle, setting it down on the desk. I find myself wanting to seek Silas's comfort because even knowing what I know about him, there is something about him that calms me. But right now, he's trying to test me to see how tough I really am. How hard I can be. How much like them—cold and emotionless—I can be. For this revenge, I can.

Without thinking, I grab his glass out of his hand and throw the drink down my throat. It burns like fire all the way down, but I quickly seal off any desire to cough or gag. And I know shooting whatever the fuck that liquid lava was is not even close to being the same as killing a man I don't know. But I'm going to fucking prove to Silas Black that I can do everything he can do.

"I can handle it. Give me a chance."

For a moment, he looks mostly offended that I just stole his drink. Then, he watches me with interest as I fight the urge to run to the kitchen for some water.

"I'll pay you," I say. "You can take it out of my father's accounts. Just let me stay for more than a couple months and teach me everything you know. Then, you can let me go. I'll do what I need to on my own. If I die, I die. But I refuse to go down without a fight."

It's quiet as he stares at me, drumming his fingers on the desk. I can see a hint of excitement in his eyes, and I wonder if he taught Gabriel everything like I'm asking him to teach me.

"Three months, but you have to do everything I say, do you understand? If you disobey, the deal is off."

I swallow. This is what I want, I tell myself, although the idea of obeying Silas Black has me feeling a little terrified. Okay, a lot terrified.

"Thank you," I mumble.

"We start tomorrow. Six a.m. I can teach you the things you need to know to keep yourself alive long enough to take down your target. If you'd like to learn hand-to-hand combat or shooting skills, you're better off asking Gabriel and Baron."

"But—"

He stands up, like he's going to usher me toward the door. I stand my ground, staring at him with my jaw open. "I definitely need to know those things. Can't you just tell them to help me? Make them do it!"

He laughs again, and it's fucking unfair the effect he has on me when I'm trying to sound tough, but he's making me want to crumble to the floor and do anything his dirty heart desires.

"No. I cannot make my sons do anything. They are adults. If you want their help, I'm sure you can think of something."

Then he rests his hand on my lower back and ushers me out of his office. Depositing me right in the living room, where two sets of evil eyes glare at me, waiting to hear what I have to ask. I've already established that Gabriel isn't interested in sex, and Baron won't even utter one word to me. How the fuck am I supposed to convince them to help me?

Surely, I can handle this. If I'm going to take down Vincent Maretti and all of his stupid goons, then surely I can handle the Black brothers.

The sour look on Baron's face assures me I won't be asking him for anything anytime soon. Gabriel is staring at me with a cocked brow, and while I'm still intimidated by his bad-boy persona, I feel like I have a better shot at convincing him to help me than Baron. "Gabriel," I cross my arms over my chest, "Do you have a minute? I need to talk to you."

"No," he quips, without even a beat of hesitation.

Something about his asshole reaction pisses me off. With Silas's words ringing in my ears, I march right over to him with heavy steps. *Prove it. Don't claim it.*

My fingers wrap around his bicep and my nails dig like spades into the skin of his arm. "I said I need to talk to you."

Baron's eyes widen in surprise and if I didn't know any better, I'd say he's impressed with my ability to take control. To these guys, I'm emotional baggage and a stranger taking up space in their domain, but I'm much more than meets the eye. I might not have an empty heart or be a trained assassin, but I do have guts and it's about damn time they know it.

Gabriel snarls, "Get your damn hands off me." He tries to

jerk away and he's strong, but I dig deeper, feeling my nails pierce his skin.

"Fine," I huff, "if you won't come with me then I'll just ask you what I need to ask right here in front of Baron."

"So fucking ask and then get your nails out of my goddamn arm."

Leaning forward as Gabriel backs away like I'm infected, I whisper into the small space between us, "Have you ever had your dick sucked?" I'm no expert on men, but I can tell that Gabriel isn't very experienced with women by the way that he tenses up when I touch him. All I have to do is blink and his dick hardens. I also know that men would do just about anything for sexual pleasure and this is all I have to offer at the moment.

Pinching his brows together, he glares down at me. "What the hell did you just ask me?"

This time I don't whisper. Screw it. He should have just walked away with me when he had the chance. "I asked if you've ever had your dick sucked?"

A loud thud from Silas's office grabs my attention for a moment, but I return my focus to Gabriel, who appears shocked by my question. "Well, have you?"

"Yeah, Gabriel. Have you?" Baron says. I look over at him and I swear I caught a glimpse of a smile before his eyes met mine and that scowl he wears so well returned.

Gabriel jerks his arm away, and this time, I let him. "Of course I have." He chuckles. "What a stupid fucking question." He heads out of the room toward the stairs, but I follow behind him. "Is there something you need, because you're getting on my damn nerves, Princess."

Trailing my hand on the banister, I shadow him upstairs. "As a matter of fact, there is. I told you. I need to talk to you."

As soon as we reach the top, Gabriel spins and pushes me up against the wall in the hallway so fast my breath hitches.

"You wanna suck my dick, Princess? Is that what you're asking?" His nose trails along the skin of my cheek as he draws in a deep breath like he's inhaling my scent and saving it to memory. Maybe for later when he's jerking off in his bedroom. Giving him something else to remember, I stretch my arm down between us and cup his balls in my hand.

His body jerks up. "Is that what you want?" I mutter as I tilt my head to the side. His warm breath hits the side of my neck, and for a moment, I forget why I'm doing this.

"No." He retreats quickly, pressing his palms to my shoulders and pinning them to the wall. "If I wanted you to suck my cock, it would already be down your throat."

Dragging my tongue across my bottom lip, I smirk. "Surely you've thought about it." His eyes dart down to my mouth and I can feel his dick harden against my leg.

He can stand here and act unaffected by my touch, but I gave him that boner.

I'll tease the hell out of him until he's practically begging to feel my lips around it. And once he agrees to give me what I want, I'll take care of his needs. I'm not going to feel bad or guilty for using sex as a bartering chip. For one thing, I love sex —always have. So it's really a win-win, the way I see it. And I have a feeling sex with Gabriel would be a big win.

I push past Gabriel and walk toward my room, but watch him as he stares back at me with hooded eyes.

Maybe he'll follow. Maybe he won't.

## Eight

LEAVING MY DOOR CRACKED OPEN, I begin stripping off my clothes, one layer at a time. Just as I turn to make myself comfortable on the bed, the door flies open then slams shut. A cool breeze hits my bare skin and sends a shiver down my entire body. In two seconds flat, Gabriel is on top of me with my back against the mattress of the perfectly made bed. His face is so close, my nose brushes his.

"I thought you might change your mind." I smirk, but he holds a scowl on his face and if it weren't for his hard cock pressing into my thigh, I'd think he hasn't changed his mind at all.

"What's with you?" His jaw clenches. "You think you can come into this house and throw yourself at me like a little whore and I'll be at your beck and call?"

While that wasn't my intention when I came to this house, it is now. I've learned a lot in the short forty-eight hours I've been here. Though my safety and protection are the sole reasons for coming here, the skills I can acquire from these men is what keeps me here. I'll do whatever I have to do to get the revenge I crave.

I stretch my hand down between us and rub his cock through the fabric of his jeans. He tenses at my touch, and I'm beginning to think even though his body reacts to me, he personally does not like me. When he lets out a subtle moan, I rub harder. "I think we can help each other, Gabriel."

He lingers over me like a moth to a flame. His blue eyes look deep into mine, like he's searching for something. "What could you possibly have that I want?"

With one hand at my side and the other still wedged between him and my naked body, I pop the button of his jeans then push my hand into the opening of his pants. My thumb grazes over his silky-smooth head, and his hips rock into my hand, begging for more.

"I think you know exactly what I can do for you. Do you need me to say it out loud?" He doesn't speak. Instead, he just nods. "I'll suck your cock so hard that everyone in this house will hear you scream when you come. And when you do help me, I might even let you stick it in my pussy. Then I'll suck it again."

When his breathing becomes labored and a bead of sweat drops onto my chest, I'm convinced he's in agreement.

"What do you want from me?"

Stretching my arm further, I take his cock in my hand and begin rubbing up and down his length in slow strokes. "I want you to teach me everything you were taught by Silas. I want the skills necessary to kill Vincent Maretti and everyone else who played a part in my father's death."

"And what makes you think I have these skills you're looking for? I'm just your average eighteen-year-old guy." The smirk on his face tells me all I need to know. Not only does he have the ability to help me, he's oozing confidence, and it's likely for good reason. He's good at what he does.

Pulling my hand out of his pants, I push his body off me then press my palms to his shoulder, shoving him down on his back. "Average eighteen-year-old guys don't tie up sixty-year-old men in their kitchen and break their fingers." I begin tugging his pants down, but his hand slaps over mine. I look up and the shit-eating grin he was wearing is gone. This time, I see something else. Realization dawns, and I tear my hand away.

*That's it. It has to be.* "Oh my gosh. I should have known. I'm so sorry." I sit up on my knees and look for something to grab and cover myself up.

"Wait. What?' He pushes himself up on his elbows. "Sorry for what?"

"For this. You're gay. I mean, all the signs were there. I just—"

"Woah, woah, woah," he cuts me off, "I'm not gay."

"It's ok. It's totally cool. I'm not judging at all. I just feel like an idiot for not realizing it sooner."

"Iris," he shouts, "What in the world makes you think I'm gay?"

I glance down at his pants that are still intact. He's unlike any straight guy I've ever been with, never making advances or taking what he wants from me. Something is definitely up here.

"If you're not gay, then why don't you..." I trail off. If he likes women, maybe he just doesn't want me. "It's me, isn't it?" Here I am, this stranger who barged into his house covered in blood and practically begged his family to protect me. Now, I'm throwing myself at Gabriel and using my body to try and get what I want from him. He probably thinks I am a whore. He did call me one, after all. Normally that shit doesn't bother me, but now that we're in this position and he's denying me, I need to know why.

"No, it's not you." He huffs, sitting up quickly and messing with the button on his jeans. "Fine, you wanna suck my cock. Have at it, baby." He whips his dick out like it's nobody's business and I'm not sure who's more surprised at his sudden outburst—me or him.

"Well, now this just feels weird."

He pushes his pants down so they're hanging around his thighs. "You asked for it. There it is. Now suck it." He drops back down on the bed and his eyes focus on the ceiling above him.

"Do we have a deal?" I ask. I have to make sure we're in agreement. Although, something about Gabriel draws me in, like I'd give him anything without him giving me something in return. I'm not sure if it's his bad boy demeanor, or the fact that he keeps rejecting me. Who am I kidding? It's both. I've always sought out the bad boys, and I've always liked a challenge.

"That depends if you can put your words where your mouth is. You said you'd suck me so hard that everyone in the house will hear me scream." He lifts his head and looks me dead in the eye. "Prove it."

What the hell is with these guys always telling me to prove shit? It's about time they learn to just take my word for it.

When Gabriel tucks his arms under his head and resumes staring at the ceiling, I get back on my elbows and knees. My fingers wrap around his cock, which isn't disappointing in the least. Giving it a gentle stroke, his body tenses up again. It's like he's never had a woman touch him before. He says he's not gay, but he sure as hell doesn't seem like he's into this.

With my hand still wrapped around him, I give him a few pumps while my tongue trails over his head, licking up the bead of precum on the tip. When I take it into my mouth, his body jolts. My eyes remain on him, but he has no interest in watching what I'm doing. Stretching my tongue out, I sweep it up and down the side of his cock before taking all of him into my mouth.

Gabriel lets out a moan then acts as if he's struggling to fill his lungs. I slide my mouth up and down his cock while I stroke the bottom half. "Holy shit," he cries out. I pick up my pace and move faster and then all of a sudden, warm liquid is shooting into my mouth. I swallow down what I can, but his timing and his aim is ridiculous.

Wiping the back of my hand across my mouth, I look at him. His eyes are pinched shut, and I swear I can see his heart beating rapidly in his chest—so fast that it looks like it could explode through his skin.

"Gabriel," I say in a calm voice, "was this the first..." I can't say it. I know he'll lose his damn mind. But, seriously. I don't even think that lasted a minute and the way he was acting—and still is—I'd swear this was the first time he's ever had a blow job. I need to know. Call me a nosey little shit, but I have to know why he's acting this way. "Was this the first time you've ever had your dick sucked?"

In one swift motion, I'm getting pushed off the bed. Fortunately, I catch myself before I hit the ground. "What the hell?"

Pulling his pants up as he gets to his feet, he heads straight for the door. Walking out before he even has his zipper up. I wanna run after him and figure out what the hell just happened, but I'm still naked. Scooping up my shorts, I pull them on without even putting on my panties first, then pull my T-shirt over my head. "Gabriel, wait," I whisper-yell as I hurry out the door and down the hall. Just as I catch a glimpse of him, his bedroom door slams shut.

Unfortunately for Gabriel, I don't leave things unfinished or unsaid. Balling my hand in a fist, I pound on his door. "Open the door." I continue to knock, louder and louder until he finally opens it. My humiliation has been replaced by anger. "What the fuck is the matter with you?" I shove my hands hard into his chest, pushing him farther into his room. I continue to shove him until both of us are standing in the middle of his gothic bedroom.

He narrows his eyes at me. "You want me to fucking help you? Fine, I'll help you. Just drop this shit and get the fuck out of my room." His finger points at the door, but I smack it away.

"No!" I yell back, "you will help me, because we had a deal. But you're also going to tell me why you ran out of the bedroom like a fifteen-year-old boy who just had his dick touched for the first time."

Gabriel nudges his shoulder against mine as he pushes past me, and for a moment, I think he's running out on me again. That is until the door shuts and he clicks the lock. I cross my arms over my chest and watch him as he fights to look me in the eye. "I was six when Silas took me away from a life of pure hell." He takes a seat on the bed and runs his hands over his face before hanging his head down. "The day after I moved in, Silas started teaching me his ways. I was just a kid, and figured it was normal."

"Wait. Silas isn't your dad?"

He shakes his head. "I never went to school. Silas hired a teacher to come in weekly to tutor me, and for the most part, I taught myself everything I know from reading all hours of the day that I wasn't being conditioned into a robot."

I'm not sure why he's telling me all this, but I'm intrigued. Part of me wants to go sit next to him, but Gabriel seems very hesitant when it comes to affection, or human touch in general. And the whole robot remark makes perfect sense to me now. It explains the void in his eyes and how he acts without emotion.

So I just stand here, and I listen in hopes that he'll tell me more. I'm not sure why, but I want to know it all. Everything about him. He holds this mystery, and I'm almost certain, I'm the first person he's ever talked to like this.

"I've never had a girlfriend. Don't even know how to talk to girls. So, yeah. It was the first time." His tone shifts and I can tell he's getting agitated—or embarrassed. "Satisfied?" He throws his arms up like he's offering me the opportunity to pick his brain.

"Actually. I am. I'm glad you told me. For what it's worth, it's nothing to be ashamed of. I mean, you're only eighteen. It's not like you're a forty-year-old virgin." I chuckle, trying to make light of the situation, but he doesn't see the humor in it.

Getting to his feet, he marches toward me and grabs me by the arm then walks me to his door. "Good. Now go. And if you tell anyone about any of this, just remember what I did to that man when we first met."

I let him push me out the door, but my hands slap on it just as he's about to close it. "How about a new deal?" There's a beat of hesitation, but his pressure on the door lessens and he allows me to push it back open. "I'll train you. You train me?"

He cocks a brow. "Train me?"

"Yeah. I'll show you what you've been missing out on. Give you some tips, and in return, you teach me your strategy. I wanna know how you get these men to talk. I wanna know it all."

When he drags his lip between his teeth and he bites back a smile, I know he's on board. Now that he's had a taste of what he's been missing, he's gonna want the whole damn meal. "Whatd'ya say?"

Looking my body up and down like he's observing said meal, he nods. "Alright, show me what ya got, Princess, and I'll teach you how to mindfuck the enemy."

With that, the door closes, and this time, I allow it. Turning around, I press my back to it and smile.

This should be fun.

## Nine

I'm in a deep, dreamless sleep when ice cold water rips me out of my peaceful nothingness, and I scream myself awake.

"I told you six a.m.," a deep voice above me bellows. "You think I have time to wait for you?"

I sit up, shaking, in nothing but my panties and a now drenched camisole. Silas stares at me, unaffected by the fact that at this point my freezing cold nipples could almost tear through my tank top.

"Well, maybe if you taught your son some fucking manners and told him to keep the fucking music down, I could be up at six!" I yell.

Another splash of cold water lands harshly against my face. "If you're not in my office in ten minutes, the deal is off." With those last remarks, he turns on his heels and heads for the door. "And clean up this fucking mess."

I'm still gasping from the last dousing, and all I can manage is a strangled scream. Who does he think he is? These guys have clearly never lived with a woman before and after what I learned about Gabriel, I'm starting to seriously doubt any of them have even been around women. They're all just cold, emotionless assholes...

But then again, I need these cold, emotionless assholes if I'm going to get what I want. So, I do as Silas says, dressing quickly and throwing my hair up into a messy bun, so I can be down in his office like he so rudely demanded. I'll just have to deal with the soaking wet bed later.

As I head down the hallway, I catch Baron's cold eyes following me from the kitchen. He doesn't react to my presence at all, and even after he was there to witness the whole blow job offer to Gabriel, he hasn't said a thing to me. I had half-expected him to come knocking at some point last night, looking for an offer of his own, but he didn't. Baron stares at me like I'm a piece of property or a pest that he's patiently waiting to be rid of.

Silas doesn't greet me as I plop down in the leather chair across from him in his office. He's typing on his laptop, ignoring me while I wait.

"You have some hard lessons to learn if you want to survive the next three months, Iris." His tone is so cold and harsh. It makes me feel bad, like I've disappointed him. I'm still livid about the water, but I find myself wanting to get in his favor again. "It was an accident," I tell him, trying to keep my shoulders back, even though looking Silas Black in the eyes terrifies me. "Gabriel's music kept me up."

He doesn't respond.

"But I did get him to agree to help me," I add.

"How?" he asks, then shakes his head. "Never mind, I don't want to know."

A slow smile creeps across my lips.

"If you can handle Gabriel, then you may just be tougher than I took you for."

My chin lifts a little higher as he says that. I search his features for signs he might be disappointed in learning that

Gabriel and I were messing around. I mean, he did sort of imply I should do what I needed to in order to get him to help me.

Suddenly he stands and walks toward the door. "Let's go."

"Where are we going?" I ask, rushing to catch up.

"A job," he answers flatly. For a moment, I almost stop him. I haven't put on any makeup and I'm hardly dressed for...assassin stuff, but he doesn't seem to care. I follow him down the dark stairs to the underground garage, which houses an impressive collection of cars, some flashier than others. He grabs a black duffle from the shelf next to the door, and I follow him to a sleek black Tesla parked in the center.

"Are you going to kill someone?" I ask when he climbs in the driver's seat next to me.

"Maybe," he answers.

I watch as he squeezes his hand around the steering wheel, shifting the car into drive with the other hand. Silas is effortlessly sexy with a confident, mature sex appeal. I can't help but wonder if he's as romantically deprived as Gabriel. Then I remember everything Gabriel told me about his childhood, parts of that story making me resent Silas for how he raised him—secluded and neglected.

"Gabriel told me that you adopted him when he was six," I say.

"That's true," he replies. The garage door opens automatically, two armed guards stand just on the other side. They nod at us as we pass.

"Baron too?"

"No, Baron is my biological son."

I let my mind wander for a moment, trying to figure out how I can ask him the burning question on my mind. Finally, I decide just to be blunt, throwing manners and caution out the window. "Did you adopt Gabriel just to make him an assassin? Like a robot?" I add, remembering the way Gabriel put it last night. I wonder if he's ever told his father or his brother the way he feels.

Silas turns his head and glares down at me with a heavy brow. "No, I did not adopt him just to make him an assassin."

"Sorry...I was just curious."

It's quiet a moment while we drive before Silas starts speaking again. "I wouldn't have taken him if I didn't think he'd have a better chance at life with me."

"What happened?"

"His biological parents were junkies who owed someone money. They kept him well-hidden, because in all of my recon, I never once saw him or even knew he existed. They never sent him to school or to a doctor. He was skin and bones and sick as hell."

"That's terrible," I mutter.

"I would have left him there, but he tried to kill me with a box cutter after I shot the crackheads who were supposed to be his parents. Almost succeeded too." With a half-smile, he holds his forearm out toward me where a long scar runs up the backside.

"I saw a fighter in him. If I had left him, he would have become a ward of the state and his life would have been one struggle after another. So, I brought him home."

My heart lurches, imagining a small Gabriel, filthy and hungry, wielding a dirty blade out of a desperate need to survive.

"Would you have...killed him?" I ask.

"No. We don't kill kids," he says it so matter-of-factly, like killing others is fine.

"Women?" I ask.

"Sometimes."

"If they deserve it?" I add, then he just glares at me without emotion.

"If we're hired to."

. . .

A few moments later, we pull up to a busy city street where Silas parks effortlessly in a spot in front of an apartment building. He stares straight ahead, and I wait for his next move.

"What are we doing?" I whisper.

"Our target leaves for work every morning at 6:45. He'll leave his apartment and walk east on Elm until he gets to the coffee shop where he gets a croissant and a latte."

"Stalk much?"

"This is part of the job, Iris. Ninety-five percent of this job is recon, knowing your targets every move. When are they around people? When are they alone? When is the best time to make the hit? What are your risks with each move?"

"Well, that sounds boring."

He glares at me with a tight-lipped expression, and I shoot him a warm smile, hoping to crack the icy exterior. Finally, there is a subtle flinch in his eye, like he *wants* to smile.

"So, we're going to kill him right here? On his morning commute?"

"Of course not," he bellows. "But he didn't show up for work yesterday, and I had planned on doing the job today. But you never complete a job when the target does something out of the ordinary."

"Why?"

"Because then things become unpredictable, and we don't like unpredictable. We stay alive and keep our business afloat on predictability."

"So maybe he's sick. Or maybe he called in sick to stay home and watch porn all day. You never know."

Ignoring me, he looks down at his watch. "Seven-ten. He's late."

"What do we do now?"

"Act casual," he says as he gets out of the car.

Acting casual around Silas Black is a joke. I'm in a pair of yoga pants and a tank top. He's in all black with dark shades and a murderous scowl. We look anything but casual. Still, I follow him as he holds open the door to the building, allowing me to walk through. We take three flights of stairs instead of the elevator—I assume to avoid cameras, finally stopping on the third floor.

It's not a nice complex, by any means. The hallway smells like cat piss and cigarette smoke. It's mostly quiet, except for the sound of someone's TV blaring behind one door. Silas stops at that door and leans an ear toward it.

I watch as he sets his jaw, looking almost angry, like he knows something I don't. Then he pulls what looks like a key out of his pocket and inserts it into the keyhole.

"What are you doing?" I whisper, watching in shock as he silently unlocks the door and opens it. "You're just going to break in?"

"It's not breaking in when you have a key," he whispers, holding up a black matte tool that looks more like tweezers than a key—a lock picker.

"You're going to show me how to do that, right?" I ask.

He shrugs at me before peeling open the door carefully. The stench hits us immediately. I wish I could say it was the first time I smelled a rotting corpse, but I accidentally snuck into my father's basement once as a kid, where I can only assume the people who crossed him ended up. It was clean, like a medical unit, but by then, the odor had been infused into every surface. I couldn't eat for a week.

Even now, my mouth fills with saliva and my tongue grows heavy, but I can't puke. I have to prove to Silas I can do this, so I peek in behind him. There on the carpet, staring lifelessly up at the ceiling, is a pale, ghostly man with gray hair and a bullet hole between his glossy eyes.

"Goddammit," Silas grits through his teeth.

I look up and notice the hole in the window, round and sharp, no bigger than a blueberry. Visions of my kitchen window the day my father was murdered come flooding back to my mind. The popping sound echoes, and the urge to vomit becomes overwhelming. The room grows cold and my vision starts to stretch, as if I'm falling down a dark hallway.

I'm about to pass out.

Suddenly, arms are around me and I'm moving, my feet stumbling to keep up. The next thing I know my face is hovering over a smelly black trash can and I'm dry heaving until my ribs ache. Silas rubs my back while the world comes back into full focus.

The street is too loud and the sun is too bright when we finally make it back to the car, and I can tell he is angry.

"What happened?" I ask, taking the bottle of water he offers me from the console of the car. He doesn't answer.

"Did someone else get to him first?"

He still keeps quiet, driving home like a maniac. He swerves in and out of traffic with his jaw clenched and his brows folded in tightly over his eyes. I give up on asking questions and just try to keep from puking again. He's never going to trust me to be able to do this if I can't even make it through seeing one dead person without losing my shit.

But it wasn't the dead guy. Well, it wasn't *just* the dead guy. Seeing those bullet holes brought up something I didn't even know I was feeling.

When we get back to the house, Silas skips the garage and parks the car right in front of the door. Getting out of the car in a huff, he bolts, and I get out to follow him. He stomps straight into the one part of the house I haven't seen yet—down the hallway and into a large room with an entire wall of guns above a large shelf. Sitting at a long black table in the middle, cleaning pieces of a large gun, is Baron.

"What the fuck did you do?" Silas barks at him.

Baron doesn't even flinch. His eyes don't move from the task at hand.

"What are you talking about?" He acts a little too even-tempered for his dad's rage.

"The Hancock job, Baron. You took out the target already, but you knew I had it planned for today. What the fuck are you doing?"

Finally, Baron sets down what he's working on and looks up at his father. "Why did you wait so long to make the kill? Better yet, why didn't you give that job to me? It was perfect for me."

When he stands up, Silas meets him toe-to-toe in the middle of the room, and I hang back by the door. It's like watching two crazed dogs who are about to rip each other's throats out.

Silas stabs his son in the chest with his finger. "Because you are not careful enough, Baron. You're reckless and impatient. I taught you better."

"Yeah, you also taught me that we worked together, but lately, it seems you want to make decisions by yourself. So I made a decision by myself." Baron's head tilts, obviously in my direction, as his unnerving golden-brown eyes glare directly at my face. It's pretty clear he's talking about me and his father taking in a stray girl who wants to fuck everything up.

"Pull that shit again, and you're done, Baron. Do you understand me?"

"Yes, sir."

Between the two, Silas definitely appears to be more assertive, a bit louder and stands taller, but Baron has a calculating expression. He's too calm, like he's already figured everything out, and that makes the hairs on my neck stand up. Manipulation is ten times scarier than violence.

Silas turns away from his son and storms out of the room, brushing past me as he goes. I stand there, staring at Baron for a long moment. He thinks he can intimidate me, but he doesn't know me at all. I won't play Baron's mind games, and I won't let him scare me into leaving.

Before I turn away, I shoot him a slow smile and leave him standing there alone. There are things I need to learn from him, but I'm not quite ready to make a deal with this one. There is something about him that draws me to him, but it's beyond clear that Baron cannot be trusted.

## Ten

Assuming my lesson for the day with Silas is complete—although I'm not sure what the lesson was—I head to my room. When I hear the shuffling of feet inside, my body stills. *Someone is in there.*

"Gabriel?" I say with a hushed tone as I push the door open. I draw in a sigh of relief when I see Carol standing over the bed fluffing the pillows. The wet sheets lie in a pile on the floor at her feet. "Thank you for doing that."

I make my way over to her side. She doesn't even lift her head to look at me. Instead, she pretends like I'm not even here as she drops the pillow into place and pulls the comforter up. "It's a beautiful day outside," I tell her, in an attempt to make small talk.

"Have a good day, Ms. Pavetta." She tilts her head, without even forcing a smile, before rolling up the dirty sheets and proceeding to walk out of my room.

For whatever reason, Silas has the staff in this house on a short leash. I suppose it's necessary when you're in the line of work they are. You can't trust anyone. I highly doubt they trust me. For all they know, I could be here on a job of my own. I get the feeling that little by little, I'm gaining their trust. Gabriel has already taken down one wall and shared something with me I'm sure he's never spoken of with another soul. Silas is opening up, too.

"Hey, Princess." His words startle me and my feet almost leave the ground. I spin around and see Gabriel standing there with both hands pressed against either side of the door frame. I spot the ball of his tongue ring positioned between his teeth. He's wearing a black T-shirt with torn off sleeves. I lean closer to get a better look when I notice splatters of red liquid on his arm. *Is that...blood?* "Silas said your lesson has been postponed. Put on something old and meet me downstairs." He waves his hand over his head and walks away.

Walking over to the closet, I shuffle through the new clothes hanging up. I don't have anything old. Everything I own in this house is brand new. Then I remember the clothes I wore on my first day here. They're balled up in the corner of the closet, and while they're clean, they are soaked in harrowing memories of a day I won't soon forget. Swallowing down the lump in my throat and fighting back the urge to cry for him, I grab the clothes and brush away any emotion. I have to stay focused. For me, and for him.

Once I'm changed, I head downstairs. The house is so quiet I could hear a pin drop. Once again, my body is tense and I'm on edge. It's only natural. It's not every day that you see a rotting corpse only days after watching the only man who ever loved you get blown away. Not to mention, the unnerving glances from the members of this household, namely Baron.

Gabriel comes stalking toward me with an expression of urgency. "Come on, we need to hurry." He trudges me toward the door and pulls it open. There's another car waiting for us, just like yesterday.

"More shopping. A girl could get used to this," I tease. I

know damn well we aren't shopping, but I tend to use humor to cover up my anxiety.

Shoving the driver out of the way like an asshole, he pulls the door open then gives me a push inside. I roll my eyes and huff, "Jerk!"

"Get us there fast," he tells the driver, before climbing in and slamming the door shut. His attention shifts to me. "Timing is everything. Remember that." He taps two fingers to his temple. "You saw what happened with Silas earlier. Time slipped away from him and Baron took the job from him. I don't fuck up, and I get the job done."

The car burns out and my body flies back into the leather seat. I fold my hands in my lap and look out the window, curious where we're going—what we're doing. I've seen Gabriel at work and it wasn't pretty. I have to keep my cool and remember this is good, this gets me one step closer to my revenge.

Watching Gabriel intently, he taps into his phone with a sinister scowl on his face. Five minutes later, we're pulling up to what looks like an abandoned building in the middle of nowhere. "Where's Mickey Barton? That's your question. Memorize it. Repeat it in your head. Focus on that question and never veer off track," he tells me, before swinging the door open and gesturing for me to get out. "Got it?"

*What the fuck?* Why is he telling me this? My question? My hand claps over my mouth. Holy shit, there's someone in there and Gabriel is planning on making me interrogate him.

When the wind picks up, I hug myself tightly and follow behind Gabriel. This man exudes so much confidence it's impossible not to be attracted to him. Although he wears this mask of mystery and darkness, I'm intrigued. I'd love to dig into his heart just to see the pain it's endured, then put a band-aid on it and lick his wounds. I still can't believe he came into this life of madness when he was only six years old. Granted, I grew up in deceit and darkness, but I wasn't part of it. It just sort of existed around me.

"What's the question?" Gabriel asks as he pulls open a large wooden door with a wrought iron handle.

"Where's Mark Barton?" My voice cracks and my displeasure in this whole situation is apparent.

"Mickey! Mickey Barton." He shakes his head then swats my arms down that are still crossed over my chest. "Straighten up. They will sniff out your fear and laugh in your fucking face. You need to walk in there and show him exactly who's in charge." Stopping in his tracks, he turns to me. "You can do this."

*No, I can't.* I want to say it. It's exactly how I feel. Hell no, I can't do this. But I lie. Because I have no other choice if I want to live a life outside of hiding. I shake my head. "Yes. Yes, I can fucking do this." Then I push past him and walk inside the dark building. It reeks of mold and mildew and I can hear someone rustling around in the distance. I follow the sound of metal scraping against concrete. My heart is pounding like a jackhammer, but I shove all fear aside and my feet keep moving. That is, until I see a small flicker of light in an open room and hear the muffled sounds of another person. Only, it's not the same sounds I heard the other day when I met Gabriel.

*No! It can't be.* Would they seriously torture a woman? All my questions are answered when I walk into the room and see the woman's long jet-black hair draped over the back of the chair. A man stands in front of her with his hands folded over his chest. His biceps are about the same size of his head with blue veins bulging out, and I can't seem to look away. There's a tray that you'd see in a doctor's office to the side and on top of it are all different sharp tools. A knife, scissors, a hammer, a lighter, a scalpel, among other items that I can't even begin to describe.

"We'll take it from here," Gabriel says from behind me. "Get the fuck out and keep your phone on. I'll be in touch once we get a location." The man nods to Gabriel then looks at me. His eyes skim up and down the length of my body and the smirk on his face unsettles my stomach. He winks as he walks past me and full-blown nausea ensues.

Gabriel gives me a shove from behind, and I swallow down the bile rising in my throat and walk over to the prisoner. She's beautiful. Her brown eyes flash a glimmer of hope when she sees me. As if she thinks I'm here to rescue her. There's a white cloth wrapped around her mouth and tied at the back of her head and her hands and legs are bound by rope. I look at Gabriel, who's chewing on a toothpick with his leg kicked up behind him on the wall. He taps his bare wrist, reminding me that time is of the essence.

"Where is…" I begin to speak, but my voice cracks. "Where is Mickey? Mickey Barton." I finally spit the words out. The girl's eyes widen in surprise and she begins squirming in fear. More muffled sounds come from behind the white cloth, and as much as I want to untie her and set her free, she's here for a reason. I don't know that reason, but I don't need to. What I do need is practice. One day soon I'll have Vincent Maretti bound in a chair, and I'll show him everything but mercy. "Where the fuck is Mickey Barton?" I repeat, louder and more sternly, as I tug the cloth down to her neck.

Leaning forward, I clench my jaw. "Tell me where the hell Mickey is or I'll…" I reach to the side and search for the scissors without looking, "I'll cut all your hair off."

Gabriel breathes out a chuckle and I shoot my eyes at him and glower before returning my attention to our prisoner. "Please, just let me go. I'll do anything," she cries out in a thick French accent.

"Anything?" I cock a brow. "How about starting with a location?" My fingers stretch between the holes of the scissors.

Once they are open, I get a firm grip on her gorgeous silk hair. I'd kill for this hair. This lady has to be in her late forties, maybe even fifties, but not a single grey. If only I can be so lucky when I'm that age. "One. Two. Three." When she doesn't respond, I position a chunk of her hair between the blades and squeeze my fingers together, watching as the strands sweep through the air and land on the floor. "Such pretty hair. Such a shame."

The woman screams, but I slap a hand over her mouth. "I've got all damn day."

"Please. I beg of you. I have kids." Something stabs at the inside of my chest and I lift my head to look at Gabriel.

He shakes his head no, but what does that mean? She's lying? What if she's not? I can't be responsible for hurting the mother of innocent children.

"Gab—"

He holds up a hand and stops me then points and bends his finger calling me over. When I'm not quick enough, he meets me halfway and grabs me by the arm, spinning me around and pinning me against the wall. Leaning close, I can hear his jaw tick. "Rule number one, never say names. Second, never engage in sob stories. They will feed them to you. You want your revenge. It starts with Mickey Barton."

"Wait a minute. Is this Mickey connected to Maretti?" I whisper into the small space between us.

"Get the location. You do whatever you have to do. No limits." He turns me back around and pushes me toward the lady. I stumble a bit while watching him. My eyes begging for answers. Answers that he won't give me.

I have to get them myself.

Grabbing the knife off the tray, my hand trembles. I give it a flick with my finger pressed on the release, as I eye her, but the damn thing doesn't open. Gabriel laughs again, so I give it another flick. "Damnit," I hiss. When he continues to laugh, frustration gets the best of me, and I chuck it at him. Of course, I miss, but I think he gets the point. Giving up on the switch blade, I grab the scalpel. The metal tip glistens under the glow of the light and this looks like it could slice through skin with just a touch. I drop it back down, realizing I'm not quite there yet. A menacing smile spreads across my face when I grab the hammer. "Where is Mickey Barton?" I ask again, but this time, I will get a response.

When she doesn't answer, I lift the hammer and bring it down forcefully on her knee cap. The sound of metal meeting bone echoes through my ears then she lets out a deafening squeal. To my surprise, I don't feel an ounce of remorse. It's sickening how satisfying that was. With no reply, I lift it again, but Gabriel comes stalking toward me with his eyebrows pinched together. I huff, "What?"

He grabs the hammer from my hand and tosses it back on the tray then takes me by the arm and pulls me to the back of the room. "Never forget the words I'm about to say. Got it?"

Looking from Gabriel to the lady, I nod. "Ok."

He leans close. His lips practically touch my ear and goose-bumps erupt down my arm. "Getting someone to talk doesn't always involve abuse and torture. That comes in later. Always start your interrogation with reverse psychology. A little therapy, if you will. Get on their good side, or at least try. If that doesn't work, then you bring out the tools. Let her sit there and wonder what you could do with them. Beat the bat on your hand while you talk, flip a knife, anything that has her attention focused on the 'what ifs.'"

I draw in a deep breath and release it rapidly. "Well, I think I've forgone getting on her sweet side and passed right to the torture."

"Oh no," he tsks. "Hitting her knee with a hammer and cutting her hair is child's play. Take this." He reaches into his pocket and pulls out the knife that I couldn't open. Giving it a flick, the blade frees. "Go over there and trail the tip around her neck while you calmly ask her questions that could lead up to Mickey's whereabouts. When did she last see him? Has he seen their kids lately? Has she seen their kids?"

With my eyes glued to the knife in his hand, I shake my head. "I don't think I can. Maybe I was a fool to think I had it in me."

Gabriel grabs a hold of my hand, pushes my fingers down and places the knife on my palm then folds one finger over at a time. "You're the daughter of Damon Pavetta. You have it in you." He walks past me over to the lady then turns to face me, waiting for my feet to make a move and prove to him that I do, in fact, have it in me.

Pressing my lips together, I close my eyes. *I'm Iris Pavetta, daughter of a mafia king.* I look down at my hand then position the knife with the blade sticking up as I walk over to Gabriel's side. A hint of a smile threatens his lips and, for a moment, I feel proud. For whatever reason, he believes in me right now.

Slouching down in front of the dark-haired beauty, I begin tracing the blade with my index finger. "Forgive me for my lack of manners, I never got your name," I say, but her eyes just roll as she turns her head to avoid looking at me. "Ok, then. I guess we're not on a first name basis." I stand up and lean in, invading her personal space. My hand rises and I let the tip of the blade rest under her chin. One wrong move and she'd commit accidental suicide.

Gabriel takes my hand and moves it to the side a couple centimeters. "Easy there, we need her alive." With his hand still on mine, he drags the tip farther around the side of her neck. Gently, without hurry. Like we have all the time in the world. I look up at him and he gives me a nod. I take it as my cue to continue the psychological part of the interrogation.

"When was the last time you saw Mickey?" I ask, as our

connected hands continue to trail along the nape of her neck. Gabriel moves the blade down to her collarbone. "I'll ask you one more time. When was the last time you saw Mickey?" When she doesn't respond, Gabriel gives our hands a subtle jerk. "Oh, fuck." I gasp as blood spills down her neck. The lady's jaw clenches to fight back the deep groan. It's just a surface scratch, but damn, that had to hurt.

My hand begins to tremble, but Gabriel tightens his grip. He nods again, instructing me to continue. "When was the last time you saw your kids?"

"You leave my kids out of this!" she snaps. "You go anywhere near my kids, I'll kill you both. Not that I don't plan to already." Gabriel jerks my hand again, and this time, she cries out. "You fucking son of a bitches. You will pay for this!" More blood rolls like dripping water, drenching the top of her baby blue sweater.

"What if I told you that I already know where your kids are?" I lie. Her body tenses up, and I feel like I hit a nerve. "In fact, what if I told you that I'll be questioning them next if you don't tell me where Mickey is? Maybe I'll bring out the wood burner and engrave Mickey's initials on their foreheads so they never forget what I wanted. And I'll also tell them that it's your fault. You wouldn't talk, so I had to move on to them. And you let me."

Dragging the knife slowly down her chest, the tip presses against it, leaving a trail of blood. Gabriel reaches over and grabs something with his free hand then hands it to me. "What's this?" I ask him as I take the cardboard tube. "Salt?"

He smirks. "I think you know what to do with that."

I peel back the metal tab on the top and hover the salt container over her, letting a little at a time fall onto her open wounds. "Stop!" she cries out. "Just stop!"

"You ready to give up that location?" I ask her for the last time.

When she doesn't answer, I dump a hefty amount onto the gash on her collarbone.

"Ok, ok. Please, just stop." She tucks her chin to her chest. "He's on an island off the coast of Italy. Elba, I think it's called. Please, whatever you do, don't hurt him. Our children need him."

*"Your* children? Mickey is your husband?" I ask her as I set the knife down on the table. Gabriel hurries to my side, bending down and picking up the cloth from the floor and wrapping it back around her mouth.

"No more questions." He shakes his head at me then nods toward the door. "Come on."

I follow behind him and we walk out of the room. Gabriel closes the door with a satisfied smile on his face. "You fucking did it. And damn, that was sexy as hell."

Ignoring his excitement, I dig for answers. "Who is she? Who is this Mickey guy?"

"That lady and her husband are employed by Vincent Maretti. The kids she mentioned? Also employed by him."

My eyes pop open. "Seriously? But, why? Why are you after this family, too?" It can't be a coincidence. Do the Blacks have a hit on the Maretti family?

Gabriel's shoulders shrug. "I'm not after Maretti. It just so happens that a hit was put out on Mickey a couple weeks ago. I took the job and lucky for you, you get to reap the benefits. You have new information, use it."

"What now?" I ask. "Do I go to Elba and hope that I can find this guy?"

"No. You don't go anywhere. This job is mine. But if Barton is in Elba, it means he's hiding. What he doesn't know is that he's been found."

"And this helps me how?"

"It doesn't. I didn't bring you here to help you find the guys you're looking for. I brought you here to teach you that looks can be deceiving. You wanted to save that woman. I saw that look in your eyes. You felt bad for her. What you didn't know is that she's conspired for years with her husband to take down entire families. You also got the information we came for. The information that *I* needed. The way you bashed her with that hammer...you've got guts, girl. I'll give you that." He turns to walk away, but there's not a chance I'm letting him walk away with all these questions swimming in my head.

"Wait a damn minute." I grab him by the arm. "That woman sitting in there works for the man who killed my father and you're telling me this doesn't help me?"

"I came here for information to help me with *my* job. You asked me to teach you what I know, that's what I'm doing."

I point over his shoulder at the closed door. "But she could have answers I need and she's right fucking there."

"She might. What do you plan to do about it?"

## Eleven

After shoving past Gabriel, I don't even hesitate to charge back in the room. Her head is hung low and I'm pretty sure she was sleeping. But the slamming of the door startles her awake. I stand there with a blank stare for what feels like minutes as I try to throw together a plan of action in my head, but I come up empty-handed. Looks like I'm winging it.

Inhaling a deep breath, I walk back over to her. Twenty minutes ago, this was for Gabriel. This time, it's for my father. Getting a good grip on the hair on the back of her head, I jerk her head and tear the cloth off of her mouth. "What do you know about Vincent Maretti?" Her pupils dilate and tears well in the corners of her eyes.

"I told you where Mickey is. If you know what's good for you, you'll let me go."

"I don't give a damn about your husband. I want Maretti. Where the hell is he?"

When she doesn't respond, I tug harder. So hard that strands of her hair tangle in my fingers. I need her to tell me. She has to. This could be exactly what I need.

"You're wasting your time," she mutters. Her voice is frail, and I can tell she's getting weak. "You can do whatever you want to me, but I have no clue where Maretti is. No one knows. He doesn't divulge that information unless absolutely necessary."

I shouldn't believe her, but I do. It makes sense that he wouldn't make his whereabouts known. "Fine." Releasing my grip on her hair, I pull out the phone Gabriel gave me from my back pocket and open the voice recording app then drop my phone onto the tray. "I want the names of everyone you know that works for him."

Circling around her, I slouch down so that we're eye level. "From one woman to another, I need the names, please."

Her eyes narrow and the next thing I know, spit is flying in my face. "Fuck you, bitch," she snaps. As if her mind did a complete one-eighty. When I was in here earlier, she was at my mercy, now all of a sudden, she's putting up a fight. Hell no. I've been told to prove myself. I'm planning on doing just that. Wiping my arm across my face, I clean up the spit then stand up and grab the metal zippo and give it a flick until the flame stills. "Give me a name."

Laughter erupts. "You're messing with the wrong woman, Sunshine."

Bringing the flame closer to her, I watch as the crimson orange touches the hair on her arm.

"Ahhhhh!" She screams as it touches her skin. I should stop. But I don't.

*Prove it. Don't claim it.*

There will never be peace in my soul until I end Vincent Maretti. If I don't, he will claim me—his pearl.

The smell of her burning flesh turns my stomach and I begin to feel lightheaded. I shout, "I don't wanna do this. Tell me the names, damnit!"

Still nothing.

Stretching back my arm, I swing my hand around and slap her across the face. Her head jerks to the side, but instead of giving me the reaction I wanted, she laughs. A deep sadistic laugh. Any empathy I felt for her walking in here is gone. She's evil. Pure evil.

The first day I showed up at the Black house, Gabriel was hard at work. The man he had in that chair was a mess, but Gabriel must have gotten what he wanted because, eventually, the man was gone. Remembering what he did to that man made my skin crawl, but now it has me wondering if I have it in me. Gabriel seems to think I do. He thinks I have guts.

Reaching for her hand, I notice that I'm no longer shaking. It's possible my body is already prepared for what my mind knows is coming. "Last chance for a name if you want that pretty wedding band to stay on your finger."

"Screw you," she grumbles.

My fingers wrap around her ring finger and I take a deep breath before I snap it back. The sound of her bone cracking stirs my stomach and my mouth begins filling with saliva. *Hold it together, Iris.*

"Fuuuuuuck!" she screams at the top of her lungs. Cries and shrieks continue as her knotted wrists fight to free themselves. "You fucking cunt. You're as good as dead."

Ignoring her threats, I grab another finger. "I might not have experience at this, but my family is gone. I have no one. I have absolutely nothing to lose. Your pain will be my victory." I grind my teeth so hard that my jaw pops. "Now, give me the fucking names!"

When her eyes shut, my faith in this process begins to diminish, but I'm not giving up. I'm so close to getting some valuable information. I bend back her middle finger and, this time, the break isn't what gets me, it's the fragments of bone that poke through her skin and the blood that pools in the palm of my hand.

"Ahhhh," she screams again. And this time, she doesn't stop. It's deafening and I'm starting to think that her body might go into shock and she'll be useless to me.

I look back at the door and see Gabriel watching through the small square glass panel. I shrug my shoulders, unsure of what to do next. Then the door swings open. He steps inside, and with hope in his eyes, he urges me on. "Don't give up."

That's all. That's his advice? But she looks like she's on the verge of passing out. I look from her to him, then back to her. I've come this far. Might as well give it all I've got. If I plan to take down an entire army of men, I have to toughen up. I have to do this.

Grabbing her untouched hand, I tangle our fingers together. Each of mine pressed between each of hers. "Remember how I said I have nothing to lose? Well, neither of us are leaving here until you give me some goddamn names. Now start talking."

When she remains silent, as I suspected she would, I pinch my eyes shut then curl my fingers, squeezing her hand in mine, and press back swiftly with intense pressure as her wrist cracks. I don't even open my eyes as she cries out in pain. I can't look. Instead, I drop her hand and step behind her with my eyes on Gabriel's, refraining from looking at what I just did.

He looks stunned, like he didn't expect me to go that far. Was it too far? Oh no. I throw my hands up in a way of asking him why he's looking at me like that, but he smiles. "Damn, girl. Do that shit again."

Drawing in a deep breath, I circle back around her then take her other hand in mine in the same position. "Last chance. After this one's done, we'll move on to ankles." It's a lie really, I don't think I could break her ankle with my bare hands, but then again, I never thought I'd be snapping wrists and cracking fingers either. "Names. Now."

When the room grows completely quiet, I squeeze and

begin pushing back. "Wait," she stops me. "I'll give you some names, but I'm telling you, you will pay for this, you fucking bitch. I will Make. You. Pay."

Pressing harder, I challenge her as her veins begin to bulge out of her wrist. "Donny." She speaks slowly, but continues, "Donny Wright. Victor Marazzi. Find them, and you'll find Vincent." I release her hand. Picking up my phone, I end the recording.

Then I leave.

Gabriel is waiting for me at the door with a wide, wicked grin on his face. "Holy fucking shit. That was the hottest thing I've ever seen." He grabs me by the waist and hoists me up against the wall. My legs wrap around him and I press my lips together, fighting back the smile that's creeping up. I did do good. And Gabriel seems pleased with my first lesson. "My turn, Princess."

"Your turn?" I question.

"You got your lesson. Now I get mine."

"Here?"

"Right here. Right now." He drops his hold around my waist and my feet catch my fall.

There is no sense in even trying to postpone this. I'm so turned on right on. I never wanna leave this high I'm on. It's time to find out if Gabriel has the ability to take me higher. "I know just the thing to start with." I tear my dress off and bend over to straighten it up on the ground, then lie down on top of it. The cement is cold against my back, but it doesn't faze me. "Take my pants off," I tell him.

He unbuttons the top and I can tell he's nervous by the shake in his hands. When he frees my legs, he tosses the pants over his shoulder. "Panties next." He takes an audible breath before he slides them off. His eyes stay glued to the bare skin of my pussy and I'm almost positive, he's never seen one before, outside of porn. "Touch me."

His eyes slide up my body and find mine, like he's searching for reassurance that this is ok. "Just touch it. It's not hard." I take his fingers and begin rubbing them against my clit. With his free hand, he wipes the sweat off his forehead then rolls his tongue ring between his teeth. When I pull my hand back, he keeps up the movements. Circling his fingers at my entrance with his rough and calloused hands. "Take control, Gabriel. Do whatever you want. Don't be scared. There's really no way to screw this up."

There's a beat of hesitation before he plunges his fingers inside me and lets out a raspy moan. "You ever touched a girl like this before?" I already know the answer, but I ask it anyway.

His hooded eyes stare back at me and his head shakes. With my bra still on, I slide my hands underneath it and cup my breasts. "Have you ever touched these before?" I tug my bottom lip between my teeth and arch my back and his fingers slide in and out of me slowly. He shakes his head again. Oh, this poor boy. He's been so damn sheltered. I get to be his first everything.

"Faster," I tell him. All of sudden, his fingers dig so deep inside of me that I can feel them hit my back wall. "Pump them inside of me." He does, and holy shit, it feels so damn good. My hips buck up. "Taste me," I tell him as I close my eyes and continue to massage my breasts.

The lady in the room begins yelling, and he begins thrusting his fingers inside of me faster, only intensifying the pleasure. Gabriel drops his knees and stretches his legs out behind him as he gets on his stomach. His tongue darts out and he flicks his piercing against my clit.

Is he playing me? Because he's better at this than half the men I've been with. I place my hands on his head and tangle my fingers in his hair, forcing his face into me, and begin rolling my hips to the movements of his touch.

"Fuck, Gabriel," I cry out as my entire body floods with an intense sensation. Every noise around me and the discomfort of lying on a cold damp floor escapes my mind. It goes pitch black as I reach my climax. His tongue sweeps up the length of my pussy as evidence of my orgasm spills onto his fingers, but he doesn't stop. He keeps going until I tug at his arm and pull him into me. His clothed body lies over my naked one as I grab him by the side of his head and force his mouth to mine, tasting every bit of what he just did to me. His tongue seduces mine and he lets out a moan. "You did really fucking good," I mutter into his mouth.

Then I push him off me as quickly as he came down. "Next time, we'll work on that." I point to his crotch where his jizz seeps through his pants. "We need to get that under control."

He jumps up quickly to try and hide his embarrassment. "Don't be embarrassed. After some time, you'll build control over that reflex."

"Fuck you," he hisses.

"What? I wasn't being rude. I'm just saying." He begins to walk away so I gather up my clothes quickly. "Would you stop walking away from me all the damn time. I'm being serious. You want my help, then you have to let your guard down, Gabriel," I shout as his feet keep moving. I tug my pants up and keep walking while I pull my shirt on.

All of a sudden, the guy from earlier with the huge biceps steps out from around a corner. "Take care of her," Gabriel tells the guy as he pushes the door open and steps outside. I know he's talking about Mickey Barton's wife, but just to be safe, I pick up my pace, following behind him. That other dude gives me the creeps.

*Taking care of her* can only mean one thing, he's either going to kill her or lock her up. I convince myself of the latter for my own sanity. She might be a bad woman who does bad things, but I can't stand the thought of another dead body showing up today.

Gabriel came here and got what he wanted, and in return, I got what I needed. It's time to start digging and find out everything I can about the names she gave me.

"Hey, what if she's lying?" I holler when he pulls open the car door.

"Get in." He gestures toward the car. "If she's lying, we do this all over again."

"But you told that man to take care of her. Is he killing her?"

Once he's in and the door is shut, he answers my question. "No, we'll keep her until the job is done. Then, we'll take care of her for good."

"Can I ask you a question?"

"No."

He should have known I'd ask anyway. "Who put out the hit on Mickey Barton?"

Gabriel glances over at me and something washes over his expression, bringing some sort of empathy to his face. Like I struck a nerve, perhaps.

"Gabriel?"

He turns his head, looks out the window and speaks, "Your father. Damon Pavetta."

## Twelve

"Did my dad say why he put a hit on Barton?" I ask while curled up in a ball on one of the chairs in Silas's office. He's staring vacantly at his computer in front of him. He does a lot of office work for a hitman.

"You know I don't ask those questions," he answers, without tearing his eyes away from the screen.

"You're no help," I mutter.

When Gabriel and I got back from torturing that woman, he left almost immediately for Italy to track down Mickey Barton, taking Baron with him. That leaves me and Mr. Cold and Broody alone for three days. He's making me sit here in his office and do all of the boring research I can on the names that lady gave me.

"It doesn't matter *why* he hired the hit, Iris. Don't focus on that. You have the names you need."

"It matters to me," I argue. My father never hired hits. I heard him say it so many times. If he wanted a job done, he did it himself.

"You're letting your emotions control you. Being upset won't help you kill Maretti."

"But this ties my dad to Maretti before the day he died. If he wanted one of Maretti's guys dead, there had to be a reason."

He stares at me blankly, and I know he's right. I know it doesn't matter, but it doesn't change the fact that I want to know—no, I need to know.

Pulling out my journal and pen, I open up to the page that has my scattered notes, none of it making any sense.

*Dad hired extra security before he died. Never let me leave the house.*

*Hired Silas to kill Mickey Barton. Why?*

*Donny Wright. Victor Marazzi.*

After a few hours of some seriously questionable methods of internet research, that I know would make some people very uncomfortable, the only thing I've discovered about the names she gave me are they both have criminal records, have done time in prison, and are both prone to visiting a sketchy corner in the city for "company." It was far too easy to acquire video footage and records that definitely are not meant to be public. I'm really not quite sure how this information helps me, and Silas is being even more quiet than usual.

"So you're still doing the job on Barton, even though my dad is...dead?" It's hard to even say it out loud. It still doesn't feel real.

"His bookie has secured the rest of the money owed to us." Finally, he looks up at me, something in his harsh features softening. "Plus, it's integrity, Iris."

There's a buzz of warmth in my belly as Silas looks at me across the desk in this dim office. "I doubt Gabriel and Baron would think of it that way."

"I raised them to put their emotions aside, not to abandon integrity. Don't you believe we can still be good men?" There's a gentle lift to the corners of his mouth and a crease in his brow. The warm buzz grows into something like attraction.

"Good men? Exactly how many people have you killed?"

"Lost count," he says, but I can see the lie in his expression.

He watches me for a moment, and I'm finding it hard to tear my eyes away from him. "I'm bored. Can we do something else?"

"What else would you like to do, Iris?"

"I don't know. Don't you ever do anything for fun?"

His eyebrow lifts. "Fun?"

"Yeah, I don't know. Just something to blow off steam?"

He watches me for a moment, and I'm expecting him to say something like 'we don't have fun, only work,' but to my surprise, he stands up and strides toward the door.

"Follow me."

Once again, we're in the garage, and I'm starting to seriously worry that we're about to go on another lame job that ends in me barfing in a trash can, but he doesn't walk toward the car parked in the middle.

Instead, he strides over to the far end of the giant underground garage and just as we pass the Range Rover, my eyes fall upon a sleek black sports car parked in the corner. I don't know much about cars, but I can tell just by looking at it, this car is fast and expensive.

He opens my door for me, and I slide in, feeling about six inches off the ground. The inside is all black, smooth, with low bucket seats and leather interior.

As Silas climbs in on his side, my eyes eat him up. I have a hard time believing any man wouldn't be sexy as fuck in the driver seat of this car, but Silas is next level sexy as he brings it to life. The garage door opens automatically as he revs the engine, the rumble so loud it makes my ears hurt.

Then, he peels out, and my stomach nearly plummets to the floor by my feet.

Now I understand why they live in the country. We speed down the long empty road and I let out a high-pitched laugh as the car hugs the winding road. Each turn and dip make my toes curl and my heart race.

As I look over at Silas with one hand on the wheel and a calm, easy smile on his face, an unexpected arousal pools in my belly. The power and control he exudes draws me to him. I want to crawl into his lap and ride him like a horse, but I also just want to crawl into his arms and let him hold me. And I've never felt that about anyone before—attraction without sex.

In fact, I've never really seen myself *being* with anyone seriously, always just assuming I would end up marrying out of necessity or to someone my father set me up with in more of a business transaction than love.

It suddenly occurs to me I'm free now, free to marry whoever I want and have any future I want—but it doesn't feel very exciting. It's terrifying. I've never been on my own before. I've never held my own future in my hands.

"You okay?" Silas asks as the car slows, and I realize my face must have fallen since I started thinking about my dad and the great unknown of my new future.

I force a smile onto my face. "I'm great."

He's quiet for a moment, looking over at me every few seconds, like he doesn't trust me. Suddenly, he pulls the car over to the side of the road.

"What are you doing?" I ask as he unclips his seat belt and opens his door.

"Your turn," he says like it's so obvious.

"What? Really?" I ask excitedly, jumping out of my seat before he changes his mind.

As I climb into the driver's seat, he gives me a stern look.

"Take it easy on the turns, and try not to wreck my six-million-dollar car."

He rests a hand on the back of my headrest, and I breathe in the scent of his cologne, sending another surge of heat between my legs. I clench my thighs, the rumbling of the motor only making me more aroused.

As I shift the car into drive and lay my foot on the gas pedal, adrenaline courses through my veins from the force. When I look down, we're going over eighty miles per hour, so I push the gas a little harder.

"That a girl," Silas says. When I glance over, his arm is still on the back of my seat; I feel so close to him and almost calm in his presence. He looks proud of me, and I love the way it feels—a strange mix of domineering and sexy at the same time that should probably feel wrong but definitely doesn't. It feels so fucking good.

With every mile we travel, the long country road stretches out before us, I shred every ounce of tension and fear I've felt this week. It's like speeding away from that terrible day when I lost everything, and the power I feel as I grip the steering wheel reminds me I'm a fucking survivor. I made it this far, and even though I need the Blacks' help, I'll be the one to pull the trigger. I'm in control. I won't be afraid of Vincent Maretti.

He should be afraid of me.

Silas's hand lands on my shoulder as I slow the car down in front of the house. "So was that what you had in mind?" he asks. "Did you let off some steam?"

"Fuck yes."

"Good."

He squeezes my shoulder, and I turn to him with a small smile, hoping he doesn't see the blush to my cheeks or pick up on the new way I'm suddenly seeing him.

## Thirteen

Pain tears through my hand as I fight to rip it away from the person holding it. They're bending it in every direction, trying to break it, but the bone refuses to snap. I can't seem to get a good look at his face, but I catch traces of him.

First, it's Vincent Maretti. His voice echoes through the darkness as he calls me his pearl while trying to snap my fingers and slice up my skin with his razor blade hands.

Then, it's Gabriel. And he's between my legs, kissing me while hurting me, my body finding some strange enjoyment in the mix of pain and pleasure.

Then, it's me. And I'm the one holding the finger, twisting, pulling, bending, trying to break it. I don't even know what sort of information I'm trying to find or why I'm doing it, but I'm in a battle with myself. It seems like an endless struggle, the pain increasing until it becomes unbearable. There's a sick enjoyment in the torture, wanting to hurt someone until they want to die, except the person I'm hurting is me—and I don't want to die.

Finally, when I can't take it anymore, I scream.

My eyes pop open, gazing into the darkness of my room. It

takes my mind long minutes to finally settle and accept that no one is hurting me and I'm safely tucked in my bed.

It occurs to me that unlike every other night I've slept here, there is no constant beat of heavy music coming from the room next door and I almost miss it. It was somehow comforting to know Gabriel was there, but now, I just feel alone.

I toss and turn for over an hour, so many questions burying themselves inside my brain.

Who is Maretti?

Why did my dad put a hit on Barton?

How am I going to survive this?

Where am I going to go after Maretti is dead?

Lying there, wrestling with my own anxiety, I think about Silas in the car again, wishing for the comfort I felt in the seat next to him. I can't explain the way I suddenly feel about him, but I like it. It's safety, and not just physical safety. It's the safety of knowing I'm not alone. That he sees me and maybe even...wants me.

This new attraction isn't like the way I feel about Gabriel. Gabriel scares me, but that excites me too, and really fucking turns me on. I never quite know if Gabriel is going to hurt me, but I know that in some sense, I'm in control.

With Silas, I know he's not going to hurt me; he's going to push me, and there's something about that I crave.

Suddenly, wanting to be near him becomes unbearable, and I peel myself out of bed. This is insane, but I don't care. So, I tiptoe silently down the hall, across the main section of the house to where I know Silas's room is. It's dark and quiet, but I gently tap on his door anyway. Sneaking up on an assassin in the middle of the night is probably not the smartest idea I've ever had, but when he doesn't answer, I push his door open slowly.

The familiar scent of his cologne hits me immediately.

Peeking inside, I can barely make out his form on the bed, but I catch the way the moonlight reflects on his bare chest while it slowly rises and falls with each breath. He's on his back, the silk sheets covering his lower half, with one arm resting behind his head.

Somehow I know he won't kick me out. I don't know how I know that, but I do. So I carefully cross the room and pull back the blankets on the empty side of the bed. He doesn't move when I crawl onto the mattress and slide between the sheets.

"What's wrong?" he whispers without moving.

"I couldn't sleep," I answer, resting my head on the pillow.

"Nightmares?"

I swallow the lump in my throat. He already knows. I imagine he probably dealt with nightmares at one point in his life, maybe after his first kill or the first instance of violence he witnessed, and I hope one day, I'm as calm and detached as he is.

Resting my head on the pillow facing him, I stare at the silhouette of his face in the moonlight. "Do you have them too?"

"Used to."

"How long did they take to go away?"

We're still speaking in whispers, even though we're the only ones in the house.

"Once I made peace."

"Peace with what?"

"With everything," he replies.

It's silent for a moment, and I'm trying to decide if Silas looks at me like I'm one of his kids or something else. He's never really touched me or flirted with me, but right now, he's lying half-naked in his bed with me—well, I assume he's only half-naked since I don't know what's going on under the sheets—and I find myself hoping he sees me the way I see him.

"Get some sleep," he whispers, extending his arm out and inviting me to cuddle in closer. I inch my way in and roll until I'm facing away from him. Other than my head on his bicep and my body against his side, he's not really touching me at all.

I wish he would. Instead, his breathing returns to a slow and quiet pace, offering the safety-like comfort I was so desperate to feel. Nestled against him and the scent of his cologne on my nose, I drift off into a dreamless, or rather nightmare-less, sleep.

This time it's not pain that haunts my dreams but the opposite. At first it starts as a subtle warmth blooming at the base of my spine, but it slowly morphs into something almost uncomfortable. I find myself squirming, moving my hips to chase the heat.

"Iris, stop." His deep, sleepy voice is so close to my ear, he's practically in my head. I can tell it's morning now. This time when I wake up, I don't open my eyes, but I peel myself out of the dream to find that I'm still in Silas's arms. His body is curled around mine, his mouth just inches away from my ear.

His hand is on my hip.

And his thick erection is pressed up between the crease of my ass.

I must have been really grinding myself against him in my sleep. Now, I just hold my hips still as he requested, but the ache of arousal is still there. It becomes hard to keep from moving, especially with his hand against my hip.

I'm torn because I don't want to make him mad and have him kick me out. But then again, my body is screaming at me, and I have a feeling his is screaming at him too.

Very subtly, I shift my hips back, causing a little bit of friction against the rock-hard bulge in his boxers. His fingers press into my hip again. This time, he doesn't stop me, and I know he's losing the battle against his will, so I place my hand over his.

"Be careful, little girl," he says, his mouth even closer. It's a warning, but it comes across more as an invitation, and it makes my heart pick up speed, hammering in my chest as I grind my ass against him a little harder this time.

A low, rumbling groan vibrates against my back. Then his hand isn't stopping my movements but urging them on, pulling my hips back, so he can crush his cock against my body. I'm soaking my panties as he does it again and again.

With my hand over his, I pull his fingers down, running them under the hem of my panties and down to the spot I'm so desperate to feel his touch. When he feels the moisture there, it urges him on, and he grinds even harder.

His lips land against my shoulder, placing brutal kisses on my skin. He moves my hair out of the way to trail his mouth up, until he's biting my earlobe while my body writhes and twists against his.

Pulling my knees apart, he drapes my leg over him as he peels my panties to the side and plunges a finger inside me. I let out a gasp, still writhing helplessly against him. He's teasing me, pulling out to coat my folds with my own arousal, only touching my clit to keep me on edge.

"Take them off," I cry, clawing desperately at my own underwear. In one powerful swipe, he tears them down, before I feel him do the same to his.

His mouth is on my neck when I feel the head of his cock at my entrance, and I fidget and shift, desperate to be filled by him. His still wet fingers are on my hip again as he pushes inside, and we both let out a satisfied groan.

With a heavy grunt, he pulls back and thrusts in again.

I'm dangerously close to coming already.

Our bodies grind together in perfect rhythm, and when he laces his fingers with mine, he pulls me even closer, so there isn't an inch of space between us. Then, he moves our linked hands down to my clit and we rub circles over the spot together. With just the sound of our heavy breathing filling the air, I come hard in his arms. My body is locked in pleasure as he holds me tightly, shuddering through waves of euphoria.

Just as I come down, my mind still blank and fuzzy, Silas shifts until he's on top of me. With our bodies still fused, he pulls back until I'm on all fours and he's on his knees behind me. He slams into me again, reaching even deeper, and by some fucking miracle, my body starts revving up again.

Then, I feel the sudden hot pain of his open palm against my ass cheek, and my eyes widen in shock. "I told you to be careful," he grunts as he thrusts in harder.

*He just fucking spanked me.* I'm in disbelief as he does it again and arousal spreads through my veins almost as fast as the pain from his hand.

I'm gripping the silk sheets in my fists when he picks up speed. His thrusts are relentless, my body feels like a string pulled tight, the pleasure a vibration with every touch. It all becomes too much as I come again, letting out a cry. Soon, his body pulses with his own climax.

We both collapse onto the bed.

He doesn't say a word as I lie in his arms, listening to the sound of his erratic heartbeat. It feels like I'm finally waking up and all of that took place in some half-waking dream. I can't bear to look at his face, suddenly terrified that I'll find cold indifference there. I'm not a needy bitch and I can do no-strings-attached sex all day long, but I'd like to think it was more than that with him. I want to be more than a warm body in his bed. Don't ask me why.

"Any more nightmares?" he says, once his breathing has returned to normal.

"No," I reply. I'm still pressed against his chest unable to gaze up at him.

Then for just a moment, I feel his lips against my forehead. "Good."

He shifts to get up and I roll away. I watch as he struts to the bathroom completely naked, admiring his unwavering confidence—and his ass.

"You should get ready. We have a job to go to today."

I immediately perk up. "A real one? The guy won't already be dead this time?"

"Hopefully."

This should *not* excite me. But it does, and I'm hopping out of the bed and running naked to my side of the house to shower and get ready.

As soon as I reach my hallway, I see Gabriel's door and something in me grows cold. I didn't even think about him while I was in Silas's bed. We're not exclusive or anything, but Gabriel is already so volatile.

Strangely, I like being with Gabriel. I love being the one to teach him everything about sex, being the first to show him pleasure, and I like his crazy, fucked-up side too, but I don't really want that fucked-up side angry with me if he finds out it took me less than twenty-four hours to fuck his dad while he was gone.

I've never had one man stick around for long, so I sure as fuck don't know what to do with two of them.

## Fourteen

SILAS DIDN'T MENTION where we're going or what we'll be doing, so I hope I'm not underdressed in a pair of blue jeans and a white cutoff T-shirt. Tying my hair up in a ponytail as I walk down the stairs, I see him standing there waiting for me. He looks striking in a pair of black pants and a dark grey button-up polo. His scent still lingers on me as I make my way down to him. His eyes focused on the skin of my stomach I've put on display. With each step, I notice his body tenses more and more. "Everything ok?" I ask, hoping that he's not having regrets about what just happened between us.

His eyes slide up to mine. "What the hell are you wearing?"

I look down at my clothes and tug my shirt a little, pulling it below my belly button. "Is this ok? I wasn't sure—"

"Go put on a longer shirt, Iris. We don't need the attention of the whole damn town. One look at you in that shirt and boys will be swarming outside."

Biting back a smile, I turn and walk back up the stairs. Fully aware he's watching my ass. I turn around and look over my shoulder, and sure enough, his eyes are plastered to it.

Something about getting his attention makes my insides sizzle. Even more so is the fact that he doesn't want me getting the attention of other men.

Pulling open the closet, I settle on just a lightweight zip-up hoodie. I don't really have anything casual that Silas would consider appropriate. I suppose it's a good thing I don't leave the house often. He might have to give up his credit card again and let me buy another new wardrobe.

When I walk back downstairs, I toss my hands out and give him a look that seeks his approval. "It'll do. Let's go." He walks up two steps and extends his hand to me. I take it in mine and I wonder if it feels like he's holding a child's hand. He can't possibly look at me that way—not now—not after what we just did.

He picks up his pace and I stumble over my feet, almost falling. "Do you plan on telling me where you're taking me?"

"I told you. We have work to do." Instead of leading me to the front door, as Gabriel did the last couple of times I've left the house with him, we go to the garage again.

"Does Gabriel ever drive?" I ask, curiosity getting the best of me.

"Why do you ask?"

"No reason. It's just that any time we leave together, he has a driver."

"Gabriel is good at his job, but he's a lazy shit. He prefers to let other people do the mundane work."

"I guess if you have the money for it, why not?" I can see the reasoning behind it. I'd rather let the hired help do the jobs they're hired for. Then again, I've been given the title 'spoiled brat,' so what do I know?

"Money is just a tool. It does not replace independence. Gabriel is young. He still has a lot to learn." He grabs the handle on the passenger side of the Range Rover, but looks at me before opening it.

"What?" I question. "Are you implying that I'm also young and have a lot to learn?" I don't like where this is going. I might only be eighteen years old, but I am wise beyond my years. I've done and seen more than most girls my age. For some reason, the idea of him calling me out for my youth after fucking me thirty minute ago, pisses me off.

"Well—aren't you?"

Crossing my arms over my chest, I snarl, "Did I feel young? Was I too tight for you?"

"There's no reason to get offensive." He pulls the door open and nods for me to get in, but I don't. I stand there glaring at him, searching for some sort of reaction that tells me he has no regrets. "The fact is, you are young. We never stop learning, Iris. Even at my age. In fact, you've taught me a rule that it seems I've forgotten."

"Oh yeah, what's that?"

"Not to mix business with pleasure. Now, get in the damn car."

After a bout of huffing and puffing, I give in, but the scowl doesn't leave my face, even when he climbs in the driver's side and leans over the center console. His warm breath hits my cheek and his cologne intoxicates me once again. Flutters ripple through my belly when he tucks a stray strand of hair behind my ear. "You also reminded me why I break the rules."

The corners of my lips lift when he retreats. I have no idea what this feeling is, but I sure as hell want it to stay. It's different from Gabriel, or even the guards back home that I fooled around with. Silas is a man. A real man, who knows what he wants and doesn't put up with bullshit. Gabriel has the ability to send butterflies coursing through my stomach, but Silas has unleashed them in my heart. Even just watching him with that domineering look on his face as he drives. One hand on the steering wheel and the other placed gently on his lap. It's taking everything in me not to climb over there and show him that, while I might be young, I can teach him a thing or two.

We pull up to the backside of a business and Silas kills the engine. "Where are we?"

"Doesn't matter where we are. What matters is where our target is."

I look around outside but see no one. There are a few other cars parked back here, and I assume they are just employees. "Ok. Where is the target?" I look back and my heart jumps into my throat when I see Silas loading a pistol. He cocks it and watches me out of the corner of his eye as he sticks it in a holster beneath his shirt. "You don't have to do this, Iris. If it's too much, just tell me. Revenge isn't always sweet. Sometimes it's bitter and leaves a nasty taste in your mouth that will haunt you for the rest of your life."

"No," I blurt out with no hesitation, "I want this. I need this. I'll live with the repercussions, but at least I'll be able to live. If Vincent Maretti is alive, I'll end up his prisoner sooner or later. I'll be forced to hide forever. That's no life for someone who is young and still has a lot to learn." I flash him a smile and my words warrant me some in return.

"That's my girl."

And just like that, he finds a way to make me feel like a giddy teenager again. I can feel my cheeks flush and my heart skip a beat. *His girl.* I know it's just a saying, but hell if I don't like the sound of it. Suddenly, any worries or fears dissipate. Silas will protect me, and not only because he has to. But also because I'm pretty sure he wants to.

His door opens and I follow suit by getting out. There's a slight chill to the October air, and I'm glad Silas talked me into a sweatshirt. Silas pulls on a black leather jacket, and I feel like I need a minute to talk my hormones down.

"When we go in here, you act casual. Until we get upstairs, we're just two customers looking at the inventory."

I nod in agreement and follow at his side. We walk through the back door of the building and the smell of burning sage hits me immediately. The store offers a very hippyish vibe. All the colors of the rainbow paint the walls behind carved wooden artifacts. There's a glass case to the right that holds different sculptures. When I get a closer look, I realize they're bongs. A man with blacked-out round glasses is standing at the counter looking in our direction. Long corn-rows cascade down his back and his smile spreads the length of his face. He looks in our direction, but doesn't even acknowl-edge us.

Silas gives the gentleman a nod and takes me by the hand, leading me to a room in the back. My eyes dance around and I want to chuckle, but it would be too much of a reminder to Silas that I am, in fact, a teenager. We're standing in the middle of a sex toy shop, connected to a paraphernalia store, and this is supposed to be my lesson. "Silas? Ummm."

"Shh," he whispers as he leads me up a staircase. Reaching into the inside pocket of his jacket, he pulls out a pair of black leather gloves and hands them to me. "Put these on," he keeps the same quiet tone, before taking out another pair and sliding them on himself.

My fingers feel slippery inside of them because sweat is dripping from my palms. I have no idea what I'm about to walk into, but I'm pretty sure it's not a flower shop. Then again, it wouldn't surprise me after this trip.

With feather-like steps, I walk up the stairs behind Silas. He gives me a look, searching for reassurance that I'm okay with whatever is about to happen. I mouth the word, "Go." My heart is plummeting in my chest and I swear the beats are visible through the three layers of fabric.

Silas turns the handle of the door and it opens effortlessly. Before I can even think, we're inside and he's walking over to the couch where a man is lying asleep on his back. One hand is draped over his head and his mustache is covered in the same white residue that's sprawled out all over the glass coffee table. The next thing I know, Silas is pulling out the gun from his holster and pointing it at the man's head. I pinch my eyes shut, but he nudges me, forcing me to open them. Without a word, he pulls the trigger and in slow motion, I watch as the bullet meets the man's forehead. The sound is muffled by the silencer. And I flashback to the shootout at home. The man doesn't even move. Not a shake. Not a whimper. Blood spills out from the hole in his head, running down the side onto the stained floral couch. My stomach turns and I swallow down the spit pooling in my mouth.

I feel faint. I'm sure I'm as white as a ghost. Everything begins to fade to black, but something grabs a hold of me before I hit the ground. Or someone, rather. Silas sweeps me up in his arms and carries me out of the room in a hurry. Cradling me like a baby as he jogs down the staircase. Once we reach the bottom, he sets me on my feet. "Eat this." He hands me a mint. I don't even ask him why. I just take it from his hand, unwrap it and pop it in my mouth. "This job isn't for the weak. But it's normal to get a little off balance in times like this. Even I need the boost of sugar after a job sometimes. Keep that in mind. Always bring something to stop you from passing out after a job. Time is of the essence. You pass out, you're as good as dead."

"Thank you." I hold up the clear wrapper as I suck in the sweetness of the mint. Suddenly, I'm feeling better. Not great, but I'm pretty sure I can walk out of here. So many questions swarm through my mind as we make our exit, but I hold back until we're both inside the vehicle.

"Who was that man?" I ask, first.

Silas pulls the gun back out and empties it before sticking it underneath his seat. "No idea."

"You killed him and you don't even know who he is?"

"That's the beauty of this job. In most cases, there's no connection. I was hired by the owner to kill his tenant who stole thousands of dollars' worth of inventory from him. I don't ask questions. As long as I'm sure it's not a setup, I do my job and collect my pay."

"Why would anyone steal dildos and bongs that amount to thousands of dollars?"

"He didn't steal his store inventory. He stole drugs."

Ahh. That makes more sense. "And how do you know it's not a setup?"

"Research. Always do your research."

Research. Of course. "Hey, can we drive by somewhere on the way home?" During my own research, I came across an address, I need to see what this place is all about.

"Where do you want to go?"

"The corner of Lithium Blvd and Hanson Ave."

His head jerks to the side. "What the hell do you want from that part of the city?"

"The guys I'm looking into are known to be in that area."

"I'll take you, but you need to make me a promise, Iris." His expression grows stern and his tone demanding. I don't agree, but he continues anyway. "Do not ever go there alone. You got it? A girl like you has no business being in that part of the city alone."

"But I'm learning from you and Gabriel. One day soon, I'll be able to handle this. Isn't that why you're teaching me?"

"I'm teaching you right now that if you go to Lithium Blvd alone, bad things will happen. You need to promise me, Iris. Or I'll turn around right now."

"Ok. Geez, I promise," I say the words, but I'm not sure that I mean them. I'm glad that Silas is concerned for my safety, but this revenge is mine, and it's going to be as sweet as this mint I'm sucking on.

Silas stretches his arm over. His hand drops on my leg and I look down where his fingers caress my thigh through the fabric of my jeans. When I look over at him, I catch him watching me. "You did good today."

Warmth radiates through me with his words. But it's his touch that is setting my soul on fire. If I keep this up, I'll be my own demise.

*Fifteen*

WE PARK outside a motel with a view of the corner where I know Donny Wright and Victor Marazzi frequent. It's not even lunchtime, so I know it's quieter than usual. There's a bus stop on one side of the intersection and a sketchy looking gas station on the other side. Right now, there are just panhandlers standing on the corner and a couple girls sitting at the bus stop, but something about the way they're dressed tells me they're not waiting for the bus.

I notice the hourly rate on the motel sign and ideas begin to brew in my head. It would be too easy to lure one of the guys here. They'd be so vulnerable in one of these rooms, on one of the beds. It wouldn't even be that hard to get them tied up if I played my cards right. Of course, I can't tell Silas this after I just promised him I'd never come alone.

My whole life has been one man after another, locking me up, keeping me safe, and never letting me do anything on my own. I want to tell Silas this, make him understand that I need an ounce of freedom now, but at the same time, I do love seeing this protective side. I like the idea that I might be his

*Gabriel.*

The brothers should be home soon, and I still haven't quite decided how I'm going to handle this with Gabriel...if it even needs handling at all. Will he just brush it off or will he freak out? And does Silas even care? I'm pretty sure he assumed that Gabriel and I have messed around already, and he hasn't said anything.

I'm lost in thought when a vaguely familiar face comes into view across the street. Silas is staring down at his phone when I spot Donny Wright get out of his car at the gas station and lean against the closed door. He lights a cigarette and just waits. He gazes every few moments over at the girls at the bus stop until one of them finally notices him.

I watch as she crosses the street to talk to him. He smiles at her, a creepy, wicked grin as she pushes out a hip and forces herself to flirt with him. Donny is the younger of the two guys I had to research, but he looks more vile than the other. It's not just the greasy black hair and pockmarked face that make the thought of touching him so gross; it's the evil in his eyes. I have firsthand knowledge of his criminal record, and I know it was more than violence that got him locked up, but his taste for young girls—too young.

I'm already looking forward to the opportunity to hurt him and not just for information.

He crosses to the motel, toward us, with the woman. Suddenly I realize I can't let him see my face since he would probably recognize me, so I turn toward Silas as they approach. Just for good measure, I grab Silas's face and pull it toward mine, kissing him deeply and hiding myself against him.

He doesn't seem to suspect anything and gladly kisses me back, his hands roaming down to my hip. Digging his thumb under the hem of my jeans, he pulls me closer. I almost get lost in the kiss for a moment, savoring the smell of his cologne in my nose and the feel of his facial hair against my lips.

When we pull ourselves apart, Donny and the prostitute are gone. They disappeared into the motel, and I decide not to tell Silas I saw him. I have ideas brewing that he wouldn't approve of. Ways of getting to Donny Wright without getting Silas, Gabriel—or even Baron— involved.

"Let's go home," I whisper, still half on his lap, and that's enough to have him throwing the car into drive, pulling away from the curb in a rush.

Looking over at him on the drive home, at the pure power and sex appeal behind the wheel, I feel myself getting too attached when I don't want to. When all of this is over, I'm leaving the Blacks' house. I have my whole future ahead of me, and I won't have to be afraid anymore, but already, I feel them pulling me in and calling their house home.

He keeps a hand on my leg while we drive, and I have a hard time not writhing in my seat. I'm so hungry for his touch. I can already see the hard bulge growing in his pants, and the thrill of anticipation hits me like lightning in my gut.

When we pull into the garage, Silas puts the car into park and grabs my face, pulling me in for a ravenous kiss. We pant and moan against each other's mouths like we're both about to combust. He tears my jacket off my shoulders and skates his hands up my crop top to grab roughly at my tits. I let out a moan as he pulls one to his mouth, biting the pink bud between his teeth.

I'm clawing helplessly at his clothes, but it's futile. There is no room in this car to do anything, but I do get a handful of his erection through his pants, and just the sound of his deep growl as I squeeze it makes my toes curl.

"Get out," he commands, and I react instantly, turning to climb out of the car. We meet at the back of the car, and he shoves me against the trunk as our mouths collide again.

Kissing Silas is like loading bullets into a pistol. The damage hasn't been done, but I still feel the power under my fingertips. It could kill me, but if it does, it will be worth it.

We fumble with the buttons of each other's pants, and he's quicker than me, yanking my jeans down to my ankles, and I climb out of them in a rush. He hoists me up until I'm sitting on the back end of the car, and he's kissing me again as he places himself between my legs. My mind can barely catch up to itself when his hot, thick head pushes eagerly at my entrance.

In one quick thrust, he's inside me, and I let out a scream, falling back on my elbows. His movements are short and forceful, fucking me fast and hard. Distantly, I notice that the garage is slowly being filled with light. I'm too distracted by the ecstasy between my legs to hear the engine rumbling into the garage.

"I want to feel you come on my cock," Silas says through gritted teeth. He's holding my thighs in his hands as he slams into me, and I'm escalating quickly toward my climax. Pushing myself toward the edge, I rub at my own clit, ignoring the fact that there are voices nearby.

Silas consumes me. My eyes, when I can keep them open, are on him, so there is only Silas.

And if there is anyone else in the garage, I assume it's security guards or someone inconsequential. Let them look. A little exhibitionism never bothered me, and maybe it's the idea that men are watching me get railed on this sleek, black car that finally sends me flying over the edge. I let out a cry as pleasure wracks through my body and I notice Silas shuddering the same way.

Collapsing onto the back of the car, I gaze up at the retreating form of Baron as he mutters something while walking through the door to the house. Then, my eyes fly open. *Baron.*

If Baron is back from Italy so quickly, then so is—

Gabriel is standing near his car, flipping a small knife through his fingers. His murderous stare is laser focused on me as he licks his lips. Silas zips himself up and helps me into my pants with absolutely no urgency, like fucking an eighteen-year-old in front of his son is the most normal thing in the world.

"How was the job?" he asks Gabriel with far too much calmness.

Gabriel glares at him now, shrugging, and I can't take my eyes off the knife in his hand.

"We had a great weekend," he mutters coldly. "It looks like you did too."

Without another word, he turns and heads toward the house, leaving all of his anger behind and me suddenly fearing for my life. Yeah, I'm so fucked.

## Sixteen

SILAS PLACES a chaste kiss on my cheek before gesturing toward the door. "I should probably find out how the trip went."

I give him a nod, then watch him walk away. My heart sinks deep into the pit of my stomach for reasons I can't comprehend. Since when do I care that I was busted screwing around with someone I shouldn't? The housekeeper once walked in when I was bent over the washing machine with the lawn boy's dick inside me. I didn't even bat an eye. She sure as hell did. She gasped, then clapped her hand to her mouth so hard that it left fingerprints on her frail wrinkled cheek for the rest of the day.

There is no way I'm growing feelings for Gabriel. That would be absurd. The guy is obnoxiously gorgeous, but he's also just plain obnoxious. He always has a sour look on his face. His clothes are usually stained in blood and he doesn't even care. His dark hair is greasy and his eyes always narrow on me like I'm some sort of toy that he wants to play with. Besides, he's a fucking virgin. Maybe that's part of the appeal. He needs me—but I also need him.

Pushing myself off of the car, I adjust my shirt and go inside to get cleaned up in the first-floor bathroom. My nerves are at an all-time high, and I fear Gabriel will be waiting for me when I go into my bedroom. Pressing my palms to the vanity, I stare back at my reflection. *What the fuck are you doing?* And better yet, why does Silas have to be so damn satisfying? He's left me with an insatiable need to get tangled in his arms and let him take on all the burdens in my heart—in my mind. He's the comfort that I need. And Gabriel—he's the challenge I've always craved.

Then there is Baron. He's so mysterious and silent, I don't think I'll ever muster up the courage to ask for his help. I'm not even sure that he'd offer it if I asked.

Once I'm finished, I crack the bathroom door and look both ways to make sure neither of the two guys I've fooled around with are anywhere in sight.

All worries are wiped away when I hear chatter coming from Silas's office. I breathe a sigh of relief and hurry upstairs to my room. It feels like my feet are moving at a pretty good speed, but when I hear the thudding of another pair behind me, I pick up my pace. Without even looking over my shoulder, I go in my room and close the door. Little good it does, because before I can even latch the lock, it's shoved back open.

Big blue eyes stare back at me. Laced with menace and intent, he pushes me farther into the room and slams the door behind him. "Miss me?" he seethes. I take a step backwards, unsure what he might do. The way his fingers are twitching at his sides, and his back is steeled, lead me to believe he'd do just about anything to me right now. He'd probably get away with it, too. No one would ever know. No one would ever find me.

"Gabriel, I can explain." I take another step back when he comes forward. My calves hit the frame of the bed and I lose my balance, falling back onto the mattress.

Gabriel eats up the space between us and presses his palms to either side of me. His face lingering over mine as his jaw clenches. "Explain what? How you let my father fuck you," his voice rises and it startles me, "in the fucking garage!"

I cower and pinch my eyes shut. "It didn't mean anything," I lie. If I told him that it actually meant everything, that being in Silas's arms feels like home, he'd probably slit my throat and laugh with my blood painting this white comforter.

His head drops forward, his mouth ghosting mine. "Did you like it?" His tongue darts out, sweeping against my upper lip. "Did he feel good inside of you?"

Shaking my head, no, I lie again. It felt like my insides were molded for Silas. His scent is stained in my memory, and his touch engraved in my skin. I liked it, and it felt so damn good. "Gabriel, I—" I'm cut off when his mouth crashes into mine. Harshly, painfully, and pleasurably. Tiny tingles shoot through my body and my legs part instinctively when his hard cock grinds into me. I may be molded for Silas, but Gabriel has every intention of breaking that mold. I feel like a whore because I want to let him try.

"Did he come inside of you?" he mutters into my mouth.

I nod my head. For the first time, giving him some truth. And I don't know why he even asked that. Is he worried I could end up pregnant? Should I tell him I have the implant so I don't need a refill on my birth control?

Lifting his head, his seductive eyes bore into mine. "I'm going to fuck you, Iris. I'm gonna shoot everything I've got inside of you and wash him away. And if he ever touches you again, I'll strap a chastity belt on you, depriving you of ever feeling pleasure again."

While that seems far-fetched, I believe him. Gabriel is intense. He might be inexperienced, but I don't think it's lack of desire, nor ability. He's been sheltered, much like I have. I was a prisoner in my own home and had to make do with what I was given. Gabriel hasn't been given an opportunity to build relationships or experience sex. He's a manipulator—an assassin—who was born and bred that way. He doesn't know how to approach women, obviously. But once he has a taste, I can guarantee that his work will take a back seat to the newfound pleasure I plan on bringing to him.

"Ok," I say, "fuck me, Gabriel." His eyes widen, as if he wasn't expecting the invitation. He wanted me to fight him off. He craves the resistance from me. A natural born savage who prefers a challenge. So a challenge I'll give him. "Later. I need to get cleaned up." I attempt to push him off me, but his body becomes a statue that doesn't budge.

Pushing my shoulders back down on the bed, his hand snakes up my shirt. With no hesitation or trembling in his touch, he takes my left breast in his hand, squeezing with so much pressure that I cringe at the pain. Lucky for him, I like to hurt. It reminds me that I'm alive. And I'm about to show Gabriel there is a euphoria he's been missing out on.

"Not yet. It's not right. I was just with Silas and—"

He slaps a hand over my mouth. "Shut the fuck up." Stretching his other arm down, he begins rustling with his jeans.

I give him what he wants. Shaking my head to try and free his hand while his fingertips press into my jaw. I give him the fight. Although my clit is already pulsating for his touch. I want this. Maybe even more than he does.

Once his pants are down, he takes his hand off my mouth and replaces it with his lips. I can taste the urgency spill into my mouth. With his free hand, he unbuttons my jeans and slides his hand down. Still dampened from my arousal with Silas. Still wet from the dripping of his cum. He shoves two fingers inside of me, and he's not gentle in the least. My body jolts up and my hips rise as he plunges them in and out. I let out a subtle moan then stretch my hand down between us. With two fingers, I begin rubbing my clit aggressively. Gabriel retracts, getting on his knees and watching the motions as he finger fucks me, and I pleasure myself at the same time.

My mind gets foggy and my hips rise and fall as I continue to rub. It feels so damn good. My body is numb and full of life at the same time. My heart begins beating rapidly and I pull my bottom lip between my teeth. Gabriel begins flicking his fingers inside of me, and just when I reach an intense high and I feel like I could float back down, Gabriel pulls his fingers out. "What are you doing?" I whimper, "Don't stop."

He pulls his shirt off and tosses it to the side of the bed then stands up, letting his jeans and boxers fall to the ground. His beautiful naked body stares back at me. Battered and scarred. Like it's been at war, but won the battle. There are a couple tattoos I can't even make out because all I can focus on is his lust-filled eyes staring back at me. I see nervousness, excitement, and an overpowering desire to claim me and fuck Silas right out of my system. While he might not succeed in that aspect, he's most certainly joining Silas's side in my heart. His jealousy fuels me, and his sexual innocence intrigues me.

Climbing back on top of me, his head presses against my entrance. I want to jerk my hips up and take all of him at once, let him finish me off. But he needs his first time to be memorable, so I let him take the lead. He'll probably go slow—savor every moment and lock in the memory. The first time is supposed to be...

Before I can even finish my train of thought, his dick rams inside of me. "Are you going to fuck him again, Iris?" Thrusting in deep, pivotal motions, he fills me up. My walls close around him as I feel my insides beat with a pulse.

When I don't answer, his fingers tangle around my throat. His pelvis slaps against mine. Continuously and rapidly. My back arches and when his grip around my neck strengthens, I nod my head. Giving him another truth. "Yes, I am."

Pulling out of me in an instant, he grabs my waist and flips me over on my stomach. There is no way in hell this is his first time. Either he's playing me, or he's watched a lot of porn. Then again, it might be neither. Gabriel has moxie and that's all you need. This isn't a shy boy who recoils. He's a fucking warrior. He has the scars and wounds to prove it.

Tugging me up by the waist, he sets me on all fours. There is no faltering when his dick reclaims its place inside of me. With my back curled, I drop to my elbows, my forehead pressing against the bed. Gabriel places both hands on my hips and pounds me from behind. There is no controlling my outburst as I cry in pleasure. "Holy shit, Gabriel." I wish I could see his face. I want to watch his eyes as he comes. Let his euphoric state collide with mine.

My entire body tingles and my breathing stills as I clench my walls and come undone around his throbbing cock. After a couple more thrusts, I feel him release inside of me.

My body relaxes, but he doesn't move. Instead, he stays completely still behind me with his dick still inside. I twist my head around to look at him, but he stares straight ahead. As if I'm an enigma. "Gabriel," I say in a hushed tone. "You okay?"

He doesn't respond. He just pulls out, letting the cum inside of me run down my leg. I turn over and watch him as he pulls his shirt back on. "What are you doing?"

Still no response. Though, he doesn't look angry anymore. I see something different this time. He looks hurt.

Jumping up, I meet him at the end of the bed where he stands. My arms wrap around his neck and I pull his mouth to mine, giving him a soft kiss. "What's wrong?"

His eyes skate up to mine, taking my breath away. "Don't fuck him again, Iris. Don't do it."

My heart sinks. But this time, it is an achy and slow slide down. "Gabriel, I—"

His hand finds its place on the small of my back. "Promise me."

My head falls and I stare at the floor between us. He's asking for something I can't give him. I can't promise I'll never sleep with Silas again. Just like I wouldn't be able to give Silas the same promise about Gabriel. "I can't. "

Without another word, he walks away. I don't follow. I don't even move. My heart feels like it's doubled in size today, trying to make room for both of them.

I don't even think about how this probably looks. Screwing Silas and then letting Gabriel give me his virginity. It doesn't matter how it looks; it's how it feels. And it feels right. These two guys are mine, whether they know it or not.

## Seventeen

CAN'T SLEEP ANYMORE. Three nights go by, and I feel like I'm crawling out of my skin. Silas is suddenly too busy at work to give me any more lessons, and Gabriel isn't talking to me. Every time I try to start a conversation with him, he walks away like he doesn't even hear me.

*Manipulative bastard.*

In his defense, the first pussy he ever stuck his dick in was still full of his dad's cum...so there's that.

Then, there's fucking Baron. His never-ending and obvious indifference is infuriating. I almost wish he would be a dick to me. Instead, he doesn't so much as flinch when I walk into a room. I went from being a pest to not existing at all, and I have a feeling the scene he walked in on with Silas has something to do with it.

To keep myself busy, I do more research on Victor and Donny. Well, as far as Silas is concerned, that's what I'm up to. But after about a day of Google searches, I got bored and hatched a plan. A plan that would probably get me killed, very likely by Silas himself.

A plan that requires getting out of this fucking fortress

Which is why I'm standing in the armory, watching Silas clean his gun. For a moment, I'm distracted by how fucking sexy it is watching his nimble fingers clean every inch of black metal. I'm sure they could hire someone to do this for them, but I find it hot as hell that they all prefer to do it themselves.

"I'm busy, Iris."

"I can see that, but I have a question." I'm standing against the door, my hands folded behind my back in a sweet and innocent posture I used to use on my dad when I wanted something from him.

"What is it?" He's a little more distant toward me now. I wonder if he's doing that on purpose, seeing how upset he made his son the other day. Fuck, I hope not.

I saunter over and lean my elbows on the stainless-steel table, pushing my tits together and trying to get his attention. "What if I want to go somewhere by myself?"

"Where do you want to go?" he asks, not looking up from his task.

"I don't know…anywhere. I just mean in general."

This time he glares up at me, and I almost fucking shiver. His dark eyes watching me from under those thick lashes is enough to make a girl forget her own name.

"You're not my prisoner, Iris. But it is my job to protect you, so if you go anywhere, have one of the drivers take you and keep a guard with you at all times. I'd like to know when and where you're going. Understood?"

Biting my lip, I look away from him and casually touch one of the pieces on the table. "Yes, Daddy," I mumble with enough sarcasm and grit that tells him I'm not exactly pleased with that answer.

He snatches away the gun part, and the next thing I know, his fingers are on my chin, lifting my face to his. "Knock it off. I'm being generous, Iris. I could have said no."

My body betrays me and hums in response to his deep

tone and rough grip, so I snatch my face away. Keeping my gaze down on the table because I don't trust myself when Silas is looking at me, I say, "My dad never let me leave the house. I feel like I went from one prison to another."

I watch him out of the corner of my eye as he speaks. "The offer still stands, Iris. We can make you disappear. Then you'll be free."

Free and far from here.

I can't help but glance up to see how he feels about that. There's a clench in his jaw and tension around his eyes. I wonder if that idea upsets him now, unlike it did a week ago. I wonder if I've slipped under his skin since I crawled into his bed.

I know he's slipped under mine.

"Is that what you want?" I almost hate myself for even asking. It's a needy thing, I know that, but I've been deprived of attention for the last few days and I'm down to desperate and shameless begging.

He scrutinizes me for a moment. "I want you to be safe." He says it like he's telling me what he wants for dinner, like there are no emotions involved. Fucking men. And just when I'm about to walk away in defeat, he snatches me by the waist and pulls me against his body. Then I'm on the table, and he's between my legs. "Of course, it has been nice having you around." There's a cruel, playful grin on his face as he leans forward and starts kissing my neck. And just like that, I forget what I came in here for.

Something about getting out of the house...something about...Donny Wright. But then his hands are gliding up my thighs, and I let out a sigh. The car. I need the car.

"Let me have a car then," I say in a breathless gasp, and he finds all the right places to turn me into a puddle.

"You want a car?" His lips are moving to my chest, and

I've been longing for his touch so much this week I don't even care about the fucking car for a moment.

"Yes, please." I squirm against the growing erection pressed against my inner thigh.

"What are you going to do for it?" he asks, yanking my body to the edge of the table. He pulls my low-cut shirt down, stretching out the neckline enough to expose my tits, just before he bites my nipple between his teeth.

I let out a gasp. "Whatever you want."

"And where are you going to go?" He bites a little harder, this time on the flesh, leaving bite marks for sure.

"I— I... don't know."

"Are you going to be a good girl if I give you a car?" He switches to the other breast this time. I'm clutching onto him, ready to come on this table just from the way he's touching me.

"Yes." It'd be a miracle if he bought that.

I open my eyes, hoping he'll take off his pants and finish what he's started. Instead, I let out a yelp as a dark figure in the doorway shocks me out of my arousal. Baron is leaning against the frame with his arms crossed, just watching us and looking bored.

"What the fuck are you doing?" I snap.

Silas pulls away and turns around to see his son standing there. He clears his throat and looks at me with a mischievous glance like we've just been caught. Which I guess we have.

"Dad, there's a client on the phone for you."

"Thanks." His face turns a little dark as he answers his son but softens when he turns back toward me. After giving me a quick kiss, he squeezes my thighs and says, "You can take the car we took to the job the other day. Baron will get you the keys. It has tracking on it, so I'll see everywhere you go." Then, he kisses me again and turns to leave. My knees are still open wide and cold from his absence and Baron's heavy stare. I hold out on closing them though. I want Baron to know he doesn't intimidate me.

"What?" I ask him when he stands there watching me a moment too long.

He doesn't respond, of fucking course.

Standing up, I walk over to him and in true Baron fashion, he keeps his face blank and doesn't react to me at all. So I get as close to him as I can stand. Once I'm against his body, I feel the cool, smooth texture of his fitted black pants against my knee and breathe in the heady scent of his cologne. It's different from Gabriel's. Baron's is potent with more spice and musk.

"What's wrong, Baron? Are you jealous? Feeling a little left out?" I trail a soft touch along the lapel of his black button-up shirt. He has every one of them done, all the way up to his neck. I'd love to unbutton them. I just want to see Baron a little unraveled. His eyes don't leave mine as I flick the top one open.

Suddenly, he snatches my hand in his, squeezing my fingers a little too tight, like he wants me to cry out or beg him to stop, but I don't, so he tightens his grip. "Fuck you," I mutter, willing my eyes not to fill with tears.

He tosses my hand away like it's garbage.

"What is wrong with you? I get that you fucking hate me, but I don't get why. I didn't do shit to you."

His lips purse just enough to make it look like he wants to say something but doesn't.

"Just give me the fucking car keys, please."

I'm so ready to get away from him. His cold eyes on me are making me more uncomfortable than I think I've ever been. Finally, he turns away and stalks down the hallway, and I take a deep breath before following him. It feels like the first breath

I've taken in a while, but the Black men have that effect on me. They seem to steal the breath out of my lungs, and I know that if I'm not careful, it'll choke me to death.

## Eighteen

It's been a few days since Silas gave me access to the car. I know I've been tracked, so covering my tracks has been a pain in the ass, but it's also necessary.

I've been walking around the shopping center for just over an hour, making random purchases to really cover my ass. If I'm going to make sure Silas believes that I've been shopping all day, then I can't come home empty-handed. Besides, there were a few things I specifically needed for today.

Leaving the car, which Silas said was being tracked, at the valet, I quickly order an Uber, still connected to my old bank account, so he won't see the charge. I'm sure it won't be long until that is also traced. When the red sedan pulls up, my hands start to shake. This is insane, but it's literally all I have at the moment, and Silas did say to prove it, not claim it.

When the driver drops me off on Hawthorne, I say nothing and climb out of the car. I'm still in my regular clothes, so with my backpack slung across my shoulder, I head into the seedy gas station and walk directly to the bathroom. It's disgusting, with piss stains and grime all over the floor, so I make quick work of peeling off my clothes, revealing the skimpy dress underneath. Then I shove the long skirt and jacket into the backpack, right next to the handcuffs and 9mm I stole from the armory when the boys weren't looking.

Taking out the bag I bought at the mall, I pull out the blonde wig and take a few moments getting it in place. With the blunt bangs and natural looking highlights, it's almost convincing. Once that's on, I spend the next fifteen minutes putting on so much black eyeliner and bright pink lipstick that I'm almost entirely unrecognizable. I don't know if Donny or Victor would recognize my face, but it's not a chance I can take. If they are tied to Vincent, they could already know who I am. For all I know, they could have been there the day my world came to an end.

Last but not least, I slip on a pair of lightly shaded sunglasses.

Once I look the part, I stare at myself in the dirty mirror. "You can do this. You're the daughter of a mafia king. You're Iris-fucking-Pavetta, and you will make those motherfuckers pay."

There are only three guys in the gas station as I walk out, and they're all staring at me as my heels click across the floor.

"Hey sweetheart," one of them says with a whistle. "You new around here?"

"Fuck off," I snap as my hands slam into the door, walking out into the cool afternoon. According to my research, and a few drive-by visits, Donny usually enjoys a little afternoon delight around two or three. He tends to get the attention of a short-haired blonde girl who looks about sixteen. I spot her immediately by the bus stop, so I head straight for her. She's alone today, scrolling through her phone and smoking a cigarette.

When she glances up at me, she does a double take. "Holy shit," she mutters as I stop in front of her. "Who are you? This is my corner, bitch." It's a weak attempt of tenacity, but I don't bother arguing with her. I just slip the two-hundred dollars I pulled out of an ATM at the mall and hand it to her. "Here."

She glares down at the money looking half-offended and half-tempted. "What's this for?"

"Two hundred to get the fuck out of here and two more if you can tell me anything about Donny Wright."

"Are you a cop? You have to tell me if you are."

I laugh. "Who told you that? No, I'm not a fucking cop."

"I don't want any trouble."

"Then take the two hundred and get outta here."

Her fingers reach out, glancing around quickly like someone is about to ambush her and arrest her for taking money from my hand.

"I don't know nothing about him," she mutters, quickly shoving the money into her bra. "He doesn't say shit when we're together."

"Does he have any special...requests?" I ask, cringing as the words come out of my mouth.

"He likes when I put my hair into pigtails, talk like a baby—"

"That's enough," I snap. "Jesus, here." I quickly pull out the other two hundred and push it into her hand. "Please for the love of God, get a better job. Go back to school, call your mother or something...just stop doing this."

She scowls at me for a moment, and suddenly I see the wrinkles around her eyes and the texture to her skin. If she's any older than me, this life has hardened her. Whereas I was born into a mansion with an entirely different set of issues to deal with, this girl has clearly been fighting her entire life, spending it at dirty bus stops and nasty motels.

We were dealt very different hands, and yeah, even after watching my father get murdered in front of my own eyes, I wouldn't want her life.

"Must be nice, Princess," she mutters as she walks away, and I let it roll off my shoulders.

I'm not a princess. A princess lets the prince slay the dragon, sits alone in a tower, waiting to be rescued and kissed. Well, not in this story. In my story, I'm going to slay the fucking dragon, starting with one of his nasty fucking henchmen.

And speak of the devil... Right on time, Donny's old car pulls up to the gas station, getting out and leaning against the door like I've seen him do at least ten times this week.

His eyes land on me, immediately, squinting as his gaze rakes over my body. He's a little too far away to make out my face yet, but I still feel so exposed, afraid that at any moment, he will catch on and call Vincent Maretti, and my life will really be over.

Luckily for me, men think with their dicks instead of their brains, and a moment later, Donny is nodding me over. Holding my bag close to my side, I saunter over, hiding the shake in my hand as I get closer to him. Seeing him this close, it takes everything in me not to break character and jam my knee immediately into his ball sack. I hate him so much without one word out of his mouth, and I hate that I will have to let him touch me at least a little bit to make this work.

"Hello there," I say, making my voice a little higher and giving it a slightly foreign drawl.

He's not even looking at my face, so I don't know why I bothered with the makeup.

"You must be one of Sal's new girls," he says in a slimy high-pitched voice, like an actual fucking weasel.

"Yes, sir," I say, tilting my head and trying to look stupid because I know he'll like that.

"How old are you?"

Bile rises in my throat. The way he asks that makes me

sick, not like he's trying to make sure I'm legal but almost like he's hoping I'm not. Fuck, I hate this.

"Umm…" I drawl, looking at the floor.

"Oh fuck, you are new, aren't you?"

A chill runs down my spine. Don't vomit, Iris. Just get him alone, so you can finally cut off his dick or shove the pistol down his throat and make him cry like a baby.

"Yeah, a little," I say, biting my lip and pushing a lock of fake blonde hair behind my ear. He reaches out and fixes it, but I flinch away by instinct. He notices me jump, and I'm afraid for a moment that he's onto me when his eyes widen, but then a creepy smile stretches across his face.

"So jumpy. Relax, darling. I'm not going to hurt you."

*Yeah, well, I'm really going to hurt you, and I'm going to like it.*

"Sorry," I mumble.

"Hey, it's cold out here. How about we head across the street and get you warmed up?" His nasty, calloused hands slide along the length of my bare arms, and I shudder again, trying so fucking hard not to squirm away from his touch.

"Okay," I mumble.

He guides me toward the motel, which looms across the street like a house of horrors. I seriously don't know how I got myself into this situation. What if I can't overpower him? What if he hurts me, rapes me, kills me? What if I just walked right into my own goddamn downfall and I can't get myself out of it?

No. I have to get those thoughts out of my head. That's the way a princess thinks, and I'm done thinking like that. Donny is the one walking into his downfall, and he doesn't even know it.

We pass by the front desk where Donny just raises his hand at the clerk, an even grosser looking old man with a greasy comb-over and dark circles under his eyes. As we reach the door to room 104, Donny pulls a key out of his pocket and smiles at me.

I do my best to smile back, still keeping my face down and avoiding eye contact. As we walk into the dark hotel room, I fight the urge to vomit again. It smells like sex and smoke with a hint of cherry air freshener.

"This is nice," I mutter quietly.

"Yeah, it is. Now why don't you get on the bed like a good girl. I don't have all day."

"Okay," I reply with a shake in my voice. Fuck, now what? Oh yeah, the bag. I have to get into my bag. He reaches for it, but I quickly pull it to my side. "I have some toys. The other girl told me you like to play with toys..."

"Not today. Get on the bed."

A cold chill fills my bloodstream as he glares at me, looking impatient and not nearly as welcoming as he was outside. Of course now that he has me cornered and where he wants me, why would he be nice?

"Let me just show you..." I stammer quickly, opening my bag, but he's too quick, snatching it from my hands. "Give me that fucking thing."

He tosses it across the room. It lands with a heavy thud, and I panic, hoping he doesn't recognize the sound of metal hitting the wall. "Now, get on the bed."

"Wait," I mutter, looking for something, anything to use against him. Then I remember Gabriel's switchblade tucked comfortably in my bra, and I back slowly toward the bed.

"I don't wait, sweetheart. Sal knows I like them young, and I don't care if they put up a little resistance, and he sure delivered this time." His eyes skim up and down my body, holding tight to my breasts. Leaving me feeling exposed and naked while still wearing clothes.

My brain is running a million miles a minute as my legs hit the mattress and I fall onto it. He closes the distance quickly, unzipping his pants and pulling out his half-hard, tiny dick. It's hanging right in front of my face, and for a moment, I actually consider going through with this. Maybe if I can just get through one nasty blow job, I can gain control over him when he least expects it.

Then, something in me snaps.

*No. Fuck this guy.* Fuck the way he treats women and whatever he does for Vincent Maretti. This piece of shit doesn't get to feel one ounce of pleasure, not today.

I lean forward, putting myself at just the right angle to make him think I'm about to shove his nasty dick into my mouth, then reach into my bra, my hand clutching the cool metal handle before I yank it out and flip it open. I've been practicing that, and Gabriel would be proud if it wasn't for me putting myself in the one situation Silas told me not to.

But that's not what I'm thinking right now. All I'm thinking is how good the shock on his face looks as I jam the blade into his side. For one moment, it's perfect. He lets out a muffled cry and his eyes turn from chilled to wide and ice cold.

His large hand swings hard against the side of my head, and I hit the floor with a thud. My wig flies off, and I turn toward him just in time to watch him pull the blade out and stare down at me with rage.

"You fucking bitch!"

I fumble quickly for the bag, but he's faster, snatching me by a fistful of hair as I feel the blade pressed against my throat.

This is it. I'm going to die dressed like a prostitute on the cum-stained carpet of a seedy motel room.

"Who the fuck are you?" he asks, his voice in my ear. His breath hits the side of my face and reeks of cigarette ash with a stench of cheap liquor.

"Fuck you," I mumble, hiding the shake in my voice.

"You think I won't fuck a dead girl?"

I struggle against his hold, trying to get my bag, but he tosses me against the bed by my hair. My stomach is pressed against the mattress, and I scramble to crawl across and get away, but he presses his weight against me, halting my movement.

I'm fucked. I'm so fucked.

With the blade against my throat again, I feel his dick against my bare leg and I fight like hell. This is not happening. Lowering my face to the mattress, I give enough space between his face and my head so that when I throw my head back, I make bone-shattering contact with his face. My head is spinning and I swear I see actual stars as he stumbles to the side, letting me up long enough to reach for the knife in his hand.

He doesn't let go of it, and I realize I should probably be running for the door, but I'm not giving up that easily. With my long nails digging into his hand, I fight to get control of the knife. But he's stronger than me.

He swipes the knife at me and I feel the cool blade sweep against the inside of my opposite arm. Blood trickles immediately onto the dingy old bed, but there is too much adrenaline coursing through my body to feel pain.

I jump away from him to avoid any more slices. Blood gushes from his nose as he sneers at me, his nasty yellow teeth in stark contrast to the red dripping down his chin.

"You're going to pay for that, sweetheart."

The bag is behind me now, and I keep stepping backward until I feel it against my heels. Any moment now he's going to lunge and our fight will continue. I have to get the gun out quickly, but I'm not faster than him. And the gun is shoved in there with clothes and other shit.

Fuck, why didn't I plan this out better?

There's no more time to think as he charges at me. I reach down to grab the backpack, swinging it at his face and praying the gun is in the right position to at least slow him down. The sound of metal hitting bone gives me so much gratification, but it's quickly replaced with pain as my back hits the wall with so much force it knocks the wind out of me.

I'm in a daze as he presses the knife to my throat again, and I struggle, fighting in vain because he easily overpowers me, and I know I'm a dead girl. The last thing I think as he tosses me on the bed again is that at least I tried. At least I didn't run and hide or die without a fight.

But I'm running out of energy to keep fighting, and he's running out of patience. As he grabs onto my ankle and jerks me violently toward him, pulling my dress up with it, I know shit is about to get so much fucking worse.

*Nineteen*

THERE'S a deafening bang just as Donny's hands wrap around my throat, constricting my airway and making my vision soften to an unfocused haze.

The next few moments become a blur. A figure in black flies across the room and a shot rings out, just as I regain the ability to breathe, gasping and choking on air. I'm still coughing and have tunnel vision when a hand squeezes the flesh of my arm, and a low voice bellows, "Get the fuck up."

My first instinct is to fight, so I thrash and swing my arms at the figure in black, trying to make sense of the face now pressed close to mine. Warm, wolf-like eyes, filled with rage and anger, glare into my very soul as he jerks and shakes me, gripping me so hard I cry out.

"Knock it off!"

That voice. It brings out a sense of hatred and not the same kind of hatred that I feel for Donny, which is really more disgust. This hatred is more akin to passion, a burning fire of hostility.

My eyes finally begin to focus, and I stare up at the last face I would ever expect to find in this dirty hotel room.

"Baron?" I whisper, just as his hand claps over my mouth. He's lying on top of me, his body heavy on mine, making it hard to breathe.

"Get in the fucking car." His breath is warm on my face, his harsh glare focused on my lips. A sudden rush of emotion pulses through my body as I shove against him. He climbs off of me as I jump up.

"I'm not going anywhere with you! I have to get information out of him!" I look down to where Donny Wright's unconscious body lies in a heap against the wall. "Fuck, did you kill him?"

"You crazy, bitch. What were you going to do, Iris? After you got your answers from Donny, were you going to kill him yourself? Did you make any plan at all?"

"Yes, I made a plan," I snap back. "I was going to...threaten him."

Now it sounds stupid in my head, and I hate that he's making me face what a terrible plan I had.

He throws up his arms and his eyes roll. "You don't fucking listen, do you? You think you're so fucking smart. Then fine, you handle it."

"Wait!" I yell, grabbing him by the arm. "How did you know I was here? Did your dad send you?"

"No, he didn't send me."

"You just..."

"Are you getting in the car or not?" His back is still to me, and the moment stretches between us. My mind is still trying to grapple with this new information.

"You followed me?"

"You should be thanking me," he replies, his voice low.

"But why?"

He spins on me, meeting me toe-to-toe, and I have to crane my neck to stare up at him. My back hits the wall before

I even realize I was stepping away from him. "Because I'm the only one who sees through your bullshit."

I try to shove him away, real terror coursing through me. Being this close to him unnerves me. I'm not really scared Baron will hurt me; it's just that I don't know what he's capable of, and that frightens me more than anything.

"Why do you care?" I ask with a shaky breath.

"I don't," he says with a sneer. The spicy musk of his cologne fills my senses, and I almost start to feel lightheaded. I press myself up to my tiptoes. Our faces are still a few inches apart, but I can see the way the contact catches him off guard.

"I think you're jealous. Because your dad and brother have already had a taste." Without hesitation, I reach down and grab a handful of his crotch through his pants, and to my complete shock, it's not exactly soft. Our eyes widen in unison, and before I know it, his hands are around my throat and I'm pressed against the wall. With his nose pressed against my cheek, he seethes.

"That's where you're wrong. I'm not jealous. If I wanted a taste, I would have had one already. You disgust me. My brother and father might be dumb enough to think with their dicks, but I'm not."

My fingers squeeze his growing erection. "Then what's this?"

He opens his mouth to answer, but we both catch movement out of the corner of our eyes at the same time. He drops me just as Donny comes flying toward us. Catching us both off guard, the two guys land in a scuffle on the floor. Donny is holding the knife in his hands, and I panic as he takes a swipe at Baron's face, nearly catching him by the eye, but the knife embeds into the carpet instead.

*Think, Iris.*

*The gun.*

In a rush, I riffle through my bag, finding the pistol and

letting a warning shot fire against the wall, sending plaster flying over the them.

"Get off of him!" I scream.

Donny flips onto his back like a turtle, dry blood crusted over his face and scalp. With my finger on the trigger, I aim the gun directly at his face, so he puts his hands up in surrender as Baron jumps up to stand beside me.

"We have to take him," Baron says.

"There's rope in my bag," I retort. He reaches into the back of his jacket and pulls out a sleek black pistol and aims it at Donny's face, with far more skill than I have. And it makes me pause for a moment because something about Baron, in all black, holding the gun with a cool, blank expression is fucking hot.

"Get it," he snaps with impatience. Letting down my gun, I rush to the bag and pull out the rope. "Tie him up. Arms behind him."

"Won't people see us?"

"It's better than leaving a dead body here where everyone has seen your face. Let me guess, you took an Uber here, walked into the gas station, and strolled past the front counter."

I don't answer him, biting the inside of my cheek and hating how right he is. I thought I was being so careful, but I wasn't being cautious at all.

"You have a lot to learn, Iris."

My eyes glance up to his face. Does that mean he'll teach me?

"Just hurry up," he barks with contempt, and I brush the thought away. I hate that I have to touch Donny, but I drag him up to a sitting position with a hand in his nasty hair. He grimaces at me as I tie his wrists together.

Once he's bound, Baron glances around the room. "Grab your stuff. Leave nothing behind." And while I'm scurrying to gather up my bag and throw the pistol in it, Baron hoists Donny to his feet. "Go make sure no one's out there. I'll pop the trunk."

There's something about Baron barking orders that has the hairs on the back of my neck standing up. He's hardly spoken a word to me all week, and now he's here, saving my life.

When I go outside, Baron's black car is parked in reverse, with the trunk only a few feet from the door. Damn, he really does think of everything.

"It's clear," I call.

A moment later, Baron leads a gagged and bound Donny Wright out to the trunk and tosses him in. Donny tries to shout and complain, but with a look of disgust on his face, Baron lands a hard punch against his face and his limp body drops with a thud in the trunk.

As he slams the trunk closed, I can't take my eyes off of him. Again, that was fucking hot.

I climb in the seat next to him. His nostrils flare in the driver's seat as he throws the car into drive and peels away from the motel. I spot him flexing his right hand, and I can see his knuckles turning red from where they made contact with Donny's face.

"What now?" I ask after a few moments of silence.

Spinning his head toward me, he clenches his jaw. "Now, we take him home, where *you* can try to get any information out of him you want, and then *you* can kill him and dispose of his body."

My blood goes cold. "I... I can't—"

He glares at me again. "You want to act like an assassin, Iris, then here's your chance. You think you know everything and you don't need our help..."

"I do need your help," I mutter. "Are you going to tell your dad?" The thought of Silas disappointed or mad at me has my stomach feeling sick, and I hate to even think about it.

He lets out a deep sigh, grinding his molars, and I can't help but notice just how much I set Baron off. He looks so angry, and it's a far cry from the brooding boy who generally looks completely indifferent to my presence.

And yeah, I can't help the way my eyes drift down his body to his pants. When he had me pressed against the wall, he was hard. For me. Is it possible Baron wants me in the same way Gabriel and Silas do? And if he does, will I let him have me?

Turning toward the window, I press my face into my hand. I should probably be worrying more about the man in the trunk I'm responsible for torturing and murdering, but all I can think about is how I seem to have yet another Black on my hands and how I might actually want him as much as I want the others. All of these men offer me something that I desire. They're like my dream man but in three separate bodies.

*WHERE IS VINCENT MARETTI?*

That's the question on repeat in my mind as I stare at Donny's unconscious body slumped forward in the chair. Baron was nice enough to at least get him out of the trunk for me and tie him up in the basement, but then he went upstairs as if he had better things to do than help me torture this stranger for information. Silas is gone, but if he comes home any time soon, I'm fucked. He's going to know I went to the motel alone, and the disappointment I already feel with myself has my stomach in knots. His disappointment in me will only add to it.

My hands won't stop shaking as I wait for Donny to wake up. I guess I could probably wake him myself, but why rush it?

Fuck, what am I doing? How did I end up here? And *why the fuck* did my dad never teach me anything to protect myself? He claimed to love me more than anything, but he lived a dangerous life and ended up dead, leaving me defenseless and alone. Is that love? If he truly cared, wouldn't he have trained me to not need a man to protect me?

Rolling my eyes at the thought, I scoff. No, of course not. In my father's eyes, I was born to a man and would eventually be married off to another man. Eventually, I would have a daughter and the cycle would continue. Stupid. So fucking stupid. I'd be better off as the hooker at the bus stop because at least she didn't need anyone to survive.

Donny groans, and I jump. Baron showed me where the tools are kept, and I sifted through them to find what I think I'll need. Pulling out the scalpel for a quick cut, a hammer if worst comes to worst, and a blowtorch because it looks fun, I completely ignored the other things that turned my stomach at first glance. I don't need or want to know when they would use the pliers or corkscrew.

As Donny starts to wake, fighting against the bindings around his wrist and legs, I quickly grab the blowtorch and stand back, keeping it behind my back. It's dark down here with only a single light in the doorway.

He and I glare at each other for a moment before I start in on my questions, but as soon as I open my mouth to ask the burning question, Donny starts to laugh. It's a loud cackling that sends chills down my spine.

"You look more scared than I do," he howls, and I clench my jaw.

"Where is Vincent Maretti?" I ask, but he doesn't stop laughing. With a flick of the nozzle on the blowtorch, it fires to life, the flame a lot longer than I expected. The room goes instantly silent as Donny's eyes pop wide open in the glow of the fire.

"You crazy bitch. You'll blow this whole place up," he snaps at me.

"Do you know who I am?" I step toward him.

His eyes squint as he looks into my face. And I watch the exact moment as realization dawns. "Oh, shit," he mumbles. And I think it's fear, before he starts laughing again.

"What's so funny?" I yell.

"You...the princess—no, the *pearl*, you're going to be the one to torture me?"

"Why did you call me that?" I bark, stepping closer.

"Because that's what you are. You're his pearl. So you might as well hand yourself over because he won't stop until you're his."

"Who? Vincent Maretti?"

Donny laughs again, this time a wild, crazed laugh.

"Stop it!" I scream, aiming the fire toward Donny's bare feet. It wasn't fun removing his shoes while he was asleep, but it was necessary for what I plan to do. Okay, I Googled torture before he woke up, but it's not like Gabriel or Baron are around to help me, and I found a little foot roasting to be a very manageable option.

His laughter subsides as he sneers at me with an evil glare.

"Where is he? Where's Vincent Maretti?" Slowly, I press the fire closer to his feet, waiting to see him react, but he manages to keep a straight face, even as the sweat falls across his forehead.

"You might as well kill me, pearl. I'm a dead man anyway. Vincent will do far worse things to me when he finds out I touched you."

"Then tell me where he is and I'll make it quick and painless."

"He threatened to rip out our tongues if we uttered one word to you. I watched him stab a man in the eye for looking too long at your picture. You don't understand what you're dealing with, Pearl."

"Stop calling me that!" I scream, holding the fire directly at his feet and watching as screams bellow out of his chest. There's a sick sense of delight in watching him hurt, remembering what he tried to do to me. Knowing what he did to that blonde girl at the bus stop. He'll never touch her again, and that's the thought that gets me through the onslaught of smell from his burning flesh.

After about three more seconds, I pull the fire away. He's gasping for air, fighting against the bindings and whimpering through the pain.

"Where is he?" I yell again.

"It's useless trying to hide. He will find you."

He screams again when the fire touches his feet, and I have to pull my sweatshirt over my face to block the smell. I can't even look at his feet because I know how charred they are.

Donny goes through three more rounds of the roasting and bullshit answers before he passes out.

"Shit!" I yell, turning the torch off and dropping it on the counter. The basement reeks, I'm sweating, and I have no new information except that Vincent is obsessed with me and I don't even know who he is. How does he even know me? And why the fuck is he so obsessed with me?

As I peel off my sweatshirt, wearing only the skimpy dress I wore as a hooker underneath, I let out a scream when I notice Baron standing silently by the door, arms crossed and watching me.

"Having some trouble?" he asks with a blank expression.

"Don't make fun of me," I grit through clenched teeth. "I'm not in the mood, Baron."

"I'm not making fun of you," he replies coolly. Stepping forward, he inspects what I've done already, barely reacting to what's left of Donny's feet. "What has he told you so far?"

"Nothing aside from the fact that Vincent calls me his pearl and is fucking obsessed with me."

"His pearl?" There's a sly grin on his face that makes me pause. I hate him for being so good looking when I want to hate him so much.

"I know, creepy as fuck. And this asshole won't talk. He's just waiting to die at this point."

"Not all of these things happen in one session, Iris. It might take time."

"I don't have time, Baron. Every second I wait is another second closer to Vincent finding me and dragging me back to whatever shithole he lives in to do God-only-knows-what to me. I'm not waiting to find out."

There's a subtle flinch in Baron's expression, and I watch him for a long second, waiting to see what he's going to say next. When he looks at me with a stern glare, I get lost for a moment in those warm brown eyes. Quickly, he snaps himself out of it, and starts rolling up his sleeves.

"Alright, then. Put the torch away and get me a plastic bag from the bottom of that box over there," he gestures toward a brown box to my left.

"A plastic bag?" I ask, looking at him.

"Gabriel won't teach you this trick because it's not bloody, but you need to make him really feel what it's like to be dying."

"And that works?" I ask, watching him open up the thick black bag, like a hefty garbage sack.

"The pain might make them want to die, but once you make them feel what it's really like, suddenly all they want is to live."

My eyes focus on him a moment, the darkness in his emotionless face, the cold brutality of his words—everything about him sends ice-cold shivers down my spine. And I want to run from it. I want to be afraid of Baron, hate him and be as far away from him as possible, but something deep inside me comes to life when I'm with him. Almost as if he brings out a dark part of myself I didn't even know existed.

I don't know if that excites me or terrifies me.

"You ready?" he asks when I hand him the bag. I don't have a second to ask him what I'm supposed to be ready for when he douses Donny with ice cold water, and the man shoots awake.

"Ask him, Iris." Baron's cold voice stuns me, and I remember my mission.

"Where is Vincent Maretti?"

"Fuck you," Donny blubbers, drool hanging off his lips, looking like the pain in his feet has him pretty fucking miserable. Then, the bag is over his head without warning. With Baron behind him, he didn't see it coming, and he struggles immediately. Something about it, watching him flail and fight for air feels so strange to me, like I want to look away, but I also want to watch him suffer.

But Baron keeps the bag on a few seconds longer than I would have, and I panic.

"Don't kill him!" I shriek, and I worry for a second that Baron is sabotaging my whole plan. If he came down here just to kill the guy, everything I did is wasted, but just as Donny looks like he's about to stop moving, Baron pulls the bag off.

The man's face is contorted in terror, eyes nearly bulging out of his head, and I have to look away.

"Iris," Baron snaps, and I quickly turn back, determination written on my face. *Focus, Iris. You can do this.*

"Where is he?" I yell, smacking Donny hard across the face. He's so busy gasping for air, looking like every inhale both kills him and gives him life at the same time.

"What...does it...matter?" Donny wheezes. "He'll get what's owed to him."

My hand clutches his throat, and I feel his panicked pulse under my fingertips. "What do you mean owed to him?"

With his bloodshot eyes trained on my face, he laughs again. "You, pearl. You're what's owed to him, and Maretti always collects."

Letting go of him, I keep my expression as blank as

possible in an attempt to mask any emotion. I nod to Baron. "Again."

Donny lets out a muffled cry this time as the bag suffocates him, stretching tightly over his mouth and nose as he fights for air. Right now, his lungs are literally starving, and again, Baron waits until the moment before Donny begins to give up his fight then pulls the plastic bag away. The whole time my mind replays his words, desperate for meaning, unwilling to accept the explanation. He's lying.

The man whimpers again. Tears and saliva soaking his face as he struggles for oxygen. This time, I don't mess around with slapping him. I grab the blunt, black mallet off the bench and swing it hard on Donny's left wrist. The bone shatters under the impact, and he lets out a soundless moan as he tries to breathe and scream at the same time.

"What the *fuck* are you talking about? Why does Maretti think I belong to him?"

It takes him a while before he can get out the words, and this time, he doesn't even try laughing. "Because you do. You always have."

Fuck that. With a yell, I bring the mallet down on his other wrist. Baron is watching with interest, a certain spark of delight in his eyes.

"Explain!" I scream in Donny's face.

"The Marettis pay their debts," he replies, and I clench my jaw.

"I swear to God, Donny, I will let Baron suffocate you all night long if you don't tell me something that makes sense. And judging by the look in his eye, I think he'll like it."

"You didn't let me finish..." he says between gasps. "Marettis pay their debts. Pavettas...don't."

I raise the mallet again, this time aiming for his femur. "You better keep talking, asshole."

"Goddammit!" he screams. "You were the fucking debt.

You were supposed to be Maretti's the second you turned eighteen, but your father decided not to pay up. And Maretti doesn't ask twice."

"My father would *never* give me to someone like Maretti. You're lying! Why would he do that?"

"Iris..." Baron's low tone pulls me out of my rage, long enough to look up at him. He doesn't say anything else, just sends me a small nod and an intense expression. And somehow, I know he's telling me to put my emotions aside and get the information I want.

"Where's Maretti?" I ask, doing my best cold and calculating Baron expression. The mallet is still resting on my shoulder, ready to break his thigh bone.

"In hell," Donny growls, and I glare up at Baron.

"Again."

"No, no!" Donny shouts. "That's what he says. It's the Inferno. He calls it hell."

I hold up my hand to stop Baron from suffocating him again. "That doesn't make any fucking sense."

"What do you want, an address? Well, there isn't one. It's only twenty miles north, off the grid. He calls it the Inferno. That's all I have, I swear."

"I don't believe you," I mutter, raising the mallet again. "How the hell am I supposed to find that?"

There's silence as Donny stares up at me, his face swollen and red. Letting his head hang back, he laughs again. "You want to go there? If you go there, you're never coming out. There's no stopping him, Pearl. He will find you. Maretti always collects."

He's rambling again, and I'm feeling frustrated and fired up, but tired of Donny's voice. "Do it, and don't stop this time."

I give Baron a harsh glare as I turn away, ignoring the sounds of Donny's muffled howling. Crossing my arms over my chest, I wait for his screaming to stop, but then I hear the bag being ripped away again, and I spin around to see Donny slouching listlessly in his chair, still struggling for air.

"What are you doing? I said not to stop this time!" I yell at Baron.

"This isn't my job, Iris." He throws the bag on the floor and walks toward the door.

"Wait! What am I supposed to do?"

Baron stops and turns back toward me, pulling a black pistol from the back of his pants. He places it in my hands, the sudden touch of his fingers on mine sends a bolt of electricity through my body.

He doesn't say a word, just leaves the gun in my palm before stepping behind me and guiding my hand up to take aim at Donny's head.

"If you're done with him, then get rid of him."

"I... I can't— I'm not ready."

"You'll never be ready, Iris. Just take the shot." His voice is deep like silk in my ear.

"Please, don't make me do this," I whisper, not bothering to hide the quiver in my voice.

As I stare at the man strapped to the chair in all his misery, waiting to die, I realize it's up to me to do it. Can I do this? It's what I asked Silas to help me with. Killing, taking a life, ending someone forever. The power in my hands echoes through my veins as I try to define how this makes me feel. I'm scared mostly. Scared that it will change me. Scared that it will ruin the very core of who I am, and I'll see Donny's bloody brains all over the wall in my dreams forever, keeping me from peace for the rest of my life.

But I'm also scared that it won't change me. That it will feel right and that I'll...*like it.* I'm scared that I will become like Baron, emotionless. A lifeless grim reaper, unable to feel anything at all. I'm afraid that this person has been inside me all along, but I've lived so sheltered that I've never had a chance to find it.

"Do it!" Baron shouts in my ear, and it frightens me to the point that I clench my hand and pull the trigger. My ears ring, and my vision narrows as I watch Donny's body jolt from the bullet to his head before falling into a lifeless pile of bones on the chair. One moment he was shaking and crying, and now he's just...nothing.

I'm in too much shock to analyze my emotions right now, and all I feel is the heavy metal in my hands, and I'm desperate to be rid of it, so I drop the gun on the floor.

"What the fuck is wrong with you?" he bellows in my ear.

"Why did you do that?" I scream.

"Do what? Finally give you the push you needed. You're so stuck in your head, Iris. So caught up in your emotions, and it makes you stupid." He's in my face now, seething anger as he looks down at me in disgust, and suddenly, all of the adrenaline and everything that's happened today comes flooding to the surface, ready to take it all out on him.

"Fuck *you*, Baron!" I yell, shoving him hard in the chest. "I hate you!"

As I try to take another swing, I realize he's letting me hit him, letting me batter him on the chest with my closed fists, probably not even hurting him at all. Finally, after a few more exhausting punches, he wraps his fingers around my throat and shoves me against the cement wall.

"Good, Iris. Because hate is about the only emotion that's going to do you any good around here." His eyes trail down from mine to my lips as I claw against his chest, trying to push him away. His fingers start to squeeze to the point where I can feel my pulse in my ears, and panic sets in.

And with the panic, something else...

My arousal hits me head on, making me feel suddenly *so aware* of my body and the way it's reacting to him. His position over me, the power in his hands and in his body; he tortures me with it. Squeezing just a little bit harder so spots begin to appear in front of my eyes, but my skin vibrates with sensation. I let out the most pathetic whimper because I can't move. He has me exactly where he wants me, and he knows exactly what he's doing. He's making me want it too.

Grasping for anything, my hands move from his chest downward, until I breeze my fingers over the rock-hard erection trying to break free from his pants. He growls, leaning in, keeping his lips just a breath away from mine. I finally grab hold of his cock as our lips collide.

He steals the air from my lungs. His hand releasing my throat and letting the blood rush back to my head. Maybe it's still adrenaline or just exhaustion, but my brain completely stops as he kisses me. All I know is his touch and the way my body feels in our unhinged, desperate movements. I don't think as I pull open the button of his pants, tearing down the zipper and grabbing his cock in my hands like it's the only thing in the world I need.

My dress is up to my waist, and my panties hit the floor before I know what's happening. Then, my legs are wrapped around him, and I'm pressed between his body and the cold, cement wall. In the dim light of the basement, I can still see the dead form of Donny Wright across the room as Baron thrusts violently into me.

I let out a scream for both the pain and the pleasure, and I cling to his neck as he pounds my back into the wall, grunting in my ear. Still, I think nothing, and rather than feel anything, I focus on the pleasure he's chasing with me. No emotions, no thoughts, just his body and mine.

The perfect rhythmic cadence of his thrusts sends me closer and closer to my climax until his hand is around my throat again and my head is pressed against the wall.

Even in the darkness, I can see his copper eyes. "Tell me you hate me again," he growls against my mouth.

"I hate you," I answer in a high-pitched plea. "Don't stop."

With the other hand clutching my thigh, almost painfully hard, he pounds relentlessly until I almost can't breathe without splintering into a million pieces. With two more brutal thrusts, I come apart. Squeezing my thighs tightly around him, it feels like I could break him. I shake and tremor in his arms, feeling his cock pulse inside me as he does the same. The sounds that come out of my mouth as I come are like none I've ever heard before, matched only by his wild groans.

We wilt against the wall for a few more moments before I finally drop my feet to the floor, and he pulls out, letting his cum drip down my leg. At this point, I don't even care. It's silent and almost awkward as he shoves himself back into his pants, and I stare again at the dead man in the basement.

"What do we do about him?"

"You'll need to get rid of the body before Silas finds him," he says picking up his gun and attaching it to the clip on the back of his pants.

A wail comes out of my mouth as I consider actually collapsing onto the floor before I can bear the thought of trying to get rid of a dead body, but before I can, Baron laughs.

Baron Black actually laughs, and if I wasn't so goddamn exhausted, fucked out of my mind, and numb from the trauma of this day, I would commit the sound to memory. Because it's a nice laugh, and the lines his smile creates in his face are worth remembering.

"Relax. We have a cleanup crew. I've already contacted them. They'll be here at midnight."

"Really? Does that mean I can go to bed?" I ask, feeling as pathetic as I'm sure I sound.

"Go shower first," he says, turning up his nose.

"Fuck off, Baron."

My body carries me up two flights of stairs until I'm standing in my room, pulling out clothes and shutting myself in the bathroom. I don't even remember turning the shower on or getting under the hot spray. I can barely manage washing myself, but as the soap runs down the drain, I lean against the white tiles of the shower and try to feel something, anything.

Today, I was almost raped and fought off a man with my bare hands before being rescued. I tortured and murdered a monster, found out my father sold me to Maretti himself, without ever telling me, and then to top it all off, I let Baron fuck me against the wall of the basement next to a dead man. I should feel terrible, lower than low, but I don't. And maybe the bad feelings will be waiting for me when I wake up in the morning, but all I feel right now is exhausted.

## Twenty-One

THE NEXT MORNING, I wake up with what feels like a hangover. My head aches, my muscles are sore, and between my legs is raw from Baron's brutal wall-banging.

*Fuck, I had sex with Baron.*

Out of everything that happened yesterday, that's the one thing that comes with a sting of regret. Well, not regret exactly. It's not like I didn't enjoy it. In fact, that was the hardest I've come in a long time, a fast and intense orgasm that bled into every inch of my body, but that was surely because of the adrenaline.

Before getting out of bed, I pull the notebook off the nightstand and write down everything I was too exhausted to jot down last night.

*My dad promised me to Maretti?*

*But he didn't pay up. Why?*

I assume the answer to that last question is because my dad didn't want to hand me over to a psychopath, but why did he promise me to Maretti in the first place, and what did he gain in exchange?

The last thing I jot down, my hand trembling as I do.

*Inferno - twenty miles north.*

Was Donny right? If I go there to finally face Maretti, am I sentencing myself to literal purgatory? One thing is for sure. I'm not ready for that. At least not alone.

There are footsteps in the hallway, and I grimace before climbing out of bed. I'm not sure I'm ready to face any of these guys, least of all Silas, who will probably never trust me again after he finds out I went to the motel alone.

Carefully, I open the door and let out a scream as Gabriel's menacing face is waiting for me on the other side. He's grinning at me with a smile that makes my stomach flip. Dressed in all black, he's leaning against the door jamb as he glares at me.

"What the fuck, Gabriel? You scared the shit out of me!"

"You're in trouble," he singsongs with that evil smirk on his face that he wears so well.

"What do you mean?" I ask, wondering just how much Baron told him. I suddenly remember how Gabriel reacted when he found out Silas and I slept together, and I feel terrible, knowing that I'm sleeping my way through his whole family, but it's not the action that has me feeling this way, it's the emotional turmoil that I feel like I'm bringing to us all.

"Your presence is requested in the kitchen." That cruel tone to his voice makes me want to scream.

Shoving him out of the way, I square my shoulders and make my way toward the main living area. The sound of someone in the kitchen has me feeling instantly on edge, and when I come down the stairs with Gabriel hot on my heels, I stare at Silas, standing behind the island and glaring at me with his dark expression.

He doesn't say anything at first, just goes about making his coffee in the delicate glass coffee press, those large hands being so precise with every small movement, and I feel like he's waiting me out. Waiting for me to confess, except I'm not quite sure what I should be confessing to first.

"Tell me what happened yesterday," he says without looking at me.

I gulp. Start with the truth and avoid the lies, I tell myself. "Baron helped me bring back Donny Wright, and I found out—"

The canister of coffee lands hard against the marble countertop, reverberating through the room and jolting me into silence. It's not fear that builds in my throat like needles —it's shame. I couldn't keep my promise, and I refuse to lie to him now. The truth might cost me his approval, but being honest with him now might save his trust, and I'd rather have that.

"You told me to prove how bad I wanted revenge, and I couldn't just sit around and wait for you to help me. So I went to the corner—"

"Did I not make you promise me that you wouldn't?" His voice is loud and there is so much anger on his face, I can't stop my eyes from pooling.

"I had to," I argue.

"I can't trust you now, Iris."

"I'm sorry," I say, biting the inside of my cheek. Gabriel is still standing behind me, leaning on the back of the couch and watching us with interest.

"What happened to your face?" Silas asks, nodding toward me, and I reach up, feeling the tender spot on my cheek where that motherfucker clocked me in the side of the head. I didn't look in the mirror this morning, but I assume it's purple by now.

"I had to fight him off, and he got me—"

"Do you understand you would be dead right now if Baron hadn't shown up?"

Pressing my lips together, hating how it feels to admit that I fucked up, I nod my head. "What did he tell you?" I ask.

This time, I really watch Silas's face. There's no sign he

knows what really went down between us, or if he does, maybe he doesn't care.

"Not much, but he didn't need to. There was a body being removed from my basement, a body belonging to one of the guys I know you wanted to question. The car I lent you was still parked at the mall, and there was a fucking mess downstairs."

Shit...did I leave my panties on the floor?

I can't help but wince, imagining what he thinks of me right now.

Without another word, he passes me a cup of hot coffee slowly across the counter. "So did you find out what you wanted?"

I wrap my hands around the cup, letting the scalding coffee burn my palms through the porcelain. "I found out my father promised me to Maretti without telling me, and when I turned eighteen, he was supposed to hand me over but didn't."

I expect Silas to react, but he doesn't. Just leans against the opposite counter and watches me with a blank expression.

"It doesn't explain why my dad put a hit on Mickey Barton, though."

"Well, Gabriel and I were doing a little research on Barton yesterday. That's where we were all day, while you were working to get yourself killed. You're lucky Baron cared enough to follow you."

"What did you find out?" I ask, my spine straightening as I look at him. Ignoring his implication that Baron cares about me at all when I know he doesn't.

"Barton used to work for Pavetta," Gabriel says, walking up and placing his elbows on the counter to look me straight in the eye.

"What? How come I've never even heard of him?"

"I assume there's a lot your father kept from you, Iris," Silas says in a scathing tone. "It would appear that Barton double-crossed your father, and he put the hit on him not long before the attack on your home."

My nostrils flare as I fight back tears. Someone my father trusted betrayed him. That must have felt horrible, and it physically hurts to think about it.

"Did you find him? Did you finish the job?" I ask, unable to hide the shake in my voice.

"Not yet." Gabriel comes up behind me and grabs a bright red apple out of the fruit bowl.

"Wait," I say. Something suddenly dawns on me as I stare at the two of them. "All of that research you did— finding out Barton worked for my dad—that wasn't to help you make the hit. You said yourself, you don't need to know why someone ordered a hit. So why did you find all of that out?"

I already know the answer, and it only adds to my already guilty heart.

Silas licks his lips as he rounds the island to come face-to-face with me. Reaching into his pocket, he pulls something out, clenched in his large fist, and drops it into my lap. Looking down, I recognize the black, satin thong I had on yesterday.

I guess I did leave them in the basement.

"We were already doing the research. Figured we could find out something helpful for you. You're welcome."

He walks away, leaving me feeling like shit as I sit at the kitchen island, clutching my panties in my hand. Across the kitchen, Gabriel is glaring at me. I can't look him in the eye.

"My brother will do anything to compete with Silas. You know that, right?"

My stomach sours. What the *fuck* is wrong with me?

"He caught me in a moment of weakness," I reply. "Besides, it wasn't a problem when it was you. Why does it matter that I fucked Baron too?"

"It always matters to me. And those two despise each other, Iris. Haven't you figured that out yet?"

"No, they don't."

A clipped, angry sounding laugh bubbles out of his chest. He doesn't bother arguing with me anymore as he tosses his apple in the trash. "So tell me everything," he says as he comes closer, leaning on the counter next to me. He pulls the blade out of his pocket and uses the tip to pry a piece of fruit out of his teeth, and my face contorts in confusion.

"You want to hear about everything that happened with Baron? It just happened—"

He quickly cuts me off. "Jesus, no. Tell me how you got Wright to talk."

"Oh." He's standing so close to me, I feel disoriented, and it doesn't make it any easier to think as he runs the flat side of his blade along my cheek.

"It still smells like shit down there."

Oops. I feel wrong for the smile that stretches across my face. "Well, the foot roasting didn't actually work. I made him pass out without getting a word out of him."

"Damn, girl. Felt good though, didn't it?" He steps closer as I turn toward him, feeling him crowd me against the counter.

"Aren't you mad at me?"

Still with the knife in his hand, he trails it across my chin and down my neck. It takes everything in me to stay still, my eyes on him, trying not to look intimidated or scared because I know that's what he's going for.

"Fucking livid," he replies with a wicked smile. "And I fully intend to make you pay for it later, but for now, I have to go to work. Stay away from my brother, Iris."

"Can't I come with you?" I ask, actually pouting because there is definitely something wrong with me, and I really should *not* want to be around Gabriel right now.

"Not today, Princess. The boss said you're spending the day with him."

My eyes widen. The last thing I want to do is spend the day with the one person who makes me feel like shit for what I did yesterday. All day with Silas's disappointment. Hard pass.

"Please take me with you."

He laughs, pocketing his knife and leaning forward. When I think he's going to kiss me, he wraps his teeth around the skin of my neck, grabbing my ass at the same time.

"I wish I could."

My body comes to life at his touch, but when I reach for him, wanting more, he pulls away and gives me a scowl. Then he turns away and walks toward the garage. I'm left alone until I hear the thump-thump of someone walking across the house. Turning toward the sound, I expect to see Silas coming, but I'm met with the sight of Baron instead.

He's back to being cold and dismissive, barely even looking at me, and all of the warmth in the room is gone in an instant. If someone would have told me when I arrived at this house that Gabriel would be the one I sought comfort from, I'd laugh in their face. Yet, right now, he's the one I want to be near.

Baron walks to the coffee maker and I can't take my eyes off of him, remembering the sound of his grunts as he fucked me, a thrill running through me and pooling like lava between my legs.

"Iris," a deep voice calls from behind me. Baron and I turn at the same time to see Silas standing at the door of his office. "Get dressed and meet me in here in fifteen minutes."

There is no humor in his expression or lightness in his tone, and I find myself swallowing down the nerves gathering in my throat. Turning back toward Baron, I see the slightest smirk play on his lips before he carries his coffee out of the room.

I'M NOT GOING to let Silas intimidate me. Well, okay, Silas *already* intimidates me, but I'm not going to let *him* know that. I have to walk in there with confidence.

I am not sorry about what I did yesterday. I don't regret going to that motel. I mean, I do feel bad about breaking my word to him, but I am not going to be a good little mafia princess anymore, and he should be proud of me for that.

And I do not feel bad about what happened with Baron. It's not like I belong to any of these men. He's not my boyfriend, and I refuse to live my life like I belong to anyone. Not anymore.

"Come in," he mutters, staring at his computer as I step up to the doorway.

With my head held high, I march over to the chair in front of his desk. He ignores me for a long moment while I sit there, waiting for him to say something.

Finally, he looks up from his computer. "What are you doing, Iris?"

I clear my throat. "I'm trying to kill Vincent Maretti—"

"That's not what I'm talking about," he bellows, his voice

deep and loud, making my confidence shrivel. "I admit we don't have women in the house often, or ever. But I refuse to cause a rift in our business—or family, because a beautiful girl steps in and fucks everything up. Understand?"

My eyes widen, and my temper starts to rise. "I fucked it up? *Me?* How about you learn to keep it in your own pants instead of blaming me?"

He looks visibly offended as my voice starts to rise. I pound my palms flat on his desk, leaning forward to glare into his eyes. "*Or*," I shriek. "Would it kill you to give your kids an actual life with girls and friends, so you don't end up with an eighteen-year-old virgin for one son and the other a fucked-up murdering sociopath!"

"Lower your voice," he growls, glaring angrily at me.

"No! I refuse to be the object of blame because you all wanted somewhere to stick your dicks!"

"Iris," he yells, trying to stop me, but I ignore him.

"And it's my fault that you wanted to fuck the girl who was also fucking your son? You didn't care then, so why do you care now?"

I stand up and spin to leave because I don't care anymore what Silas thinks or how angry he is at me. I won't sit here and listen to him calling me a fucking *rift in his business.* But he's on me before I can slip through the door. His arm wraps around my waist and he spins me quickly, holding me against his chest. I'm lost as to what he's doing until I'm draped over his knee and he's tearing my pajama pants down my legs. I gasp and fight to get out of his grip, just before his hand lands hard against my ass.

"What are you doing?" I scream, struggling to get away.

He doesn't say a word as he spanks me hard again and again; this time, the pain wakes up something raw and dirty at my core. With each strike, my screams turn into raspy cries.

"I wouldn't pick you even if you made me choose," I yell.

"Oh really?" he growls, smacking my sore flesh again. "You sure about that?"

"Yes," I snap. "I don't want any of you. You're all fucking psychopaths, and I wish I never ended up in this stupid house. I'd rather be with Maretti—"

The next smack is harder than all the rest and it shuts me up pretty fast. I'm more than just aroused; with every blow of pain, my body edges closer to a climax I didn't see coming. If he keeps this up, I might come right here on his lap.

"This is for raising your voice at me." His hand lands hard again on the opposite cheek. My body jolts, but the fight in me dies. Instead, I cling to his body, feeling his erection grow against my belly.

"And this is for what you did with Baron." This time, after laying down another blow that makes me cry out again, he grabs my ass cheek in his hand, massaging the flesh. His fingers are so close to exactly where I want them that it has me writhing and twisting for more.

This attraction to Silas feels so wrong yet so right at the same time, and this foreign desire to have him spank me then fuck me feels so dirty, but so fucking good.

No. No! I can't keep letting these men get in my head and in my pants because I'm weak to the pleasure they bring me. This is how I keep getting myself in this mess, falling into bed with one and then another. And if I keep it up, they're going to tear me apart.

"Silas, stop!" I scream.

He freezes, and in the next breath, my pants are up, and I'm off his lap. My chest is still heaving as I stare at him, wild fury seeping from my pores as I glare angrily at him. I'm half-aroused and half-raging mad.

"What is wrong with you?" I say through gritted teeth.

His eyes travel downward from my face to my breasts, and after a moment, I look down at them too, noticing the stiff peaks of my nipples through my loose-fitting pajama shirt—a clear sign of my arousal.

"Admit you liked it," he says with a smug expression I want to slap off his face.

So I do, whipping my hand hard across his cheek. He barely reacts.

"I was wrong about you," he whispers harshly as he takes me by the chin. "You aren't a rift at all. You're a fucking bomb, Iris."

Tearing my chin from his grip, I bite back, "It's not my fault, you know. And I'm not going to break my deal with Gabriel because you can't keep your hands off me."

"And Baron?" he asks, his eyes narrowing as he watches for my response.

What the fuck can I say about that? There is no rational explanation for what happened with Baron. It wasn't something thought-out. It was adrenaline and passion and lust. That was it. The sex between us had the same energy as a gruesome murder.

"I have about as much control over Baron as you do."

His thumb swipes gently over the bruise on my cheek, and I flinch away from his touch.

"He didn't do this, right?"

He has a lot of nerve asking if his son hurt me after he just turned my ass red.

"Of course, he didn't. He saved my life."

"What the fuck happened between you two?" I snap, angry with all of the secrets in this house.

With a sigh, he turns away. Running his hand through his hair, he crosses the room to his desk and drops into his chair. He's trying to find the words, and as mad as I am at him, I want his body close to mine. I really am a fool for these guys.

"Baron doesn't think I should be in charge anymore. He

thinks he knows best, and I'm afraid he's outgrown this family."

"What does that mean?" I ask.

"It means he probably won't be here much longer."

"Where will he go?"

He doesn't answer, but his eyes stay on my face. Then he gestures for me to come to him, but I stay in my place, working hard to hold onto my anger.

"No," I snap. "You hurt me."

"You liked it."

I roll my eyes and avoid responding. What am I gonna do? Lie? Of course, I fucking liked it, but I can't tell him that.

"Iris, come here so I can kiss it better."

"You're going to kiss my ass?" I say, lifting my eyebrows with a serious expression.

He lets out a subtle laugh. "Close enough, right?"

And fuck him and how hot he is in that chair, behind that big desk with those dark eyes and wicked grin because I'm powerless to him. Moving reluctantly to his desk, I hop up on the surface in front of him.

Rolling his chair even closer, he slides between my knees and runs his hands softly against my thighs in a soothing rhythm. It blows my mind these men have gone so long without a woman around, but it's very clear by how deprived they all are for physical touch. And I'd be lying if I said I didn't love that they are all getting what they need from me.

"Answer my question, Silas. If Baron leaves, where will he go?" I don't know why it bothers me so much, the idea of him leaving.

"That's what worries me, Iris. Not just where he will go, but I'm afraid he's already gone."

Reaching down, I take his face in my hands. "Have you talked to him?"

He glares, and it's enough of an answer.

"You should."

He doesn't reply as he rests his head in my lap. When I run my fingers through his hair, he lets out a long exhale, and I see the weight he's carrying for this family. The burden on him is heavy, this strange mix of family and business while constantly having to think ahead, worry for his boys' safety and never, ever make a mistake. And now he's taken me on as well.

My nails soothe their way across his scalp and down his neck, feeling him relax against my touch. The last thing I should want right now is to help him, but I want to ease his tension, carry some of that burden for him, but that's insane. I've only been in this house a couple weeks now. This isn't my family, and when everything is done here, I'll leave, and the Blacks will be nothing more than a memory in my history.

And just as that thought crosses my mind, Silas's hands run up my thighs to circle around my hips as he pulls me closer, burying his face even deeper into my lap. I feel him shifting closer and the effect he has on me is so intense, I can't fight it anymore. My body is still blazing hot from when he had me over his lap.

His lips are soft against my legs as he mumbles, "I should have sent you away that first day, Iris. Because I don't know if we'll be able to let you go now."

I let out a gasp as his fingers dig into the waistband of my pants, lifting my hips and tearing them down my legs until I'm sitting naked from the waist down on his desk. I'm so power-less against him that when he brings me to the edge, draping my legs over his shoulders so he can devour me like a meal on his desk, I don't fight it.

Does this make me a fool? Probably.

Am I falling more and more into their hands every day? Letting each of them wield so much power over me that it will probably be the death of me.

But why would I fight this? Why push any of them away

when being with them finally gives me the freedom I never had before? The thought of being his—no, being *theirs*, doesn't make me feel like the prisoner I was at my father's. With them, I'm so much more than that.

Silas is turning me into a leader—making me smarter, stronger.

Gabriel is teaching me to take what I want without asking permission, to stand up for myself, and to never accept defeat.

And Baron, I don't know yet, but I'm not as afraid of him as I was before. I'm not afraid of anything as much as I was before.

I should probably be ashamed of myself for thinking about all three of them as Silas tongue-fucks me on his desk to the point that I'm screaming his name. I come with my thighs clenched around his head—my nails clutching his hair in my hands. But of course, I'm not ashamed.

Nothing has been conventional since I got here, and this whole family is pretty fucked up when you think about it. But with every passing day, I'm becoming more and more a part of it, and I don't hate that idea so much anymore.

## Twenty—Three

WITH MY HAND in a bowl of buttered popcorn, I'm right in the middle of my fifth episode of the latest graphic Netflix show—a juicy sex scene too, when Gabriel walks into the living room.

"Oh, what are we watching?" he asks as he leaps over the back of the couch and lands next to me, spilling my popcorn all over my lap.

The couple on the TV are going at it. He's got a fistful of her blonde hair as he rails her from behind. Her orgasm screams are fake as fuck, but otherwise, it looks pretty legit.

"Some stalker drama," I reply, watching as he kicks her leg up on a chair to get a better angle.

"Goddamn," he mutters next to me, grabbing a handful of popcorn and shoving it into his mouth.

"You should take notes," I mumble, without looking away from the scene.

"Fuck you."

"You have to teach me something first," I reply with a playful smile.

"Oh I'll teach you something," he growls, throwing his

body over mine. I let out a scream as he wrestles each of my wrists into one of his hands, pinning them to the couch over my head. I squirm and fight against his hold, my laughter echoing through the living room as he kisses my neck and tries to weasel his hand into my shorts.

I finally manage to land a hard kick to his groin, and he freezes before rolling off of me, falling hard onto the marble floor. Turning toward him with a cruel smile, I gaze down at him.

"You okay?"

"Good kick," he wheezes.

"Hey, this gives me a good idea on something you can teach me."

He pops an eye open, suddenly interested in whatever might result in him getting laid again. "I'm listening."

"I almost got my ass handed to me yesterday by Donny. I need to learn some self-defense moves."

There's an obvious pique in his interest as his eyebrows arch to his hairline. "I'll teach you moves—you teach me moves."

A laugh bubbles out of my chest. He's still lying on the floor, and with those tattoos creeping up his neck and the piercing in his lip, I can't tell him I'd be willing to show him some moves even without the trade. Gabriel is starting to soften up to me, not as cruel or as scary as he was when I first got here, and I honestly can't tell if that is making me more or less attracted to him.

His eyes meet mine, catching me staring, and for a moment, there is no tension between us, but he breaks the connection as he hops up, throwing up that dark facade like he had before.

"Alright, get up." He shoves the coffee table to the side, and I stare back wide-eyed.

"Right here?"

"Right here, Princess."

There is a plush gray rug in the middle of the room, so at least there's a small amount of cushion for the sparring, but I hope he doesn't expect me to fulfill my end of the bargain out here too.

Taking me by the arms, he puts me across from him. He walks me through a few basic punches, a neck strike, and how to properly hold my fist, knuckle out, to get the best results. Too quickly, I remember how it felt being pressed against the wall with Donny's giant hand around my throat. So I make Gabriel show me how to get out of that when I accidentally elbow him right in the face after he shows me how to pivot out of the move. He's about to have a matching purple bruise on his cheek.

After about an hour, we're both sweaty and breathless.

"Alright, get on the floor," he says.

My heart starts to race and I glance toward Silas's office door. "Right here?"

His brow knits together as he stares at me in confusion. "I wanna show you another move. Although, you know I'm not opposed to bending you over this rug after we're done. Not like you and the old man cared much about discretion when we rolled up in the garage last week."

As I lie down on the rug on my back, I roll my eyes at him. "I'm not fucking you on the living room rug, Gabriel."

"Be that way then," he mutters as he lowers down to climb between my legs.

"We're still doing self-defense moves, right?"

He winks. "I want you to know how to get out of this one. Ya know, just in case *Baron* ever tries to touch you again."

At that very moment, the devil himself walks past the living room and into the kitchen. It would explain why

Gabriel chose to say his brother's name so loudly. He must have seen him coming.

"She didn't need those moves last night," Baron says flatly from the kitchen.

I swallow, staring up at Gabriel to see his reaction. His jaw clenches, and his eyes narrow.

Ignoring his brother, Gabriel walks me through how to hook my leg around his head and twist out of this hold, letting me practice it a few times to the point where I'm almost able to actually do it on my own against his full strength. By the end of the maneuver, I have his arm between my legs and in the perfect position to snap it at the elbow, which he shows me how to do by leveraging from my hips.

Is it terrible that I almost hope I get the opportunity to actually do it to someone one day?

Maybe. I wish I could go back in time and properly defend myself against Donny Wright, making sure to really snap his arm at the elbow. I can almost hear his screams of pain in my memory.

"Get up, Princess," he says, pulling me up by the arm. "We both need showers before dinner."

Baron is still standing in the kitchen, browsing through his phone as he watches us leave. I can't help the way my gaze is caught on his face, looking for any reminder of what we had yesterday or any sign that he's jealous of Gabriel.

There's nothing. He watches me leave without one fucking expression on his face, and it makes me hate him more.

As Gabriel and I get upstairs and stop by the bathroom, he continues on to his room. "Come on," I call after him. "Take a shower with me."

I can tell there's still some sourness in his expression as he tries to leave me in the bathroom by myself. "Gabriel, come on."

"Nah, I'm good. I don't want your pity fucks."

He spins to walk away, and I grab him by the arm to pull him closer. "What are you talking about?"

Pushing me against the bathroom counter, he glares angrily into my eyes. "What do you think I'm talking about, Princess? You fuck my dad while I'm gone, and then turn around and fuck my brother. But in order to sleep with me, you need to make a fucking trade. So what's the trade off with them, huh? Are you whoring yourself to them, too?"

"Gabriel," I whisper softly, reaching for his face, and he quickly swats my hand away. I see the pain in his eyes, and I hate it. He spins on his heels, marching angrily toward his bedroom. I hate that just a couple hours ago, he was the fun Gabriel that I love to be around, but one reminder from his brother that I'm not exclusively his, and he snaps—naturally so.

I keep on his tail as I follow him to his room before he shuts me out. "I'm not sorry that I slept with them, Gabriel, but I am sorry that you think I only sleep with you because of our trade off. I mean, sure, in the beginning that's how it was—"

"Stop with your bullshit!" he yells.

"It's not bullshit!" I huff. "Fine, if you want to stop trading sex for favors, we'll stop."

"Fine!" he snaps back.

We're both still sweaty from the sparring and panting from the heated exchange as we stare at each other. "I know you're feeling self-conscious because you were a virgin."

He lets out a frustrated groan.

"But the reasons I like being with you have nothing to do with the deal."

"Oh, fuck off," he yells, as he tries to get by me, but I block the doorway.

"No. You can't keep shutting me out when shit gets

uncomfortable. Just because I'm not *just* yours, doesn't mean I'm not *still* yours."

He freezes in front of me, shaking his head with an evil-looking sneer. "You're just a slut without a family."

I react on instinct, slapping my hand hard against his face —the second Black I've hit today. But instead of stopping the way Silas did, Gabriel fights back, grabbing my arm and tossing me on the bed. When I expect him to land on top of me, I feel a surge of disappointment as he turns to walk away.

I jump up quickly to stop him, squeezing myself between his body and the door.

"Will you fucking move?" he shouts.

"No! We made a deal." I reach for his basketball shorts, trying to peel them down, but he grabs my wrists and tosses me to the side. I don't let up, though, and maybe I come across as a crazy bitch in this moment, but Gabriel doesn't listen with words. He wants to fight and play dirty, so that's what I'm doing.

I don't let him leave, and he can act fed up with me, but I'm noticing the way his cock is growing in his shorts. And he's losing his will to fight as well, so when I lean up to kiss him, he doesn't fight me as hard anymore. Instead, he slams me back against the door and assaults me with his mouth.

I grab eagerly at his pants, and this time, when I reach in and get a hold of him, he doesn't slap me away.

"Get the fuck off me," he growls, but I don't listen. Dropping to my knees, I tear his shorts off completely, letting his cock point directly at my face. And I don't hesitate to pull him into my mouth, making it hard for him to fight me off.

"Fuck," he grunts as I slide my lips and tongue from the base to the head, giving it a little squeeze at the end, which makes him groan even louder. After a couple pumps, I feel the head tighten, and remembering the way his first blow job went, I loosen my grip on his cock and reach for his balls, pulling them down with force.

He lets out a moan, deep and guttural, suddenly taking control of the situation. His hands land in my hair, clutching tightly as he fucks my mouth, but I don't let go of his balls, keeping him from coming sooner than he wants to.

My eyes start to brim with tears, so I stare up at him. I want Gabriel to see my face, to see that I want him as much as the others. And as he thrusts into my throat, causing the tears to roll down my cheeks, I see the pleasure on his face.

Finally letting go of him, I run my hands up his legs, under his shirt and let my fingers slide across the rigged plane of his abs and up to his pecs. I still have my eyes on him as I feel him tighten in my mouth just before he yanks me off of him again.

With a hand in my hair, he drags me up to standing. Pressing my front to the door, he tears down my pants and yanks my hips back against his. Aligning his cock to my entrance, I shove backward, impaling myself on him. He lets out a low groan.

Immediately, I'm hit with the sudden soreness from where Baron pounded into me last night and the bruising from where Silas spanked me this morning. But even this pain makes me feel alive, and I welcome it. This feeling of my body being so used and wracked with pleasure brings an addictive energy I can't get enough of. I may never get tired of this.

With his hands on my hips, he presses me against the wall, thrusting hard and breathing his grunts into my ear. The more I shove back toward him, fighting him for my own pleasure, the harder he thrusts. It quickly becomes a battle for control, and we both reach our climaxes fast and hard, the room echoing with our grunts and cries of pleasure.

We're catching our breaths when he finally pulls away, dropping onto the bed and staring up at the ceiling. As I turn back to look at him, I notice the satisfaction written in his features, so much more than the first time we did this when he came so fast it made my head spin. He's finding confidence in sex, confidence I'm giving him.

Pulling my pants back up, I step toward him. "I know you're angry I was with Silas and Baron, but maybe I like seeing you jealous." His chest is heaving as he bores that crystal blue stare right through me, and I feel pinned in place. Leaning down, I put one hand on the bed next to his head as I say, "I like the fight in you."

Silently, I slip out of his room and head to the shower. I really should not feel as proud of myself as I do right now, and I really shouldn't get used to the idea of having all of them to myself. These guys are still as dangerous as they were when I first got here, but I no longer feel threatened by them. Now, I feel like one of them. They are letting me in on their secrets, opening up their hearts to me. And, I'm doing the same for them.

## Twenty-Four

It's Donny's face just before the bullet penetrated his skull and sent him into a lifeless slump in the chair that wakes me up in the middle of the night. I don't feel bad about killing him. The man was a monster, but I have a feeling that pulling that trigger is going to haunt me for a while.

Slipping out of bed, I tiptoe silently down the stairs and across the house toward the warm bed that has welcomed me more than once since I've arrived here. But there are a pair of menacing amber eyes that stop me in my tracks as I pass the kitchen.

Baron is standing in all black, drying his hands on a towel as I skid to a stop in front of him.

"Your bedroom is the other way," he mutters darkly.

"I couldn't sleep," I whisper.

"Running to Daddy's bed after a nightmare? What are you, five?"

My forehead wrinkles as I glare at him. "What do you care?"

"My brother cares."

I scoff, spinning toward him and planting my hands on

the counter. "And if Gabriel mattered at all to you, you wouldn't have done what you did the other day."

He doesn't respond as he folds the towel precisely and places it on the cold surface.

"My little brother is the only man in this house with any heart left, so don't stomp all over it, okay?" He doesn't look up at me as he speaks. He begins to walk away from me, but I'm quick to stop him, grabbing him by the arm and turning him toward me.

"Bullshit."

His face twists in confusion as he smirks down at me. "Bullshit?" he asks, as if he's toying with me. Being this close, I get a whiff of his cologne but something else. Crisp night air, a hint of sweat, and, maybe, gunpowder? Did he just return from a job?

"Yes, Baron, I'm calling bullshit. You and your dad can pretend all you want that you're stone-cold killers without emotions, but I'm not buying it. I think you've just gotten very good at hiding them."

With a menacing step toward me, I feel him back me into the wall, glaring down at me.

"Would you like to put that theory to the test?"

"How would we do that?" I ask, barely able to take a steady breath with him this close.

His hand snakes up my body, goosebumps erupting in the wake of his touch until he reaches my throat, laying his broad hand around it and giving a gentle squeeze. "I could snap your neck right now and not feel a thing."

It becomes almost impossible to keep from swallowing, but I refuse to let him see me tremble in his presence. He thinks he's intimidating me, but it's all just a front, a way to keep from showing emotion, and I'm ready to call his bluff.

"Go ahead then," I whisper in return, tilting my chin up a little higher.

There's a subtle squint to his eyes. Traces of surprise in his expression. His fingers squeeze a little tighter, and he presses me against the wall with force, cutting off my windpipe, but I don't react. Then, I feel him rubbing against my leg, and the stiffness there has my heart beating a little faster. Fighting against the urge to knock his hand away, I reach down and stroke him through his pants.

He lets out a groan, inching his face closer to mine until I feel his breath against my face. Then, he pulls back his hand just enough to allow my lungs to fill up.

I'm playing with fire. I know Baron could easily kill me with his bare hands right now, and I'm testing the one person in this house I should not be testing, but what the fuck do I have to lose at this point? He wants to play games, then I'm ready to play.

When his hand drifts away from my throat, his mouth moves closer to my ear. "Let's be very clear. This is not emotion I'm showing. It's mercy, and not for you but for my brother because I do think he likes you. And he deserves better than a whore who will fuck every cock in the house."

He wants a reaction out of me, but I don't give him one. He thinks calling me a whore will hurt my feelings, but it won't. Mostly because he likes me more than he's willing to admit, and I like toying with him just enough to watch him dance around that admission.

Pressing my hands against his chest, I shove him far enough away to look him in the eye.

"That's very kind of you." When I give him a wink, he grinds his molars, and I know I'm getting to him. "So, why are you just coming home at three in the morning? Did you have a job?"

There's an incredulous expression on his face, and I know it's a long shot, expecting him to talk to me about his jobs, but Gabriel and Silas talk to me, so it's worth a shot.

"Why would I tell you anything?"

"Who the fuck am I going to tell, Baron? I literally have no one."

"You don't need to know, so you don't get to know. It's that simple."

There's something strange in the way he says that that grabs my attention, almost as if it's a little rushed as he turns away from me. Like he's hiding something. What would he possibly be hiding from me?

"Was it Mickey Barton?" I ask, following him down the hall toward his room.

"No. Go to bed."

My curiosity is too strong now. I haven't heard Silas talk about any other jobs, and I mean, I know they have other jobs, but there's something strange about Baron coming home in the middle of the night—keeping secrets and avoiding questions.

"Who was it?" I ask again, putting myself between him and the door to his room. When he stops to stare down at me, it's not the anger in his expression that alarms me but the fear. It's subtle, but it's there.

"Are you keeping secrets?" I whisper, and something in him snaps. In a swift violent motion, he snatches me by the waist and throws me hard against the wall across from his doorway. One hand holds me firmly against the chest as he points the other in my face, a biting hatred on his face as his voice booms so loudly it makes me flinch.

"You mind your own fucking business, or I swear to God you won't wake up in the morning, Iris. Do you understand? I will feel nothing. I won't miss you and life will go back to the way it was. Do you have any idea how easy that would be for me? So, if I were you, I'd leave me the fuck alone, and unless you want to wrap those lips around my cock, just keep your mouth shut."

In a rush, he spins away from me, slamming the door to his room behind him, and I have to fight the urge to cry. In a silent tip-toe run, I head straight for Silas's room, climbing into bed with him and letting him wrap me up in his arms.

"Nightmares again?" he asks in the silent room.

"Yes," I reply with a shake to my voice as I press myself closer to his body, letting him smother me in comfort and safety. If Baron is hiding something, there's nothing I can do about it now, and I think I've been playing with fire enough for one evening.

## Twenty-Five

SIFTING through my journal for the hundredth time this week, I start to feel restless again. The business has been crazy busy this week, so I've been distracted by helping them out where they need me. Gabriel and I played a little good cop/bad cop with a guy in the basement. We ended up getting the information a lot faster than he normally does, and it put him in a good mood. When Gabriel is in a good mood, everyone is in a good mood.

Silas took me on two business deals this week, trying to teach me the business side of things. During meetings with clients, I would sit quietly next to him, absorbing every word and the clients never suspected I was even paying attention. Then in the car, Silas would quiz me on every detail, rewarding me with kisses and orgasms, and that was before we got home.

For the most part, we've settled into a rhythm, and it's actually been nice. Formal dinners together like a family, coffee and breakfast at the island before everyone disperses for the day, and then me discreetly sneaking into one of three beds sometime in the middle of the night.

Okay, one of *two* beds. I don't sneak into Baron's bed. He and I are still holding each other at arm's length, and except for a few *accidental* run-ins and very few words, we don't actually have much of a relationship.

Gabriel is still holding onto so much resentment regarding our little arrangement, if you can even call it that. The sex between us has been mostly filled with spite and jealousy, but on the bright side, I think that makes it better. Being jealous of Silas makes Gabriel work harder for my attention, and he loves when he finally gets it. I never would have thought something like this could possibly work, and call me crazy, but it kind of is. It's not like anything else the Black family does is conventional, so why would their relationships be?

As my first month at the Black house comes to a close, there are three things that have become abundantly clear to me. One: I love this job. And no, I don't mean just killing people. That's morbid as fuck. But I love the business part of it, the time and skill that goes into it, and yeah, the money, because it is a lot. And the people who get whacked by the Blacks usually had it coming, had plenty of warning, and would have probably died a way more gruesome death if they didn't handle it.

Two: I don't really want to leave. Considering my alternate plan for life if my father hadn't died was to be married off to some psycho who would have probably shut me in the house, pumped some baby making juice in me, and then let me get old in perpetual boredom for the rest of my life, I actually like this option far more. These guys actually value me, and not just for sex. They teach me things, and it's so fucking *nice* to be helpful.

The last thing I know for certain is that Baron Black is keeping secrets. I can't tell if Silas knows his son is keeping something from him or if he's in denial about it. Even if I manage to get all three of them in the same room, the tension between those two is thick. Baron is always busy with work that I don't see Silas assigning to him, and when I ask about it, he doesn't tell me anything. I have a feeling he's working on his own and doesn't have the heart to tell his dad.

And as much as I hate to admit it, the idea of Baron leaving makes me a little sad. I mean, don't get me wrong, most days I hate him. He's rude and cold and selfish, but he's also the only one who can look me in the eye and it feels like I'm seeing someone just like me looking back. We connect on a deeper level, and I know he feels that too, even if he won't admit it.

Which is what brings me to his door at ten in the morning on a Sunday—his day off. I wouldn't normally sneak in on Baron because I don't actually trust that he wouldn't kill me by accident, but I'm desperate, so I take it slow. First, I knock, and when he doesn't answer, I turn the knob and enter.

The room is dark, almost pitch black from the thick light-blocking curtains. I can see his form under the black comforter, so I approach him carefully, sitting on the bed near his feet.

"Baron, wake up," I call to him softly. He rustles just enough for me to know he at least heard me.

As he turns onto his back and my eyes adjust, I take a moment to admire how stupidly handsome he is. With that heavy brow and strong jawline, I wonder if he knows how much he would slay with the ladies if he actually tried to live a normal life. I mean, let's be honest, all three of the Black men would be drowning in pussy if they took even one day to just be regular, warm-blooded men.

"What do you want, Iris?" he groans, covering his eyes with his arm draped across his face.

"I need you to show me how to shoot."

He lifts his head, peering up at me with skepticism on his face.

"You're kidding, right?"

"Do I look like I'm kidding? Your dad's taught me the business. Gabriel taught me interrogation. I still have not learned how to properly shoot a gun. So I need you to show me."

"I'm not your fucking mentor, Iris. Have one of them show you. They know how." He rolls away from me, hiding his face in his covers.

Squaring my shoulders, I reply, "Well, I want to learn from the best."

He laughs. "Nice try."

"Come on, Baron! What do you want? We can make a trade like I did with Gabriel."

"We already had sex," he deadpans, and my insides dance a little when he says that. Why do I get so hot and bothered by Baron? Because he's the biggest asshole of all of them? What is wrong with me?

I know I'm an idiot for what I'm about to say, but it's all I have. I've barely gotten anywhere on my own revenge case since working with them on their hits, and it's starting to worry me that we will never really solve it. I'll never get to kill Maretti like I want, and we'll just sweep it all under the rug.

So, I'm pulling out the big guns.

"Fine. Then help me and I won't tell your dad that you're keeping secrets and doing side jobs on your own."

There's one beat of silence before I'm flying toward the bed, landing flat on my back in the darkness with Baron hovering over me, a look of pure fury in his eyes. "Did you just fucking threaten me?" he says with a sneer.

*Keep your cool, Iris.*

"Yeah, so what if I did?" I lick my lips in anticipation as his eyes dart down to my mouth.

"I don't think you're really in the position to threaten me, you little bitch."

That one earns a laugh. Baron has himself so convinced he hates me, but it's starting to become blatantly obvious that he doesn't. In fact, I'm starting to think the opposite.

"Why not? You can't just snap my neck and toss me out anymore. People in this house actually care about me now, and like it or not, they'll listen to me. And by the way you're reacting to my threat, I'm even more certain you have something to hide, so just let me go and I won't bother you again. But I might have to talk to your dad."

He lets out a throaty sigh, blowing his nasty morning breath right in my face.

"So you're telling on me? Am I hearing this right?"

I let out another laugh. "Yeah, I guess I am." As he rolls off of me, he groans before throwing a little temper tantrum, flinging the covers off and stomping to his en suite bathroom.

"Meet you downstairs in an hour then?" I call, but of course, he doesn't answer.


We're standing behind the house with a long stretch of land between where we're standing and a couple shooting targets about fifty yards away. Baron has hardly said a word since I woke him up. He's being broody and quiet again. Probably because I threatened him, and he doesn't like that.

He walks me through loading the pistol, moving way too fast for my comfort. Then, he gets behind me, wrapping his arms over mine as he raises my hand, aiming the gun at the target.

"Stare down the barrel, and don't take your eyes off the target."

I feel his breath on my ear and his hard body against my back. It's hard not to be a little distracted by his proximity.

With his hands resting gently on my arms, I pull the trigger, and the bullet punctures the target toward the edge and nowhere near the outline of the body.

"Focus," he whispers next to my ear. "Clear your mind and think only about the target. See the bullet hit right where you want it. Then on the exhale, pull the trigger."

The softness of his voice and the smell of his skin so close to my body starts to infiltrate my mind so that it's no longer distracting. Instead, it grounds me. Baron clears the noise in my head until it's only him and me standing together. He becomes an extension of me, his body a shield against mine.

Shutting my eyes for a moment, I do what he says. I focus. And when I open them, I imagine the bullet hitting where I want it before letting out a long exhale that comes from somewhere deep in my chest. Then, I pull the trigger.

The bullet doesn't hit the center, but it gets close. A hell of a lot closer than last time.

"Good girl," Baron whispers in my ear, his voice low and sultry, and a shiver runs down my spine. *What is he trying to do to me?*

He steps away after a moment, leaving my body feeling cold without the contact. I turn to him as he busies himself loading a second gun.

"Who taught you to shoot?" I ask.

"Silas." The way he says it, so cold and emotionless, sounds strange to me.

"You mean your dad."

"Yes, my dad," he mutters reluctantly.

"What happened between you two that you seem to hate him so much?"

I notice the way his shoulders tense and his jaw clenches. "Nothing happened."

"Do you," I ask, pushing him out of curiosity, "hate him?"

"No, I don't hate him."

"Well, you clearly don't like him very much. All you guys do is fight. He seems to think you don't even want to be a part of the family anymore."

Baron slams the gun on the table. "No, what my father's problem is, is that he has confused family and business."

Biting my cheek, I watch him, seeing so much anger coursing through him. Baron is clearly at war, but with who, I don't know. His father. Himself. In some sense, I see the way he struggles with me, and it's almost like he has himself guarded, afraid to let go around me. I wish he would.

"How old were you when you started working for him?" I ask tentatively.

He scoffs. "You mean my first kill? Or when he stopped looking at me like a son and more like an employee?"

"Baron," I say, reaching for him.

"It doesn't matter, Iris. I don't know why you even bother prying. You're going to kill Maretti and then be gone, right?"

"That's the plan," I mumble. "And I'm not prying. I just hate to see you two so angry with each other."

He turns toward the target without responding, unloading the magazine rapidly, each bullet puncturing the target right on the center dot. When his arms relax, I notice a subtle change in his posture. His shoulders hang a little lower, and the tension in his neck has softened.

"I was thirteen," he says, and I wait in silence for him to explain. "When I made my first kill. And he didn't make me do it. I wanted to. It was a long-range sniper shot, and the guy was a known murderer. Killed a whole family in their home because of drugs, so I didn't feel bad when I made the shot. I think he did that on purpose, and gave me a clean job. It was something I could be proud of, and I was."

"He was proud of you too," I whisper like a question, finishing his thought.

"I guess so." He's staring down at the table again,

reloading before he clears his throat and adds, "Gabe came not long after, and we became a family. His little workforce family."

When he hands the loaded gun to me, nodding to the target, telling me to fire again, I hesitate. "Are you going to leave, Baron?"

"Don't worry about it."

"He's worried about it, you know."

"Just shoot, Iris."

There's a lump in my throat, and I hate how attached I'm becoming to this family. How the thought of Baron leaving has my insides twisting, unable to process how the idea of him abandoning Silas and Gabriel makes me so sad I want to cry. Why do I even care? Like he said, when all of this is done, I'm leaving. It doesn't matter how much I like it here or how bad I want to be a part of this family business. I'm just a guest, and my time here is temporary. As soon as I get my revenge on Vincent Maretti—or the Black family gets sick of me, which-ever comes first—I'm out of here. Free to start my new life. My boring, free life.

After another few rounds, I start to get the hang of this and I've come so damn close to hitting the target numerous times, but have yet to land a bullet on it. Each time I pull back on the trigger, I can feel Baron tense up as much as I do. As if he's anxiously waiting for me to hit the bullseye. Dare I say, he believes in me?

With the gun gripped tightly in my hand, I slowly pull back the trigger, exhaling as soon as the bullet expels from the chamber.

My arms immediately fly in the air. "Fuck, yes! I did it!" I shout with an excitement I didn't know was possible just from hitting a bullseye with a bullet.

The next thing I know, Baron is swooping me up in his

arms from behind me and squeezing my body tight against his. "Yeah, you did."

My neck twists to get a look at him as his hold on me loosens. Our eyes catch and his expression drops. For a brief moment, I thought I'd be turning around to see wonder in his eyes, but I see nothing. Cold and empty orbs stare back at me.

Baron takes a step backward, as if he's ashamed with himself for even touching me. Or, because he let me see a side of him that wasn't calloused and demanding. A side he never wanted anyone to know existed.

My joyful outburst fades as fast as it came. I take a step forward, reclaiming the space that Baron just stepped out of. My eyes are laser-focused on him when I place my free hand on his cheek. My fingers are still wrapped tightly around the gun that hangs freely from my other hand.

Baron looks down at my arm that's stretched out to him like every part of me is infected. "You're allowed to be excited about things, Baron," I tell him, as if I'm trying to explain something he didn't already know. It shouldn't be something that needs to be explained. But, in his case, it is. Baron and Gabriel were not raised; they were trained. Emotions are frowned upon. Connections with people outside of business are forbidden. I should be forbidden. Yet, here I am. In this house with these three men; all of whom are slowly making a home inside of my heart while I'm tearing down walls in theirs.

His head cocks to the side and he looks at me like I'm a puzzle he's trying to piece together. Confusion sweeps over his expression and something shifts inside of him. Slowly lifting his hand, he places it over mine and for a moment I think that he might kiss me—respond in a way that shows me a glimpse of the warmth that I know is hidden inside of him somewhere. That is, until he begins peeling my fingers off his face, one at a time.

"What—" I start to speak, but he squeezes all four of my fingers together. Harder, and harder, and harder. Until bone is grinding against bone. "Baron, that hurts." I jerk my hand away.

"Don't touch me again," he hisses through his clenched teeth.

"I'm...I'm sorry. I thought—"

"You thought wrong." He snatches the gun from my hand and stalks past me with thunderous steps.

"Baron, wait!" I shout as I chase after him. "I'm sorry. Let's just go back to shooting."

I catch up to his side, but he doesn't even bother acknowledging my presence as we walk hurriedly down the marble white flooring of the corridor.

"We're finished." He heads upstairs, but this time, I don't follow. I stand at the bottom and watch him leave, wondering what he meant when he said *we're finished*. Finished shooting? Finished fooling around?

Baron might be able to end this thing between us as fast as it started, but I'm not sure I can ever quit him—or any of these guys for that matter.

*Twenty-Six*

Once I'm finally alone in my bed, in my own thoughts, I chase away the feeling of defeat with these guys. It seems like I'm always saying or doing the wrong thing, and I guess I sort of am. I've slept with all three of them, and as wrong as it is, I have no regrets. Life is too short for that bullshit. I loved every minute of every time I was with every one of them. Worrying about my heart potentially breaking in the end is redundant. My heart is already shattered. I'm fighting this life of mine alone, and it's my fight.

Not Silas', not Gabriel's, not Baron's, and not my father's.

Heaving a sigh, I curl my legs up to my chest and wrap my arms around my knees on top of the still-made bed. How could my father promise me to Vincent Maretti? How dare he even think he had a right to choose who I'd marry. I miss him fiercely, but I can't help but feel anger boiling inside of me—hurt, rather.

Regardless of whether or not he recanted on his deal, at one point in my life, he looked another man in the eye and promised me to him. I wonder how old I was when that deal was made. Was I just a child? A teenager? Maybe it's best I don't know. I still love him and I will avenge his death and save my life. Vincent Maretti will still pay for what he did and the only pearl he'll come close to is the strand of them that I just might wrap around his neck.

I stayed in bed all night, not even bothering to sneak or peek into the rooms of my housemates. Then, I stayed in bed half of the day while none of them made an attempt to visit me either. It's crazy how I can feel on top of the world when I am near any of them, but also like an inconvenience at the same time. I imagine that's the way they all look at me. Like, I just waltzed into their lives and rattled things up. I suppose that's exactly what I did.

It's half past noon when there's a gentle knock at the door. "Ms. Pavetta, your presence is requested in the dining room," Carol says with a crack to her voice. She was given strict orders to steer clear of me, so I'm not a bit surprised that she does just that.

"By who?" I shout from under the covers. I've been lying on my back, deep in a mess of thoughts since eight o'clock this morning.

"Mr. Black, dear."

Well, that's not exactly saying much. It could be any of them. It could be all of them. Still lying stiff as a board, I retort, "Ok. I'll be down shortly."

I tug the blankets up tighter to my chest, unsure if I'm ready to face today's music. Speaking of music—now that I think about it, Gabriel didn't have his speakers shaking the walls last night. Aside from when he was in Elba, he's played his music every night.

Now that my wheels are spinning, it's also odd that Silas didn't wake me up this morning. Whether it be with a glass of cold water or some morning wood that needed attention. Tearing the white down comforter off of me, I spring out of bed. My bare feet pad across the hardwood floors as I head straight for my en suite bathroom.

Once I've brushed my teeth, ran a comb through my hair, and tied a black plush robe around my waist, I head straight out of my room and down the stairs. I could have put on something a little more presentable, but as soon as this little meeting is over, I'm retiring straight back to my room to think about the next phase of my plan.

With my feet still bare, I walk briskly toward the dining room. My feet smack against the floor and there's no doubt that the sound alerts my presence to whomever is waiting for me.

As soon as I catch sight of the very large table, my movements freeze. I tug the ropes around my waist snugger and my mouth drops open. I'm not sure if it's out of confusion or humiliation.

"I'm...I'm sorry, I didn't know we had guests," I say with nervousness on my tongue. Yep, it's definitely humiliation.

Silas, Gabriel, and Baron all sit on one side of the table. Directly across from them are two other men who I've never seen before. Both of whom are wearing snazzy suits with slicked back hair, not a single strand out of place. The room reeks of testosterone and I know immediately that whatever has taken place in this room was not pleasant.

Silas waves a hand, gesturing for me to join them. "Sit down, Iris. We'd all like to have a word with you."

My thumb shoots over my shoulder. "Maybe I should just go and change into something more...appropriate."

"Nonsense, darling. You look simply delightful." One of the strange men says as his eyes skate up from my bare legs to my breasts, finally meeting my eyes. He pops a toothpick between his teeth and the corner of his lip curls up in a sick and twisted grin. "As a matter of fact, I've saved you a seat." He pulls out the chair directly beside him and my stomach twists in knots.

The tension in this room is so thick it's suffocating. Gabriel lets out a heady breath and I watch as his posture stiffens. His eyes cemented to the man who's watching me and waiting for me to take a seat beside him.

*It's ok. Silas, Gabriel, and Baron would never let these men hurt me.* Feather-like steps lead me over to the chair. I take a seat and slide it closer to the table. My hands fold in my lap as I focus on the three men sitting across from me.

"Iris," Silas lifts a hand and gestures toward the men, "these men are here to cut a deal for Mr. Maretti."

My heart sinks as I sit my ass on the chair. "A deal?" My eyes trail from Silas to Gabriel, then from Gabriel to Baron. Baron doesn't even look at me. His eyes are in his lap and I can only assume he's texting someone. Wouldn't surprise me if that son of a bitch was playing Candy Crush while these guys are cutting deals at my expense.

The man beside me places a hand on my shoulder, which sends the legs of Gabriel's chair shooting back. Gabriel stands up, smacks both hands to the table and leans forward with a hiss. "Hands off! Now!"

"My apologies," the gentleman says as he sweeps my shoulder off with his fingertips and returns them to his own personal space. He then twists his body to face me and extends a hand. "Name's Buzz. It's a pleasure to meet you, dear Iris." I gaze at his hand like it's the plague before gently laying the tips of my fingers on it. He slowly raises my hand to his lips and places a delicate kiss on my knuckles. My stomach turns and if I allowed myself, I'd probably vomit all over his lustrous black suit.

Snatching my hand away, I rub it on the material of my robe.

Gabriel doesn't sit back down. His hands remain plastered to the table. Even when Silas gives a tug on his black jacket and grumbles something under his breath, Gabriel completely ignores him. In a weird way, it makes me feel important to him. There is no doubt in my mind that these men came to collect me for Vincent Maretti. But I know Gabriel will not let them take me without a fight, and neither will I.

As for Silas—he's a businessman. There is a very good chance that he will make a deal. Baron is here, but I'm not sure he's really here. He couldn't care less. Gabriel, though, he cares, and it squeezes my heart. I offer him a half-smile and he nods, assuring me he will not let anything happen to me.

"Mr. Maretti is willing to spare an all-out war with the families if you kindly let us take what is his," Buzz says to Gabriel.

It's so strange seeing a full-grown man trying to barter with an eighteen-year-old boy. It goes to show that Gabriel has pull, even being so young. People fear him—admire him and respect him.

With his eyes dead locked on Buzz, Gabriel raises a brow with his jaw clenched tightly. "There's not a damn thing in this house that belongs to Vincent Maretti. Unless, of course, you're referring to the bullet from my nine-millimeter. In that case, I'll gladly deliver it straight to his fucking head."

Buzz slides his seat back in the same manner that Gabriel did and takes the same stance, with his palms plastered to the tabletop. "If you know what's good for you, you'll sit your ass back down, boy."

Gabriel makes a quick movement that has everyone in a state of panic. Silas and Baron are on their feet, and this time, it's Baron watching me. For a moment, I swear I see worry in his expression. As if he's ready to fly across the table to protect me.

Baron's eyes shift to Silas and I watch the movement in

slow motion. Silas gives him a nod, and it's as if I could almost predict what was going to happen next. Baron looks back to me, but before I can even collect another thought, Gabriel is rounding the table so fast that no one has a chance to react. He takes hold of the other man by wrapping his arm around his neck. When he reaches in his pocket of his jacket, I gasp.

He pulls out a hand-sized gun and holds it to the man's head.

The next thing I know, I'm being pulled in the opposite direction of the men. Frozen, unable to think. I'm dragged out like a ragdoll. "Walk, damnit." I look up and realize that it's Baron taking me away. "Hurry the fuck up. We need to get outta here."

"But...what about Gabriel. And Silas?" I choke out.

"They can take care of themselves. You cannot. So if you wouldn't mind walking yourself, that'd be great."

I'm still trying to gather my thoughts that are a scrambled mess. All I can think about is Silas or Gabriel getting hurt and, for some reason, my body puts up resistance against Baron. We can't just leave them.

"God damnit, Iris." Baron sweeps his hands under my ass and lifts me up, throwing me over his shoulder. I stop fighting. I just stare into the space in front of me, hoping that one of them will come out before gunshots begin sounding. That other guy is going to attack. There is no way that he will allow his friend to get shot in the head. This can't end well.

Baron pulls open the front door and steps outside. "Baron!" I shout, "we can't leave them." Tears begin streaming down my cheeks, falling onto the shoulder of his jacket.

"Calm your ass down. I said they'd be fine. Silas has security watching every move they make."

I'm still flung over his shoulder and still in my robe when we approach a black car with a gentleman standing at the back door. He pulls the door open and Baron tosses me in like I'm a bag of trash. For a moment, I consider that he's just sending me away and he's going back in to help, but he climbs in beside me. I'm not even sure how I'd feel if he did leave me. On one hand, Silas and Gabriel would have backup. But, on another, Baron would be in harm's way, too. I care about them all so much and the idea of losing any one of them hurts fiercely.

I'm fiddling with the straps of my robe in the back seat of this spacious car—still too stunned to begin asking questions —when Baron hands me a bottle of water. I look from it, to him, in confusion. "What's that for?"

"It's water. You drink it," he deadpans.

Taking it from him, I just hold it in my hands and stare straight ahead. "They were coming for me, weren't they?"

"Drink," he demands.

"I'm not thirsty."

"You need to stay hydrated. I'll get you some food later, but right now, drink the damn water."

I was almost taken by two mobsters and he's concerned about my hydration. "Baron, I—" He cuts me off by snatching the water bottle back out of my hands. Unscrewing the top, he tosses it to the floor and then hands the bottle back to me. This time, I don't take it. I just stare at it dumbfoundedly. "This is ridiculous. I told you I'm not thirsty. What I need right now is answers. Who were those men?"

It's a stupid question because who they are doesn't matter. It's who they work for that is important. I already know the answer to that question, though. They work for Vincent. Pretty much said so themselves. What I really need to know is how they found me.

"You drink, and I'll answer. Deal?"

"Why are you so concerned with me drinking this damn bottle of water?" I grimace, "Are you trying to drug me or something?"

"Don't be ridiculous, Iris. If I wanted to drug you, I'd shove a pill down your throat myself."

I crane my neck, a bit taken back. "Ok, then."

"We have a long drive ahead of us and we're unable to stop. You haven't eaten breakfast, so the least you can do is try not to get dehydrated."

"Since when do you care about me or my health?"

"I don't care. But, my family does. For some reason, they've gotten quite attached to you." He turns his head to face me. "I think we both know why."

Tipping the bottle back, I take a long swig, so I don't have to respond to that. Little good it does, because he's still looking at me when I swallow down the water and bring the bottle back to my lap. "What?" I hiss at him.

"Nothing? No sly comeback about how you're falling in love with my brother and my father? Or how they got a piece of that golden pussy?"

Choking on the last swallow, I cough it back up and water flies out of my mouth. "Excuse me?" I wipe the back of my hand across my mouth.

It's not like I owe any of them an explanation. "You weren't complaining when you got a piece of it." Then I tip the bottle back and take another drink.

"What's to complain about? It was free."

My eyes go wide, and I suddenly feel the intense desire to spit this water right in his face. "I know what you're getting at. You think I'm a slut, don't you?"

His shoulders shrug and he finally turns away. Is it because he doesn't want to answer, or is he hiding his face because... "You're jealous, aren't you?"

His gaze snaps back to me. His eyebrows furrowed, his jaw locked. "Fuck no, I'm not jealous."

I smirk. "You are. I can tell." I take another drink and smile into the rim of the bottle. He can deny it all he wants, but part of him is a tad jealous that I've slept with a guy raised as his brother and his biological father. Even if he doesn't care much for Silas, they are still family.

"Has anyone told you that you're an annoying little shit?"

"Yup. But it doesn't change the fact that you felt something toward me when we slept together, and it bugs the hell out of you that you weren't the only one."

His head angles toward me and his expression grows serious. "Let's get one thing straight. The only thing that *bugs the hell out of me* is the fact that you parade around our house in skimpy clothes just to grab the attention of every member with a dick—being every member of our household—and the only reason that you're doing it is because you want something from us. You may have gotten under the skin of Silas and Gabriel, but you won't get under mine."

He turns back and faces the back of the seat in front of him. I don't say anything for about thirty seconds, but the gnawing desire to push him a step further is intense. "Yep. Definitely jealous," I mutter under my breath with a smirk.

"What'd you just say?"

"Oh, nothing," I singsong as I pick at the chipped polish on my fingernails.

Before I can wipe the shit-eating grin off my face, his strong hands are gripping my cheeks. His chest presses against mine and I don't even let out a breath before his mouth is devouring mine. He tastes of bourbon and bitterness. But the further his tongue slides in, the sweeter he becomes.

I resist for a moment. Pulling back and trying to eye the driver around Baron's head. "The driver," I say.

"Fuck him," he says point-blankly.

I can feel his growing cock press into the side of my hip. My back arches and I heave, "Baron." I'm not even sure why I just said his name, or if I planned to follow it with something. But I don't. I just let his name linger between us and hope that he takes it as an invitation to do whatever the hell he wants with me.

Wrapping an arm around my waist, he slides me down so that my back is pressed to the cushion of the seat. His body cloaks mine and I'm, once again, thankful that this car has so much space.

There's something special about getting this sort of attention from Baron. It's obvious that he doesn't let many people see an ounce of vulnerability in him, but for some reason, he's offering it to me. I could easily push him and humiliate him, but he knows that I won't. I'll succumb to his desires, because they mimic mine.

Our mouths part while his lips still ghost mine. "I think they're the ones who are jealous." He speaks in an undertone before crashing his lips to mine again. His knee comes between my legs and presses aggressively against my crotch. I grate myself against it, begging for more as my entire body floods with the desire to feel him inside of me.

With both hands, I pull down the sleeves of his jacket until they linger around his forearms. He slides one arm out, then the other, and lets it drop to the floor.

I lean forward, trying to get a look at the driver. Wondering if he's watching us right now, or if he cares what is happening—or about to happen.

"Don't worry about him," Baron says as he comes up just enough to undo the ties of my robe. His hand slides under my shirt and he cups one of my breasts. Still grinding his knee abrasively against me, he begins rolling my nipple between his thumb and forefinger. Tugging, pulling, and driving me fucking wild. I buck my hips up to gain friction when he rubs his knee harder. I can feel myself dampen between my legs and I just remembered that I don't even have underwear on underneath these shorts. Not even giving a damn, my chin tips up and my eyes close as I relish in the way he makes my body feel.

"You like that?" he grumbles as he tugs harder at my nipple, stretching it to the max.

There's a sting, but it's more pleasurable than painful. "Mmmhmm." I stretch my hand down between us and rub his rock-hard cock through the fabric of his pants. "Take these off," I tell him.

He doesn't hesitate. His hand slides out of my shirt and he braces himself up with one arm while he undoes his belt and pops the button on his pants. I give him a hand and help slide them down along with his briefs. Once his cock springs free, I take hold of it and lock my fingers around his girth. Sliding up and down. I come forward a tad and get a glimpse in the rearview mirror in the front and catch the driver's eyes on mine. He's definitely watching.

My strokes cease. "Baron," I whisper. He looks at me and I gesture toward the front seat. When he follows my stare, he sees the driver watching us in the rearview mirror.

"If I catch you looking at her again, you're fired," Baron snaps. "Take the fucking mirror off." When the driver does nothing, Baron snaps again, "Right fucking now!" I hear the snap and drop of the mirror and my eyes widen. Did he seriously just make him break the mirror from the window so we could have sex back here? "Better?" he asks.

"Yeah. But he wasn't just watching me. He was watching us."

"He was watching you. Everyone watches you, Iris. How could they not?" He takes my bottom lip between his teeth and tugs it gently.

His body slides slowly down mine as he kisses the nape of my neck. He moves lower and lifts my T-shirt and kisses my stomach, then my side. His fingers rim the hem of my shorts. In one swift pull, he jerks my shorts down, then continues sliding until his head is between my legs. He kicks his pants the rest of the way and drops his knees to the floor then shifts my body so that half of my ass is hanging off the seat.

Darting his tongue out, he licks me up and down before sliding a finger inside of me. I bite the corner of my lip when he sucks my clit between his teeth. He slides another finger in and begins pumping them inside of me. My hips buck up and down to his movements as I ride his face.

Fisting his hair, I guide his movements as we both find a rhythm. Everything that happened before we got in this car escapes my mind and, right now, Baron is all I can focus on. This is all I care about. The euphoric state he's bringing me to. His face between my legs while he tastes me. His dick hard for me. His hands gripping my hip bones as he sucks me, licks me, tongue fucks me.

"Oh god, Baron," I cry out in pleasure when he slides yet another finger inside of me. Stretching me and hitting every wall. He pumps faster and harder and begins teasing my clit. I tug at his hair tighter and ride the hell out of his face as my entire body fills up with an undeniable urge to combust. "Fuck!" I moan. Feeling my arousal spill down my ass. He keeps going until my body relaxes, then he licks me from bottom to top as his eyes watch me.

Something unforeseen comes over me. Something I didn't expect. Seeing him look at me that way—my heart fills and warms at the same time.

Baron positions me so that I'm completely back on the seat but still lying down. He slides up and comes between my legs and with no notice, he slams his dick inside of me. My body jolts upward and my head hits the door. He grabs my legs and lets them dangle over his forearms as he lunges inside of me repeatedly. I let out a gasp when my head ricochets off the door again and again. It doesn't hurt; in fact, it only adds to the intensity of this moment.

His mouth gapes open while his eyes stay fixated on mine.

Burning into them like a punishment for awakening something inside of him. "Do I look jealous now?" he croaks.

I shake my head. He doesn't. He looks confident and in control. Masculine and mysterious and so fucking sexy.

My legs drop and his body lies on top of mine. He slows his pace but still watches my face like he's searching for something. Rocking back and forth inside of me, he scoops my head in his hand and presses his lips to mine. So gentle. Not at all forced or rough. Just a slow and steady kiss. His tongue glides into my mouth, sweeping it up and tangling it with his.

Bringing my hands up, I cup his head and my entire body burns with desire.

Then he breaks the kiss and begins fucking me like he hates me again. Ramming so hard into me that my neck twists as my head presses against the door.

"What the fuck are you doing to me, Iris?" he says with a raspy voice. I wrap my arms around him and hold him tightly, feeling the head of his cock swell inside of me as he comes undone. A couple more thrusts and his body drops heavily onto mine. His head resting on my chest.

Just when I start to think that this moment couldn't be any more perfect, he pulls back and sits up—the expressionless gaze returns as he refuses to look at me.

One step forward, two steps back.

## Twenty-Seven

WE PULLED over at a rest stop so I could clean up, then resumed the drive. It's been an hour and the only words I've spoken to Baron were to ask where we're going. His response was a bottle of water in my face. I figure he's not going to tell me, so I don't bother to try again.

Tucking my legs to my chest, I stare out the window, trying to make out where we are, but I lost track while we were having sex and I have no idea what direction we're headed in.

Baron seems to be deep in thought and it's a different look for him. Usually when I see him, he's either engaging in conversation with Gabriel or Silas, coming or going, or on his phone. Stealing a glance, he doesn't notice my eyes on him. His square jaw is clenched and his eyebrows are dipped into a V. I'd give anything to know what he's thinking about right now.

Breaking the silence, I clear my throat. "Has Gabriel or your father tried calling?"

His eyes snap to me. "Don't know. My phone is off."

"Could you turn it on and check? Just for a minute? I'm really worried about them." We don't know what happened when we left. They could have been in the middle of a battle zone while we were orgasming and that realization has my heart aching.

"Too risky," he quips. Shifting his gaze out the window on his side, he folds his hands over the jacket that's laid neatly in his lap. So proper and so robotic. It hurts me to know that Gabriel and Baron have lived their entire lives like this.

Hugging my legs tighter, I let my head fall against the door. My eyes close and my thoughts slowly drift away from me.

When my eyes open, I startle myself, forgetting where I was for a moment. Looking over at Baron, I notice him watching me. Still holding the same expression and statue-like posture. "How long was I out?" I ask him.

"Only about thirty minutes. We should be there soon."

I go to put my legs down and notice my robe draped over them. My fingers graze the plush fabric and I look at Baron. He's resumed looking out the window, but something pricks at my chest. He covered me up.

It's a small gesture, but any act of kindness from Baron is huge.

"Baron," I say his name softly, "I'll have that water now."

Stretching his hand down, he grabs a bottled water off the floor and hands it to me. Maybe he really is just trying to look out for me. In his own fucked-up way, he cares. I twist the top off and take a long drink then screw it back on. "Thank you," I tell him.

He gives me a subtle nod and looks away. But I slide down closer to him. Inching more and more, hoping I'm not making him uncomfortable by invading his personal space. I know these guys have never been given much affection, therefore, they probably do not welcome it. Once my outer leg hits his, I curl my legs back up to my chest and rest my head on his shoulder.

I can feel his body tense up and I'd swear I can see his heart beating through the fabric of his white button-up shirt. Taking a deep breath, I close my eyes and find comfort in being near him. No matter what happens, I now know these guys would do anything to protect me. Baron might spew hate at me, but I know that deep down he just doesn't know how to behave any differently.

"I'm scared," I mutter into his arm. He doesn't respond. Doesn't move. So, I lift my head to look at him. "Baron," I say, trying to grab his attention.

His back is steeled against the seat. His mind and body in sync with one another.

He finally looks down at me. "Don't be scared."

Taking us both by surprise, he lifts his arm and wraps it around me. Nuzzling closer, I draw in a deep breath, saving his scent to memory. Something about it makes me feel safe—secure. I imagine not many women, if any, get this close to Baron and it takes away from some of the disdain I feel in his presence.

"Do you think they're ok?" I ask him.

"I know they are. Silas and Gabriel are fully capable of defending themselves. We're the bad guys, Iris. Always remember that."

That's what they think. It's what they've been trained to believe, but I see something inside of each of them that they don't see in themselves. "No. No, you're not. You just have a job that portrays you that way."

"Our jobs are our lives. This," he looks down at me, "this is *my* life." His big brown eyes bore into mine. So empty. So dark. But, beyond that, I see someone who wants so badly to feel emotions that aren't credited to a successful hit.

"You really believe that, don't you? You truly think that you're defined by your line of work?"

"You have to be heartless to do what we do."

Straightening up, I level with him. "Baron, I killed a man. I held a gun to his head and I pulled the trigger. It will haunt me for the rest of my life, but you know what? I don't regret it. Does that make me heartless?"

"You killed a bad guy in your quest for revenge. You weren't paid to do it. Taking lives doesn't put food on your table or a roof over your head. Silas built our empire by killing others. One day, I'll build my own the same way. As will Gabriel."

"Oh yeah? And who will you share that empire with? A maid? A henchman? Where is the happiness? There's no joy in living your life alone because you shut off all emotion and won't allow yourself to grow attached to another person."

Jerking his arm away, his voice rises. "You think I don't feel happiness, sadness, or even loneliness? Of course I do. But what will those emotions bring but a few short-lived seconds of feeling something that will only disappear to be replaced by anger? Why seek them out if you know they will fade away?"

"What happens when those feelings find you and you aren't even expecting them? Do you ignore them or do you allow yourself that fracture of a second to feel alive?"

"They have. And I do."

Is he talking about me? Baron is so hard to read and he talks in riddles, so I have no idea what he's referring to. "You do? Who?"

"Isn't it obvious?"

"Umm, no." I chuckle. "Not really."

"Good. We'll just leave it at that."

I grab him by the arm, needing more. Hungry for the words. "Tell me. Are you talking about me?"

"It doesn't matter. Life has a way of fucking me at the most inopportune times, so even if I did allow myself to feel anything at all, it's too late. Which is exactly why I should have never let my emotions win."

"You talk as if there's a war going on between your head and your heart and if that's the case, you waged that war. Maybe it's time to stop fighting it all so much."

"Like I said, it doesn't matter. It's too late."

Throwing one leg over him, I straddle his lap. With his eyes on my lips, he watches as I speak. "You're still here. That means you still have time."

Trailing his index finger over my lips, his eyes keep watch on the movement. "Time is running out. In this line of work, loyalty is everything." His finger slides between my lips and I allow my mouth to close around it as he slides it in and out. "The respect of others is everything. When you make a deal with the devil, you don't dare cross him."

Practically spitting his finger out, my eyes widen. "Who made a deal with the devil? You?"

The car comes to a stop and before he can answer me, his mouth crashes into mine. Seductive and unwarranted. Not fragile or empty of emotion, and it feels a lot like goodbye.

When he breaks the kiss and pulls back, he takes my face in his hands and stares back into my eyes. "It was never supposed to be like this. It was a job and I never leave a job unfinished."

The door opens and I'm faced with a slew of burly men. They're directly outside the car door and there are four others behind him. All wearing the same black suits and sunglasses like they just stepped out of the movie, *Men in Black*. "Baron, what's going on?" My heart begins to beat thunderously in my chest and I can feel the tears welling in my eyes. He doesn't respond. Doesn't attempt to move his body or mine. "Baron?" I say his name again as a question.

Two hands wrap around my waist, but they're not his. "Damnit, Baron. What the fuck is going on?" I shout as the man begins to lift me off Baron's lap.

His chin drops to his chest. He can't even look at me as he lets them take me away. "You're a coward," I shout. "You don't lack emotion, you're just scared of it. Do you fucking hear me?" I scream as I'm pulled out of the car.

My feet never touch the ground, even as they kick back and forth, trying to land on someone or something.

"I'm sorry," Baron says, before he stretches his hand out and pulls the car door closed.

He helped them. He helped Maretti. All this time that I felt safe with him, he was on their side. For a moment, I really felt like I was starting to see a side of Baron he's never shown anyone. A part of him he didn't even know existed. At that moment, I thought that one day, I could love this broken man. All this time, he was just gaining my trust so that I didn't doubt him. Just so he could hand me over.

He made a deal with the devil. That devil has a name—Vincent Maretti.

## Twenty-Eight

TWENTY MILES NORTH. That was a crock of shit. We drove for at least two hours and I don't think we were heading north. Though, I can't be sure. Once the burly man carried me inside the castle-like structure, he stuck a blindfold over my eyes and took me down a long flight of stairs then a very cold hallway that smelled like wet cement.

Now, I'm sitting in a room surrounded by stonewalls with only a bed and a thin white sheet. The door consists of parallel bars that resemble a jail gate. Basically, I'm in my own personal prison.

"Hello," I call out. Knowing that it won't do any good. I've been shouting for almost an hour, at least I think it's been an hour. It could have been longer. I don't even know. I'm hungry and thirsty, and I really wish I would have drunk more water like Baron told me to.

*Baron.*

Tears stream down my cheeks again, as I try to choke them down. I can't believe he betrayed me this way. But, was it really a betrayal? Baron owed me nothing, offered me nothing, and made no deals with me. He never claimed to care and he never pretended. Gabriel and Silas, though, they care. There is no way that they can be part of this and I refuse to believe that they are. They are my only hope at getting out of this situation and I just need to pray like hell that they find me.

My stomach growls in anticipation of food. I could eat just about anything right now. My throat is coarse and swallowing feels like I'm downing pine needles.

"Is anyone here?" I shout again, with my fingers clenched around the wrought iron bars of the door. "Please. Can somebody answer me? I'm hungry and I need to use the bathroom."

I take a step back when a new man shows his face. He's much smaller than the guy who manhandled me earlier. His lip curls up and there is something so familiar about him. There's more stubble on his face and his tan is more pronounced, but I've definitely seen this guy somewhere before.

"Ms. Pavetta, we meet again."

Is this...is he? "Vincent Maretti?" I choke out his name in question.

He lets out a throaty rumble of a laugh. "No, my dear. You'll soon meet your future husband, but first, you meet me."

*Future husband?* My heart drops into the pit of my empty stomach. So, this is how it ends? Me, the wife of a mafia leader who killed my father just so that he could claim me as his wife. I'll be a prisoner for the rest of my life. Much worse than this hellhole I'm stowed away in right now. I'll likely be put up in a lavish mansion and given anything my heart desires, aside from freedom. And I'll pay for those desires with my soul and my body. He will own me. I will be Mrs. Iris Maretti.

I take another step back, my head continuously shaking. "I won't marry him. I will get away," I snarl before my voice rises so loudly that it echoes off the stonewalls. "I'll kill you all before he touches me!"

An airy laugh leaves his vocal chords and, this time, it's frightening. His expression drops, his eyes laser-focused on me as if he can see right through my tough-girl facade. "Mr. Maretti gets what he wants, and he wants you."

Taking another step back, my calves hit the small twin-size bed and I drop down onto it. "But, why? Why me?" My face falls into my hands and I let out all the tears that I've fought to keep hidden. For the first time in a while, I finally break.

"Because you, my dear, are his pearl. He will wear you proudly for the world to see. He's been waiting many years for you, and now, it's time for him to collect what was rightfully promised to him."

*Many years?* Vincent isn't much older than I am. Maybe six, seven years. "How long has he been waiting for me?" I have to know when my dad made this deal with this monster.

"Since you were thirteen years old."

Everything in my body stills. My thoughts, my heart, my blood flow. I can't think, and suddenly, I can't breathe. I attempt to draw in a breath, but it's ragged and unfulfilled. I exhale, only releasing tiny spurts of air. "I can't breathe." I stand up quickly, placing my hands on my chest as my panic attack peaks. I begin pacing the length of the room in an attempt to distract myself. My head feels faint and my body off balance.

"Ms. Pavetta, please sit down."

Gripping the sides of my head, I tug aggressively at my matted hair. "I can't breathe," I repeat again as I try for another deep breath. Frantically, I pick up my pace, paying no attention to the man on the other side of the door.

I'm going to pass out. I'll be limp and lifeless and this man and his friends will be free to do whatever they want with my body.

I stop walking. "Please. I need water. Something," I say in a plea, before I drop to my knees on the cold cement floor. I sit down and tuck my head between my bent legs. I begin rocking back and forth to try and calm myself, but it does little good.

"Ms. Pavetta. What on earth are you doing?"

My heart is racing, my palms are sweating, and my entire body feels as if it's getting pricked with a thousand pins.

"What's going on over here?" I hear another voice. It's familiar and I don't have to look up to know it's the man that carried me in here.

"She's having some sort of fit," the smaller guy retorts.

Still rocking back and forth, I begin to slowly feel my lungs fill fully and my heart rate decrease. Coming back to reality and able to think logically. I hear the gated door open, and I think. This could be my only chance to escape. But how?

Without looking up, I hear footsteps approach me. "What do we do?" The bigger guy asks.

There's a devious bout of laughter, followed by a heinous remark. "I could think of a lot of things I'd like to do with this pretty girl."

"You and me both," one of them responds. There's a brief pause before he continues, "Jerry had to run some errands before the boss gets here. The others are probably taking a nap. We could make it a quick one."

My heart stills. But I don't let it get the best of me. These men will not touch me. I'll die first.

I continue to rock with my head locked firmly between my knees.

There's another beat of silence before I'm scooped up with my arms still hugging my legs. I lift my head and look into his dark eyes. It's the big guy, the one who brought me in here. He looks sardonic and horrifyingly pleased with himself.

As soon as I'm set down on the bed, I unclasp my hold on my legs and bring my knee to his balls in a swift movement.

He lets out a whimper, but it hardly fazes him. Eyeing the door that's still open, I think quickly. There are two of them and one of me. I haven't had nearly enough training to take these guys down, but I think back to some of the techniques that Gabriel taught me in the living room.

My thoughts are interrupted when the bigger guy pushes my back down onto the bed. *Oh my god, this is happening.* "Please. Don't do this." I hold up my hands to stop them from coming any closer. "If you touch me, I'll tell Vincent and he'll kill you."

The smaller guy laughs and it's getting really fucking annoying that he thinks everything is so damn funny. "He'll never believe you."

"I'll be his wife. Of course he'll believe me."

He laughs again and I really just wanna knock this son of a bitch out, so I never have to hear that sound again.

The bigger guy slides a hand between my legs and pries them apart while his other hand slithers up the leg of my shorts. Nausea ensues and my entire body feels like it's on fire when I hear the zipper come down on the pants of the smaller guy. He takes a step closer and his dick smacks the side of my cheek. "Open up, pretty girl."

I pinch my eyes shut, locking my lips tighter as he trails the head of his penis over my mouth. I can feel the tip of the bigger guy's finger at my entrance and I give up. I'm defeated. I can't win. They will have their way with me and I'll live a miserable life at the beck and call of Maretti and his goons. Tears slide down my cheeks and I give up the fight.

"I said open up, you little bitch." His dick slaps my face harder, but that's one fight I will not give up. He will have to pry my mouth open before I ever let him stick his cock in it. And when he does, I'll bite him like he's a cheap piece of steak.

I hear the clank of a belt hit the floor and I know immediately that the bigger guy just dropped his pants. His body positions between my legs and he's so big that I feel like my ligaments are going to snap. He tugs my shorts to the side and more tears fall as all of my hopes and dreams crumble.

Just when I brace myself for the fact that these men are going to rape me, I hear a muffled pop and the full force of a body crashes down on me. Then another, and the bigger guy falls backward and down on the ground. I scoot myself up and push the lifeless body off me.

Then I see him.

He came back for me.

"Are you ok?" Baron asks as he hurries to the side of the bed. His warm hands cup my cheeks and for a moment, I feel as if he really is concerned about my wellbeing.

That is, until I remember that he's the one who brought me here. "Get away from me." I stretch my foot out and kick him in the stomach.

"I know you're mad, but we have to go now." He grabs me by the hand and begins pulling me off the bed.

Snatching my arm away, I sneer, "I'm not going anywhere with you. Do you think I've forgotten that you fed me to these wolves?" I stand up and push past him. Ready and willing to defend myself. Starting by getting the hell out of here.

"Iris, wait," Baron hollers as he walks steadily behind me.

I don't stop. I keep walking as fast as I can down the maze of walls. It's damp, cold, and I feel like I'm walking through a dungeon from the Medieval Times. My breaths are labored and unfulfilled; I have blood drying into the skin of my arm, and I feel like my legs are on the verge of giving out on me.

"Iris," he whisper-yells, "would you wait a damn minute?" He's at my side now. His hand grabs ahold of my arm in an attempt to halt my movements.

"Get off of me." I pull back and look him dead in the eyes. "I hate you, Baron Black!"

With regretful eyes, he tries to take my hand in his, but I snatch it away. "I came back for you. Doesn't that count for anything?"

My voice is low, but loud enough to make my point very clear. "I. hate. you."

"Please, just come with me. There are others up there and you will be caught. This time, I might not be able to save you."

My blood begins to boil. Unable to connect my mind with my body. Clenching my fist, I cock my arm and plant my knuckles right on his nose.

His hands cup his face as he lets out a few muffled groans. "Damn, girl. That fucking hurt," he bellows.

With the upper hand, I continue walking briskly through the dark hall that is only lighted by a couple lanterns about six feet apart attached to the stone. Baron catches up to me and in one swift motion, he scoops me into his arms and turns around. Cradling me like a baby, I kick and squirm to try and free myself.

His mouth ghosts my ear as he whispers, "You're going the wrong fucking way. Now do what I say or you'll be getting us both killed."

I slowly give up my fight, because as angry as I am right now, he's right. I have no idea where I'm going, and as soon as Maretti finds out that I've escaped, they will be searching high and low for his precious *pearl*. Ugh, my stomach churns at the thought of ever being his bride and bedmate.

Baron stops abruptly when chattering voices draw near. His eyes dart to mine and widen, his way of telling me to be quiet. Holding my breath, I try not to make a sound as he presses his back to the wall and listens.

"He'll be arriving in an hour. We need to clean her up and have her presentable for him." I hear one guy say.

*Maretti isn't here?* Regardless, he's coming for me.

Footsteps thud against the cement floor and Baron sets me gently to my feet. "Stay here," he says, before pressing a finger to his lips and taking a step away from me.

My eyes widen and I shake my head. *He's leaving me here?* I have nothing to protect myself. I can barely even hold myself up on my own two feet, and he's leaving me?

Baron rounds the corner and I lock myself to the rigid stonewall as if we are one.

"Hey, boys. Is he here yet?" Baron says casually to the guys.

Another man retorts with a thick French accent, "An hour. What the hell happened to your face?"

Baron huffs. "She's a feisty thing. Popped me right before she was taken out of the car."

"What the fuck are you doing down here anyway? Thought you took off?" the French guy asks.

"Just had to make sure they got her nice and settled," Baron replies with such confidence and certainty, it makes me sick.

"Might as well stick around for a bit to see the boss. He's pleased with your work. Even mentioned bringing you on full-time. That is, if you're fully prepared to turn on that old man of yours."

"Just might do that," Baron says.

This entire time, Baron has been working against Silas and Gabriel? He wants to work for Maretti? This doesn't make any sense. Silas and Gabriel are his family. Who is that monster standing around the corner? And how the hell didn't I see this sooner?

Slowly inching myself down the hall, I attempt to put some distance between me and the men—including Baron. He says he came back for me, but I don't believe a damn word that comes out of his mouth.

My bare feet make no sound as I slide down the rigid wall

with my eyes held tightly to the corner. A little further. And further. *Fuck.* My head smacks hard against the lantern attached to the wall. There's a slight sting, but that's not what worries me. Seconds later, three sets of glowing eyes are on me and I'm hauling ass down the hall. Round the opposite direction of where the guys just came from, I grip the corner of the wall, turn then book it down the other hall with no idea where I'm going.

When I reach the end, I look left, then right. *Damnit. Where am I?*

"Get her!" The French guy shouts. He's much bigger than I imagined, which can play to my advantage. I might not have a lot of strength, but I can run like hell.

Deciding to go right, I keep running toward a closed door, hoping like hell that it's unlocked and will take me somewhere far away from these guys.

I can hear their footsteps come closer as I reach the door. *A little further.*

Unable to slow my steps before I reach the door, my body slams full force into it. I grab the handle and turn, then defeat washes over me once again. It's locked. I turn around with my back pressed to it, and there they are. All three of them.

All staring at me—Baron wearing a look of remorse as he stands behind the other two. I watch as he reaches into the flap of his jacket, my eyes widen with anticipation and hope that he's retrieving a gun. Then for assurance that he's not planning to use it on me. When he pulls out the palm-sized pistol, I gasp. He doesn't hesitate before putting a bullet into the back of the French guy's head.

He drops carelessly to the ground, watching me as he falls. His eyes dark and full of fear. I pinch my eyes shut, unable to watch another person die. It never gets easier.

There's another pop and the thud of the other falling body. I open one eye, then the other, and see Baron still standing there. This time, the gun is on me. I hold my hands up in surrender. "Baron, please. Don't do this."

With the gun held tight with both hands, he gestures it to the side. "Walk."

Stepping away from the door, I keep my hands in the air. With each step I take toward him, worry is replaced by fury. Heat rises from my toes to the tips of my ears and I clench my jaw so forcefully that I'm surprised I don't crack a tooth. "You're the devil, Baron Black."

I walk in front of him while he trails behind with a loaded gun pointed at the back of my head. "No, Sweetness, I was just raised by him."

Stepping around the bodies on the floor, I make my way to Baron. "Why are you doing this?" I choke out. "How could you betray your father this way?"

"Right now, all I care about is getting us both out of here alive. You don't seem to want to listen, so this is the only way to ensure that happens."

"Why should I believe anything you say? Everything has been a big lie."

He nudges me from behind when my steps become smaller. "You're right, it has. Up until now. Now, walk."

Aside from being angry, my heart hurts. It's like he shattered it into tiny pieces and stomped on them all. Now he thinks he can just come back and try and put it back together like nothing ever happened? No. No way. Once we are out of here, I'm going straight to Silas and Gabriel and telling him what Baron has done. I could care less if he suddenly had a change of heart. I have no interest in hearing his excuses.

It shouldn't surprise me at all. Baron was always standoffish with me. The closer I felt like I was getting to him, the more he'd pull back. It was like he was fighting against himself, because I know that, deep down, he was just scared to get attached to me the way Silas and Gabriel have. Now I know why. All this time he's been working for Maretti—the man who killed my family. The man I sought revenge on.

So many questions linger in my mind. So many irrational thoughts and unwanted emotions. But there's one question— one thought— that needs to be said. "Baron," I say in a hushed tone.

"What?"

I stop walking, then turn around and face him, placing my hand on his arm to lower the gun. He watches me with intent and I can feel myself choke up. "Did you know Maretti was planning on killing my father?"

He doesn't respond. Just stares at me blankly. His silence is deafening. Louder than any noise or thought in my head.

"Baron," I say again. "Were you..." My words trail off. It's ridiculous and totally far-fetched. But I have to know. "Were you at my house the day of the ambush?"

Watching him, reading his expression, waiting for a response for what feels like the longest seconds of my entire existence, I shake my head slowly. "No? Baron, please tell me you didn't know." Tears slide down my cheeks.

Nothing else matters at this moment, I just have to know. A thousand men could come charging at me and I'd fight them off just so I can hear Baron's response. Just so I can know that he was not at my house when Maretti came for me and killed my father.

His expression grows solemn. With eyes that threaten tears, it's impossible to look past them. Is this man even capable of tears—pain, sorrow, any emotion?

"We have to go," he says calmly. That's it? That's his response?

I shake my head. "No, I'm not going anywhere until you answer my question. I'll die before I marry Maretti, and I'll marry Maretti before I let you get away if you had even the smallest part in my father's murder."

"Iris," his chin drops to his chest, "this was all before. Everything is not as it seems."

I let out an airy and sarcastic chuckle. "No shit!" Sweeping away the tears, I toughen up. This is the last time I'll be made a fool. In a swift movement, I snatch the gun out of Baron's hand. Holding it up, I point it right at his face.

"Iris, don't do this. Let me explain."

Pressing my lips into a thin line, my hands tremble uncontrollably, causing the gun to shake as I aim it at him. I feel like I'm on the verge of a complete mental breakdown. I could shoot him, but then I might as well turn the gun on myself because I'll never forgive myself. As much as I hate what he's done, I would never be able to forget the man that I thought he was. "You were right," I tell him.

He's taken aback with no idea what I'm talking about. "About what?"

"On our way here, you told me that you have to be heartless to do what you do. You were right. You are heartless. Unfortunately, I am not." I lower my arm and let the gun slide out of my hand. It hits the cement with a thud. Baron doesn't make a move to grab it, instead, he reaches out for me.

Shoving him back, I hiss, "Just because I didn't kill you doesn't mean I don't want you dead. But you deserve to live a painful and miserable life after what you've done. Karma is a fucking bitch, and she's coming for you." I turn on my heels and walk down the hall.

I'm getting out of this place on my own, because in the end, I'm all I have.

Baron will pay for his sins. He just killed four of Maretti's men and freed his prisoner—me. I have every intention of telling Silas and Gabriel about his betrayal and then Baron, too, will be alone. Left to fend for himself. To fight the monsters in the dark all on his own. Just as I have to do.

*Twenty-Nine*

WHEN I REACH the end of the hall, I'm, once again, at a standstill. Looking left, looking right, unsure where the hell I'm going.

"Left," Baron says from behind me. I let out a huff before going left. Part of me wanted to go right, just to piss him off and do the opposite of what he said, and on a normal day, I would have. But, if I want to live, I need to suck up my pride and let him lead me out of here. At this point, I think that really is what he's trying to do.

"Straight to the door. It'll lead us up a staircase." He steps in front of me, blocking the door before I can pull it open. "Before you go up there, you need to prepare yourself for the possibility that men will be waiting at the top of that staircase. Stay behind me and if I say run, you run like hell."

"Just move out of my way. I can take care of myself." I push past him and pull the door open.

"Yeah, you've proven that." I can't see his expression, but his tone was sarcastic as hell.

Completely unprepared, even though I was given a warning, I walk out the door. Being stubborn has gotten me in trouble many times, but this takes my stubbornness to an entirely different level. I was so focused on getting away from Baron, or even just proving that I can take care of myself, that I didn't even put any thought into the fact that there would most definitely be people up here.

They don't see me, but I see them. Three guys talking amongst themselves with their backs to me. They're standing together in a sitting room that is decked out with a gothic appeal. Everything is blood red and crow black. A large black crystal chandelier hangs from the vaulted ceiling. A red shag rug sits in the middle of the room beneath the black leather furniture.

One of the guys laughs and another raises his voice so I use this as my opportunity to slide around the corner. Baron is hot on my trail with his hand on my waist. I turn to look at him and he's expression is loaded with concern. Just as my back presses to the wall where they can't see me, someone hollers, "Baron, what the hell are you still doing here?"

Baron steps out from around the corner, closes the door and leaves me.

"Just making sure everything was taken care of with the girl. Wouldn't want to piss off the big man. He here yet?"

Someone else chimes in, "He's about twenty minutes out. She's a hot little number, ain't she? Maretti's a lucky guy."

"Oh yeah. She's something alright," Baron responds.

My eyes roll as I slide down the wall slowly, carefully, without a sound, with my eyes glued to the corner where Baron and the men are.

My movements are halted when I crash into something, or someone rather. "You lost, little lady?" He doesn't make any attempt to whisper, which tells me that this guy is not going to play nice with me.

In a matter of seconds, more people come into view,

including Baron. I look at him in hopes that he has a plan because I've got nothing.

"What the fuck is she doing out of the basement?" one of the men that Baron was chatting with around the corner says. He's younger, probably not much older than me. But his expression is fierce and there's fire in his eyes. "Why are you all just standing around?" his voice rises, "get her back down there."

"I'll take her," Baron says as he comes over to my side. He gives me a look that tells me to follow his lead. He grabs a hold of my arm. "You sure do like to cause trouble, don't ya?"

"What a minute." The younger guy holds up his hand. "You were just down there, Baron. Where the fuck are the guards?"

Baron looks down at me and in that moment, I might as well be ash at his feet. I'm not even sure that I'm breathing when he mouths the word 'run.' My feet don't move. My body doesn't allow it.

I'm not even sure what happens next. Right before my eyes, guns are pulled. A knife is swung, grazing Baron's arm. I gasp, staring at the blood dripping to the floor.

"Run!" Baron shouts so loudly that the word echoes continuously in my ears.

I'm finally able to react, and even though I have no idea where I'm going, I run like hell down a long narrow hallway. Once I reach the end, I look over my shoulder, and I see him. In slow motion, I watch as the bullet leaves the gun held by a tall man with a ponytail and a leather jacket. It's as if time stands still and I want to reach out and grab the bullet before it pierces any part of Baron's body.

He drops slowly—taking my heart with him. His eyes never leave mine. "No," I scream at the top of my lungs. I start moving toward him, but in slow movements, his head shakes. He's still alive—for now.

All eyes dart to me. "Get her!" the man with the ponytail demands of the others.

Peeling my gaze off Baron, I turn back around and run. My bare feet slide across the waxed hardwood floor, but I keep going toward a set of open French doors.

Still hot on my tail, the men don't give up. They'll probably never give up. I'm kidding myself to think I'll get away from here. But I have to try.

Once I'm outside, I hurry down the stairs of a wooden deck, through the fresh cut grass of the lawn, until I reach rows of trees that are lined up perfectly. I don't even stop to take in my surroundings. When I hear them drawing closer, I pick up my pace.

There's a large log in the way, and before I jump over it, I look behind me to see how much space is between us. They're close, but I can do this. Lifting one leg up, I jump over the log. As soon as I'm back on the ground, a stick jams into my foot. "Fuck!" I cry out, tears falling carelessly down my face. Blood trickles off my foot, leaving a fresh trail as I continue to run like hell.

Minutes pass. I'm not sure how many. So many turns. Left, then right, then left again as I make my way quickly through the maze of trees.

Every couple of seconds, I look over my shoulder and watch as the people chasing me fade farther and farther away, until I no longer see them. I still don't stop. Now is not the time to be naive and assume that I'm safe. Am I ever really safe? Will I ever be safe again?

My feet hurt so fucking bad. They are raw, cut, and bleeding. My bare legs are scratched up from the grass that has gotten taller the farther into the forest I get.

Once I feel confident that I've put enough distance between us, or hopefully lost them all together, I stop.

Bending over, I press my hands to my knees and catch my breath, or at least attempt to.

My body aches. I'm tired. I'm hungry. I'm scared. But nothing compares to the pain inside of me.

*Baron. Silas. Gabriel. Are they ok?*

Dropping to my knees, I buckle. I break down. For the second time tonight, I lose all control. One moment I feel strong and in control, the next, I'm lost again. Defeated and ready to just give up. Marry Maretti or die.

As if those are my only options.

No. Hell no.

I'm a fucking Pavetta. My dad might have made a deal with the devil, but my bloodline is strong. We are not quitters. We fight, and we fight hard.

Pressing my palms to the dried grass, I push myself up. I straighten my crown, and this time, I don't run. I walk. With my head held high and rage running through my veins. Snapping a strong and sturdy stick off from a tree, I carry it in my hand. It's the only protection I have. If it comes down to it, I'll stab any son of a bitch in the eye.

They want me; they can try and catch me.

# Thirty

THE SUN IS STARTING to set. The sky is painted in cotton candy colors—baby pink and blue. The air is still and it's so quiet that it's eerie. I've been walking for over an hour and I still haven't managed to find my way out of these woods. I'm so damn thirsty. My throat feels like I'm swallowing sandpaper. Stopping for a moment, I allow myself a break. I drop to my ass and press my back against a tree.

Tilting my head back, I look at the sky. "Daddy, you got me in this mess, please get me out of it," I whisper to the clouds.

My tears have run dry. I feel as though I'm on the verge of spilling them again, but they don't fall.

I can't even begin to wrap my head around what I'm feeling. As angry as I am with Baron, he took a bullet for me. He tried to right his wrong and came back to save me. I got away, but he did not.

My entire body trembles as I take in a shallow, hitched breath. "Please don't die, Baron," I mutter under my breath.

He betrayed his family. Went against them and started working for Maretti. He was at my house when we were attacked, and he was even aware that my dad was a target, but for some reason, I still want him to live. What the hell is wrong with me?

I've spewed the word revenge for the last month. It's all I've wanted, but this whole time, it wasn't just Maretti that should have been my target. It was all of his men, including Baron. Maretti put the plan in action, but his men carried it out.

Baron was right; it is necessary to be heartless to do what they do. If only he knew that he does, in fact, have one. He would have never come back for me had he not.

I just want him to be ok. I want them all to be ok.

Climbing to my feet, I look around again. It's sort of a guessing game at this point. I choose right this time. Pressing my stick to the ground, I use it as a walking cane. One thing is for sure, if I do get out of here alive, I'm soaking in a bathtub for an entire day and eating my weight in food. Assuming I even have a home to go back to.

I don't know what happens next, but I hope I have my guys by my side to help me figure it out. *My guys.* I like the sound of that. They might not even know it, but they are mine. Even Baron. At this moment, I hate him, but he's found a home in my heart and I'm not kicking him out just yet. The idea of him lying helplessly in a pool of blood in that house has my heart breaking in two.

Stopping in my tracks, I stare straight ahead when I notice the rows of trees coming to an end. *Could I have finally found a way out of here?* Hope swims through me as I continue walking. Picking up my pace until I'm full-on running. I reach the end, but take a step back.

*No. It can't be.*

"No!" I mutter under my breath. That hope is quickly diminished as defeat returns, once again. The house that I ran from hours ago looks back at me. I walked in a circle. All this time and I'm back where I started.

My heart drops when I see the figure of another person. I take another step back and trip over something on the ground, falling right on my ass. The mysterious person catches a glimpse of me and hurries in my direction. Scooting on my butt, I crawl back into the maze of trees before I get up and begin running again.

"Iris, stop!" he shouts. Only, it's not a stranger's voice.

Turning around, I gasp, "Gabriel?"

It's him. He's here.

"Oh, my god, Gabriel." I run into his arms. Letting him wrap his arms around me, feeling safe. Finally, I feel safe. Tears fall down my cheeks. "Gabriel, they shot...they shot Baron."

He pulls back and cranes his neck to look at me. "I know. Are you ok? Did they hurt you?" There's deep concern in his eyes that has me back in his arms. Never wanting him to let me go.

"I'm ok. But, Baron—"

I can feel his head shake above me. "He'll be fine. For now. I'm so fucking sorry, Iris. We had no idea."

"It's not your fault."

"Come on. Let's get inside." He takes me by the hand, but I don't move.

"I can't. I can't go back in there. They'll be waiting for me. We have to get out of here," my voice rises, "we have to go, now!"

"It's ok, babe. They're gone. Silas is waiting for us inside."

I look up at him. Searching for answers. "They're gone?"

"We took care of them. Maretti caught wind of our arrival and he's...he's somewhere. But, not here."

There's a pang in my chest. "He's coming for me. He'll never stop until I'm his. He will find me."

Gabriel's eyes light up as he grins and it's exactly what I need right now. "Not if we find him first."

Our feet begin moving steadily as we walk up to the backside of the mansion. Squeezing Gabriel's hand tighter, I put my trust in him. "I'm so glad you're ok. I was so worried when we left you and Silas," I tell him.

Tilting his head, he looks in my eyes. "We're survivors, babe. Never worry about us."

I give him a fractured smile. He can tell me that they're survivors, but I'm sure those guys who planned to rape me earlier today thought they were survivors, too. We all have our moments where we feel invincible, until we're not.

"And Silas?" I question. "Is he ok, too?"

"Still a pompous asshole with nothing but hate for the world," he snickers. "He's fine."

Oh, Silas. He's the glue of this family, but I know that holding it all together isn't as easy as he makes it look. His heart pumps blood the same as the rest of ours, and I know it has the capacity to be filled with more than just hate. I long to be the person who shows him that. The one that he lets in and never lets out.

My palms begin to sweat as we walk up the stairs of the back deck. Gabriel must have sensed my resistance because he stops and faces me as he stands on the top step. "You're safe now. But, just a heads up, it's not pretty in there."

I give him a subtle nod. I can handle this. Blood and bodies are becoming a part of my day-to-day life. Though, no amount of mental preparation could have readied me for what I see when we step inside. Blood splatters the walls like red paint. Bodies lie lifeless on the floors. One. Two. Three. Four of them directly in front of me.

"Silas!" I beam, as I run over to him. He doesn't open his arms to greet me, but that's just him, and I don't take it personally. Still, I throw my entire body into his and hug him. One hand pats my back before he takes a step to observe me.

"Are you hurt? Did they touch you?" he asks with a stern expression.

"I'm ok. A little scratched up and very dirty, but I'm not hurt."

"Take her to the hotel," Silas tells Gabriel.

"But...but, Maretti. We have to find him. I'm ready to do this. Where is he? He has to be near."

Silas shakes his head. "You're not ready, Iris."

"What?" I cry out. "But, I am ready. If I don't do this now, he's going to find me again. And next time, I might not be so lucky."

Silas places his hands on either side of my shoulders. "This is not luck. This is a catastrophe. For you, and also for my family." He looks behind me at Gabriel, I presume. "Take her. Now."

Looking around the room, I search for Baron. "Where's Baron?"

Gabriel comes up behind me, sets a hand on the small of my back and leads me forward toward the main doors. I stop and turn back around to look at Silas. "He came back for me. I think he regrets what he did," I tell him, in hopes of swaying his decision if he plans to kick Baron out of the family.

"Baron will be dealt with once he's well."

"Where is he?" I ask. There's a beat of silence, so I turn to Gabriel. "Is he at the hospital?"

Gabriel nods toward the door. "Let's go."

Stomping my foot to the floor and jerking my body away from Gabriel, I shout, "Damnit, would you two quit being so vague with me? I'm not leaving this house until someone answers me. Where the hell is Baron?"

They share a look and then Silas addresses me. "He's being

cared for by one of my doctors at a local hospital. He's in surgery now."

"Surgery," I gasp, clapping a hand over my mouth.

Silas continues, "the bullet lodged directly under his heart. If anyone is lucky, it's him."

"Oh my god. But you said he'll be ok, right?"

Silas nods slowly. "Now, go."

With no choice, I allow Gabriel to walk me outside. There's a car waiting and I shouldn't be surprised to see an army of men standing around with guns nestled under their arms.

"Let's get you a warm shower and some food," Gabriel tells me as he greets the driver standing at the back door with a nod.

Shuffling across the seat, I make room for Gabriel. He slides in and the driver closes the door.

"Ok, it's just us now. How bad is this?" I ask immediately.

Gabriel clicks his tongue on the roof of his mouth. "Not gonna lie. It's pretty bad. What started off as a man wanting to collect a debt has waged a war between two families—his and mine. One member of our family has turned against us and he intentionally put you in harm's way."

It's my fault. All of this is because of me. With a downcast gaze, I whisper, "I'm sorry." Gabriel will try and assure me it's not my fault, but we all know the truth. Silas' cold encounter minutes ago was warranted. He sees it, too.

Gabriel takes hold of my arm, pulling me down the seat so that I'm closer to him. "What are you apologizing for? You did nothing wrong."

"I knew you'd say that. But I did. None of this ever would have happened if I'd just stayed away. Went somewhere else to hide out after my father died." Those tears that were once dried, return. Falling carelessly down my face and into my lap.

"First of all, you coming to us was probably the best thing

that could have happened. You made our house feel like a home. Instead of just walls housing members, life was brought into it. Second of all, Baron chose his side long before you arrived."

"How do you know that?" Sure, Baron brought me to Maretti's men and I figured it all out, but how does Gabriel know this?

"The men who came to see us this morning. Silas killed one immediately when he tried to flee after you and Baron. I got to play with the other one for a bit." There's a sinister smirk on his face and it's eerie, but it's also totally Gabriel.

"And, what did he say?" I still haven't gotten the entire story of why Baron did what he did. All I know is that he tried to amend the situation and got shot.

"Told me that Baron has been trying to join Maretti's men for months. Took on his first job when..." he trails off and looks at me in a way that tells me I don't want to hear the rest.

I do, though. I want to hear it all. "Tell me," I demand.

"His first job was to assist in the elimination of Damon Pavetta. His job was to collect you and deliver you to Maretti. Things didn't go exactly as planned, and you escaped. Then you fell right into his lap by showing up at our house."

My eyes close and I drop my head down. "But, why?" I say, though I wasn't expecting an answer. It was more for myself. Why would he do this to his brother and his father?

"Baron's a hothead. Thinks that rules don't apply to him. He's got the patience of a toddler and the skills of a ninja, but he's his own worst enemy. He's always looking for more. He wants to rise to the top immediately and disregards anyone that stands in his way. Silas announced a few months ago that when he dies, he's leaving everything to Baron and me, both. He wants us to take over his legacy and keep the Black name one of respect and admiration."

"Ok, that's normal. You're both his sons. Why would that come as a surprise?"

"Because I'm not technically a Black. Their blood doesn't run through my veins. Up until a few months ago, Baron was to get everything. Apparently, the idea of sharing threw him into a childish fit. He probably thought that he could go work for Maretti, gain the trust of his goons and then take him out and step in as the rightful new leader."

"So stupid," I spit out. "Sounds like Baron wasn't thinking at all."

"Actually, he probably thought long and hard about it. I mean, it's not a bad move if you don't mind throwing your entire family under the bus—literally. Maretti doesn't have a family. No heirs, no blood relatives to take over once he's gone. His dad died when he was sixteen years old and he's been raising hell ever since."

"He wanted to marry me to give him an heir, didn't he?"

"For sure. He'd knock you up the second you're married. Probably make you spit a couple out just in case something happens to the other."

Oh my god. He talks as if we're discussing vegetables in a garden. Not kids. When I do have kids, it will be with a man that I love. I look over at Gabriel, thinking that he could quite possibly be that man. He'd be a good dad. Sure, he'd teach him his ways, but with me, I could teach him kindness and show him all the love that he needs. *He.* As if it would be a boy.

The car comes to a stop in front of a high-end hotel. Neon blue lights illuminate the circle drive and cottonwood trees sit on either side of the entrance. I stretch my head up, trying to look at how tall this place is, but my vision is restricted in the back seat. "This place is huge," I say. It's at least twelve stories. Yet, the parking lot is empty, aside from a few expensive cars.

Gabriel's door opens and the driver steps aside, making

room for his exit. Once Gabriel steps out, he reaches his hand inside and I place mine on it and follow suit.

"Are we the only guests here?" I ask, unsure why this place wouldn't be packed full of cars.

"I'm sure there are others. This hotel is limited to VIP members."

"Ah, I see." It makes sense now. Dad used to take me to ritzy hotels like this when I'd tag along on business trips with my former nanny. He'd disappear for the day, only to return at night when I was already asleep, or so he thought. Oftentimes, I'd wait up for him, worrying that he'd never return.

Gabriel leads me up to the entrance, still holding my hand tightly. His skin feels soft and his touch reminds me that I'm safe. I'm not sure when I became such a scaredy cat, but I really need to get past that because I still have a task to accomplish. Maretti might not have gotten me like he wanted, but I will get him.

It seems that the kingpin and I have more in common than I thought. Maretti has no living blood relatives, and neither do I. At least, not any that I'm aware of. Dad was never close with his family and I was just a kid when Mom died. Our family consisted of servants, tutors, and groundskeepers. A few of which, I grew quite fond of.

When we walk inside, I expect us to check in at the front desk, but there is no one behind it. Gabriel leads me to an elevator and presses the arrow up. "There's fresh clothes on your bed. I'll have room service bring you food. Try and get some rest when you get to your room."

My posture dampens. "You're not staying with me?"

We step on the elevator and the doors close. "I have my own room."

"Please. Please, just stay with me."

He's silent for a moment then finally obliges. "Ok. I have some business to take care of, but I'll come to your room tonight. I'm in 1003 if you need me, just call first. I might be out."

Once we come to a stop, we step off the elevator in unison. The doors close behind us and I'm not sure why, but it startles me. Gabriel places a comforting arm around my waist and leads me down the narrow hall. "What business do you need to attend to?" I ask him out of sheer curiosity.

"My brother," he deadpans. Stopping, he swipes a card in front of the door and pushes it open. "There are guards outside. Don't worry. You're safe here."

I step inside and watch as the door slowly closes. Giving it only a couple of minutes, I pull the door back open, look both ways, then shut it and change quickly.

He's attending to matters that involve Baron, and I need to be sure that he doesn't plan to harm him. I'm angry with Baron, too, but I'm going to make damn sure that he stays part of this family. I will not be the reason that they fall apart. Everyone can tell me this has nothing to do with me, but I know the truth.

I was the domino that fell, and they all came tumbling after.

## Thirty—One

THANKFULLY, there is a brand-new pair of Converse shoes in a box waiting for me on the bed, along with some comfy sweatpants and a hoodie. I'm still filthy, but at least I'm warm now and my scoffed-up feet are covered. My stomach growls, but I ignore it. Food can wait; I have more important things to do right now.

Using the landline phone in my room, I was able to call for an Uber that was instructed to pick me up at the gate, instead of driving up to the hotel. I don't have any cash or cards on hand, but I was able to convince them to let me pay over the phone by offering a very hefty tip. It's a good thing I have my personal credit card numbers memorized. I'd probably get ridiculed for using it because it's an easy way to be traced, but my options are limited.

Apparently, there is only one hospital in the area—about fifteen minutes away—and I'm sure that's where Baron is. I have to see him.

Gabriel said that he needed to take care of business with Baron, and I have no idea what that means, but I can't imagine it involves going to see him in person. He's likely plotting something that will take place over a course of time, and it's my mission to make sure his plans are never carried out.

Tiptoeing down the hall with no phone of my own and no idea where the hell I'm going, I figure the elevator is a good place to start. I'm waiting anxiously, tapping my toe to the carpeted floor as the light moves from three, to four, to five...finally, it stops at ten and the doors open. For a moment, I contemplate the possibility that someone will be waiting for me inside, but thankfully, it's empty. I get in and press the first-floor button.

I'm fully aware that my escape from this hotel is not going to be an easy one. Gabriel mentioned that there are guards outside. I'm sort of just winging it in hopes of being sneaky, but in the off chance that I get caught, I do have a plan. It won't be the first time I've had to flaunt my tits and whisper sweet nothings to get what I want. If I had to guess, this won't be my last either.

Instead of going out the doors we came in when we got here, I follow an exit sign to the end of the hall on the opposite end. To my surprise, the door is unlocked. Once it closes slowly behind me, I give it a pull, sure enough, it's locked. Getting out was easy, getting back in will be another story. I'll deal with that when the time comes.

Hugging my arms to my chest, I walk briskly around the outskirts of the hotel, keeping a safe distance from the building. There are trees lining the property, so I stick close to them in case I need to hide behind one. Once I'm past the building, I pick up my pace until I'm running through the lawn and heading straight down toward the entrance of the property.

It's a long drive away and I don't dare step out onto the cement. Instead, I walk through the trees until I'm faced with a wall. Looking right, I notice the lights of a car coming into view. Pressing my back firmly against the wall, I wait until the gate opens. Once it does, and the lights fade into the night, I slither out before it closes.

The Uber has not arrived yet, thankfully. If he had, whoever just left may have seen him and it would have raised suspicion. I get the feeling that the people who stay here do not want to be found.

Pacing back and forth in front of the gate, I wait impatiently.

Lights shine in the distance and I stop walking. "Come on. Hurry the hell up," I grumble. Looking down the driveway, I make sure no one is coming.

The car comes to a stop and the driver rolls his window down. "Ann?" he asks.

I nod in response at the fake name I gave him. It's not totally fake per se, it's my middle name and also my mother's name. He gestures toward the back seat and I open the door and get in, closing it behind me.

"Alcott Memorial Hospital?" he asks.

"Yes, and the agreement was a return ride about thirty minutes after drop off. I paid over the phone."

"That's correct. Appreciate the tip. Most I've made all month." He chuckles.

Nervously, I fiddle my thumbs, feeling very uneasy about this entire situation. If Gabriel finds out that I've left my room, he will no doubt send out a search party for me. It's worth it, though. Baron is lying alone in a hospital bed and I need to see him. I need him to know that he's not alone. That I do forgive him, if forgiveness is what he wants.

About ten minutes later, the car comes to a stop. "I've got a quick run down the road and I'll be back in about thirty minutes," the driver tells me.

"Thank you," I say as I open the door and step outside beneath the carport to the emergency room entrance.

There's a chill in the air that has me stuffing my hands in

the pockets in the front of my hoodie. The doors slide open and I step inside. I'm greeted by an older woman at the front desk. "May I help you?" she asks.

"I'm looking for Baron Black's room."

Tapping into the computer, she nods her head. "Yup, Baron Black. Take the elevator around the corner to the second floor. He's in room 211. There is security watching his room as his own doctors were called in. I'm not sure that you'll be able to see him unless you're family."

"I am," I lie. "I'm his sister."

"Good luck." She smiles back at me.

Without another word, I follow the instructions she gave. Once I've reached the second floor, I don't even have to look at the room numbers to know which one is Baron's. There's a man in a security uniform standing outside his door in a military stance. Getting past him might be a problem.

Tucking into a corner, out of view, I try to come up with a way that I can get in the room without going through the hassle of dressing up as a nurse. But it's the only thing I can come up with. I need a pair of scrubs or something that helps me blend in.

My eyes dart to an x-ray room on the other side of the nurses' station and I think I have an idea. Taking the long way around, avoiding being seen, I walk to the door, push it open and as if the gods of luck are on my side, the room is empty. Letting the door close behind me, I begin my search for anything that I can put on that will disguise me. There's a small, open office behind a wall and draped over the chair is a long, white lab coat. I snatch it up and pull it on. I'm still wearing sweatpants and black Converse shoes, but I have to make do with what I've got. As I'm walking out of the office into the x-ray room, I see a box of masks hanging on the wall; I take one and put it on before exiting the room.

With my head held high, I strut over to Baron's room.

"Excuse me, I just need to check on Mr. Black. It shouldn't take long."

He stares straight ahead, not even blinking. "He has a visitor."

*A visitor?*

"It's not a problem. I'll work around them."

Reaching around the guard's back, I go to open the door, but he grabs my arm, startling me. I'm sure he can feel my body shake under his touch and my labored breaths are no mask for my discomfort. Reaching into his pocket, he pulls out a small notebook. "I need your name."

"My name?" I say in question.

"I was given strict orders to keep note of everyone who enters or exits Mr. Black's room. Your name?"

"Dr. Ann Writhe," I spit out. It's my mother's maiden name, so it was easy to come up with.

After he scribbles it down, he gives me a nod of approval and steps aside. I push open the door and instantly gasp when I see Gabriel standing over Baron's bed. Forcefully shutting the door behind me, I hurry over to his side, but I'm not quick enough.

Baron's sad eyes stare back at me as Gabriel's fist plants in his face, forcing his eyes shut. Baron's hands draw up immediately, cupping his nose. "That's for Silas," Gabriel growls, "and this is for Iris." His arm cocks back again, but I grab it just in time.

"What the hell are you doing?" I hiss. "Have you lost your damn mind?"

Gabriel swings around to face me as if he was completely unaware that someone had even entered the room. "Iris, what the hell? You're supposed to be at the hotel."

"Well, it's a good thing I'm not." I give him a shove back, away from Baron's bed. Hovering over Baron, I take all of him in. "Are you ok?" I try to pull his hand down to get a look at his face, but he doesn't budge.

"Get away from him," Gabriel hisses, as he tries to maneuver between me and the bed that Baron lies on. "He doesn't deserve your kindness."

There's an IV connected to his arm, dripping fluid into his veins. His face is battered, his forehead holds a row of stitches, and his arm is wrapped. And that's only the visible trauma. Underneath his gown, I imagine he's stitched up where they had to remove the bullet. My heart aches. It hurts so bad seeing him lying here like this in such a vulnerable state. I just want to lie beside him and put my arms over his chest and tell him that everything is going to be ok. But how can I do that when I'm not even sure that it will be ok?

"Just leave, Gabriel," I demand, though it's useless.

He huffs. "Like hell I am. I'll never leave you alone with this fucking monster."

Baron shrieks in agony as he tries to scoot himself up. I place a hand on his shoulder. "Take it easy."

He opens his mouth to speak as blood trickles down from his nostrils. The skin beneath his eye is swollen and already threatens a bruise. "Water," he chokes out.

Grabbing a Styrofoam cup off his bed tray, I hold the straw up to his mouth. He takes a long drink then pulls away. I set the cup down and sit on the very edge of his bed. Taking his hand in mine, I look into his red-rimmed eyes. "How are you?"

His voice comes out raspy. "Why are you here? You should hate me for what I did."

"Yeah. yeah, you should," Gabriel chimes in, agreeing with Baron.

I look back at Gabriel and furrow my brows. "I'm here because one bad move doesn't stop someone from caring."

"He fucking handed you over to Maretti on a silver platter.

Not to mention, he was part of your dad's assassination. You want your revenge," he grabs a pillow from a chair beside the bed and extends it to me, "here you go. Get your revenge right fucking now."

I grab the pillow and tuck it in my lap. "You boys may have been raised not to forgive, but when someone shows you they are sorry, instead of just saying it, I take the high road and forgive them. Especially when it's someone I care about."

Gabriel lets out an airy chuckle behind me. "The only road Baron should be on is the road to hell after what he's done."

"I didn't..." Baron begins speaking, but stops in the midst of a coughing fit. Once he's calmed down, he continues, "I didn't think it would be as hard as it was. I was never supposed to get attached," he says. His eyes are deadlocked on mine. "In the beginning, you were just a stepping stone to something more. Something I thought was better. Now I know I was wrong. I don't want more. I want this." He takes my hand in his. His eyes hold remorse. But deeper than that, they hold contempt. He knows he was wrong and I can see that it's painful for him to admit it.

"I'm still completely shocked about everything that happened, but how can I be mad at you when you took a bullet for me? That's all the proof I need to show me you care and you really are sorry. I can never hate you after that. We'll get past this." I turn and look at Gabriel. "We will *all* get past this."

Gabriel sweeps the air with his hand and grumbles, "Fuck if I will." He walks over to the window, parting the blinds and looking out into the night but continues talking. "Baron's never fucking liked me. From the minute I stepped foot in that house at the age of six, he viewed me as a threat. Why should I show him any grace?"

Baron scoots himself up farther on the bed, cringing with

every movement. "You're right," he says. "I've been awful to you. I've been a bad son, a bad brother, and I don't deserve to be part of this family. You both want me out, I'll leave. But she's coming with me."

I can feel the tension in the room thicken with each passing second that brings Gabriel back over to my side. His eyes are locked on Baron's and the crystal blue in them is glossed over with something dark and menacing. "Gabriel, don't." I step in front of him when he looks as if he's ready to lunge at Baron.

Gabriel points and shouts, and it has my nerves rising, "Stay the fuck away from her! You hear me?"

"Would you stop it! This is not the time nor the place. He just had a bullet removed from his body. You've already punched him. Just leave him alone."

Baron brings a hand up to stop me. "It's ok, Iris. You don't need to defend me. Gabriel's just a little pissed he's not actually a Black and doesn't have a say in anything that happens in my family."

"Baron!" I snap. "Stop it! Both of you." With one hand braced on Gabriel's chest and the other descended toward Baron, I lower my voice. "This is ridiculous. Blood does not make you family, loyalty does. Gabriel is just as much a Black as you are. He's proven that."

Gabriel doesn't stop. He pushes further. "If loyalty makes a family then it's pretty damn obvious he's not part of it."

Baron grows silent. His eyes holding tight to the wall behind us. I look over my shoulder to see what his focal point is, but there's nothing. He opens his mouth to speak, then closes it again. Bringing both hands up to his head, he begins rubbing circles on his temples and his eyes close. "I know I fucked up. Not just today. But every day. It's what I do. I fuck things up." His eyes open back up and he looks at Gabriel. "Every day I'm reminded of why you're here, and he's not."

Who is *he*? Looking at Gabriel, I search for the answer, but he gives me nothing. In a swift motion, he's stomping away and out the door, slamming it so hard behind him that it rattles the wall.

"What are you talking about?" I ask Baron. "Who isn't here?"

He shakes his head. "Forget I said anything."

Reclaiming my spot on the edge of his bed, I place my hand on his. "I can't just forget something like that."

"We made a promise not to talk about. I've already fucked up enough, don't need to add to the list."

"Ok." I nod. I get it. Family loyalties and all that. I won't push for answers right now.

"I really am sorry. When I made this deal with Maretti, I was in a bad place. I've been in a bad place for a while. Feeling like nothing made sense. There was no point to anything that I did because I got nothing in return. Silas and I have barely spoken for years. I don't have friends, don't have relationships, so I figured it was time to try something new. Step into a new adventure and start planning for my future. Then you came along and shook everything up."

My chin drops to my chest and I watch as I weave my fingers through his. His knuckles are cracked and bruised and I feel the urge to kiss them. "I'm sorry I messed everything up."

"No. You didn't mess anything up." He pulls his hand away and pushes my chin up with his thumb. I avoid eye contact by closing my eyes. Fearing that the tears will spill again, but he catches on to my apprehension. "Look at me, Iris." Opening them slowly, filled to the brim, my tears escape. "When I said you shook things up, I meant inside of me. You stirred emotion I didn't even know existed. Feelings I thought were just in fairy tales. The first time I saw you, I knew I was in trouble. It's why I tried to stay away. I was so unequivocally drawn to you it scared the shit out of me."

"You were?" That doesn't make any sense. I thought for sure that he hated me and looked at me as a child.

"Without a doubt. But now, I'm not fighting it anymore." A smile grows on his face, sending swarms of butterflies through my stomach. "Run away with me, Iris. Let's leave this fucked-up life behind and start over somewhere, together."

For a sliver of a second, I almost say 'yes.' A life with Baron sounds like a dream. This softer side to him is something I've been waiting for. I knew it existed, but he put on this tough guy facade and it had me doubting I'd ever see it. There is no doubting the chemistry between us. His touch alone ignites something inside of me. But it's the same something that Gabriel ignites—and Silas.

"Baron, I—"

"It was a stupid idea." He shifts his body away from me. "They've got me on some pretty potent pain killers. Just ignore me."

"Baron, I want to be with you."

His head snaps around, and his expression wears his surprise. "You do?"

I nod my head with a smile. Not one that's forced or faked. A real smile. "I do. But I don't want to leave. I want to stay."

"With Silas and Gabriel?"

"With all of you."

He huffs. "That's absurd. There is no way that either of them would allow you and me to be together under that roof. And you certainly can't have all of us."

I raise a shoulder. "Why not?"

"Why not?" He laughs. "Because we don't even like to share guns. There is no way in hell we'd be able to share you.

Besides, I don't want to share you with anyone. I want you to be mine, and only mine."

He's right. There is no way this could ever work. It's a crazy idea to think I could have them all. Only, I could never choose. Gabriel is my home away from home. Silas is my comfort. Baron is my safe place. They all offer me something that I lack without them. Each one of them has one-third of my heart and no matter what I do, I'll lose a piece of it. "I can't leave with you, Baron. But I'm begging you to please stay. Work things out with Gabriel and Silas. With time, I know they'll forgive you. You belong here." I lean forward and ghost his lips with mine. "You belong with me." He leans forward a tad, connecting our mouths. When he cringes, I pull back. "Are you ok?"

Smiling through the pain, he bites down on his bottom lip. "I'm perfect."

That he is. Perfectly imperfect, and all mine.

Lying down next to him with half of my body hanging off the bed, we talk about life. We talk about our past, our child-hood and I try to dig for answers to the person he mentioned earlier, but he gives me nothing. Two hours have passed when I shoot out of bed. "Oh shit! I forgot that an Uber driver was waiting for me in the parking lot."

Baron chuckles. "Well, I doubt he's waiting anymore. Looks like you're spending the night."

"Actually, I should probably get going. I need to patch things up with Gabriel and make sure he's ok." Baron rolls his eyes, but I swat at his arm gently. "Stop it. He's still your brother."

"Not by choice."

"I really do need to get back, though. I'll come back and visit you tomorrow."

"No!" He shakes his head with a stern voice. "It's not safe for you to be wandering around. That asshole is still looking for you. Stay with Gabriel and Silas, they'll keep you safe. I'll be outta here in a couple days then we'll get started."

"Get started?" I quip.

"Your revenge? Have you given up?"

"Well, no. I guess I just haven't thought much about it. So much happened today."

"I want to help you. My way of trying to right my wrongs. Besides, Maretti will be after us all now, so he needs to be taken down."

"Really?" I beam with excitement. "You'll help me?"

"Of course, I will. We all will. That's what family does, right?"

"Yes." I nod. "That's exactly what family does."

## Thirty-Two

Iт's after eleven o'clock when I finally get back to my room. Baron made arrangements for one of the family drivers to come pick me up. I walked through the main doors and no one questioned a thing. I'm sure Gabriel gave them a heads up that I'd be arriving, again.

I don't have a key card to get in the room, but apparently, I don't need one. As I near the door, I notice that it's open a crack. Looking left, then right, I stick my head in the door. "Hello. Is anyone there?"

There's no response so I push it open farther. I should be scared to death, but I'm so tired and so hungry that all I care about is collapsing on that bed with room service.

I'm pulling my hoodie over my head when my heart jumps into my throat. "Oh my god, Gabriel. You scared the shit out of me." My hoodie falls to the floor and I kick both shoes off. Making my way over to the bed where Gabriel lies with his hands perched behind his head and his ankles crossed, I notice the deep scowl on his face. "Why the sour face?" I ask him, knowing the answer, but playing dumb.

Tipping his chin up, he scoffs. 'What took you so long?"

"Baron and I had a lot to talk about." Dropping onto my back on the bed, I let out a pent-up breath. *Ah, it feels so good to lie down.*

Gabriel gets on his knees and presses his palms on either side of me. His face hovering mine. "Did you fuck him?"

"What?" I sneer, "Of course I didn't fuck him. He just had surgery. Are you serious right now?"

"What'd you two talk about?" I turn to look away from him, but he takes my chin in between his forefinger and thumb and turns my head back to face him. "You're a damn fool if you forgive him."

Crystal blue eyes stare back into mine and I'm under his spell. I try to look away, but he doesn't allow it. "I don't see how that's any of your business."

His eyebrows dip into a V. "What kind of game are you playing here, Iris?" Warm breath hits my neck, sending chills down my entire body. To them, it may seem like I am, in fact, playing games, but the truth is, I can never choose. They've all won me over.

"My own. Wanna play?" It was supposed to be a joke, but part of me is dead serious. I've already explained to Baron what I want, and he didn't shoot down the possibility that we could make this work. I'm not so sure that Gabriel will be as accommodating.

"I don't play games and it's in your best interest not to play them either." His hand sweeps down my leg, then back up between my thighs. Cupping my crotch, he seethes, "This is mine. I do not share."

My back arches and the desire to devour his mouth is tantalizing. In doing so, I feel like I'd be agreeing with him, and I refuse to do that.

"Agree with me," he continues, "tell me it's mine and only mine."

Pressing my mouth into a thin line, I shake my head. "Uh-uh."

His hand slaps the mattress, startling me. "Damnit, Iris. Tell me!"

"I can't. Because it would be a lie. I care about all of you equally."

"Since when does caring about someone have anything to do with who touches your pussy? I care about people, but I don't fuck em'."

"You do? Who?" I say, trying to change the subject.

"That's beside the point. I need to know I'm the only one who gets to touch this." He rubs my crotch aggressively through the fabric of my sweatpants. "And the only one who tastes these." His lips press to mine. Ravenous, unruly, and so damn delicious. He tastes like sin, but fuck if I wouldn't go to hell just to do this again and again.

My legs part instinctively as his body dips between them. Sliding himself up and down as he grinds against me, he takes my tongue hostage before dragging my bottom lip between his teeth.

I throw my head back and run my hands up and down his bare arms. "Fuck me, Gabriel."

"You want me to fuck you? Then promise me they'll never touch you again. Tell me you're all mine."

"No," I blurt out. Pushing him off me and taking control. He has no right to give me ultimatums. My palms press to his shoulders as I shove him down on the bed and take what I want. Bracing himself on his elbows, he watches me watch him as I slide down his pants and boxers. I throw them off the bed and don't even blink before taking his cock in my mouth.

His blue eyes bore into mine as I lick up the length of his cock. Cupping his balls in one hand, I massage them as I flick my tongue underneath his shaft.

He bites the corner of his lip and places a hand on my

head, guiding my movements as I take all of him in my mouth. In and out, up and down, while watching his expression. Popping his head out of my mouth, I stop. Wiping the back of my hand over my mouth, I climb off the bed.

"The fuck you doing?" He grunts.

I pick up his sweats and his boxers and toss them on his stomach. "Goodbye, Gabriel," I say sweetly, but my words are loaded with intent. There is no way in hell he will let me leave.

"Wait a damn minute." He jumps off the bed. His cock sticks straight out, tempting me. Grabbing my wrist, he stops me. Just like I knew he would. "Where are you going?"

"Back to my room. If you can't accept that all three of you are in my heart then I guess I have to let you go."

A laugh rumbles from his throat. "So, you're choosing them?"

"I'm choosing me. For once in my life, I'm doing what makes *me* happy. I'll never choose between the three of you, and if I'm forced to, then I choose none of you."

"You really are serious? You think this will work. You're delusional, Iris. Baron hates both me and Silas. Not to mention the fact that they are blood father and son. Neither of them will ever agree to this."

My arms cross over my chest and I pop a hip out. "Maybe they already have."

"Liar."

"Baron and I talked about it tonight. He's coming home and he's willing to give this a try because he doesn't want to lose me."

"Baron doesn't have a home. Since when do you get to call the shots?"

Licking my lips, I drape my arms over his shoulders. "Since I have something you all I want."

"What's that? A golden pussy?"

My lips press to his neck. "Is it worth it to you?" Trailing my tongue up, I sweep it around the lobe of his ear.

I can feel the goosebumps on him cascade downward from my mouth.

"How do you expect this to work? We each get a day of the week? That's fucking absurd."

Moving down to his collarbone, I suck his skin into my mouth. "It's fucking beautiful. What we have is beautiful." I lift my head and look at him. "We don't live normal lives. We don't have to pretend. Just let this happen naturally. I promise I'll never give them more than I give you and vice versa. I'm still yours. I'm just theirs, too."

Weaving his fingers through his hair, he's silent for a moment as he thinks, then he grumbles, "On the fucking bed, now!"

Smiling inwardly, I oblige. Throwing myself onto the bed, he shreds every last piece of clothing on my body.

Gabriel pulls his shirt over his head and dives between my legs. I let them fall to the side as far as they'll go and grab a fist full of his hair. Arching my back, I force his face into me as his tongue sweeps up and down. He sucks my clit in between his teeth and I let out a subtle groan. "Ahh, baby."

"Fuck, you taste so good." His tongue muscle flexes as he darts the tip inside. With one hand pressed against my left thigh, he uses his free hand to rub circles around my clit. An intense tingling sensation swims through my body.

I buck my hips up and down and ride his face while still gripping his hair forcibly. Sweeping my fingers up my stomach, I cup my breast in my hand and massage as I throw my head back and close my eyes, relishing the pleasure he's bringing me.

When he slides two fingers in, my body jolts. My arousal pooling around his fingers that pulsate against my walls. "Ugh, Gabriel," I moan. He pushes harder and faster. His tongue flicking my clit and causing me to fill with an intense need to release. "I'm gonna come." I whimper before more groans escape me.

He licks me up and down before raising his head. His lips are swollen and wet and his chin is tinged pink. Sliding his body up on mine, he smirks before sliding his fingers into my mouth. My eyes widen as my tongue tries to force them out. "See how fucking good you taste." He slides his fingers in and out of my mouth before taking them completely out and replacing them with his lips on mine.

Before his mouth even leaves mine, his dick is sliding inside of me. It's a good feeling knowing I'm the only one Gabriel has ever been with, but I can't take credit for his skills. He's done that all on his own. He's so smooth and amazing, hitting just the right spot. As if he's done this a thousand times.

His hips rise and fall in a repetitive motion. Pressing himself up, he gets on his knees and locks my legs under his forearms, bringing my ass off the bed before he starts pounding into me.

With my mouth agape, he lets out a few muffled groans and watches as his dick slides in and out of me.

My body inches backward, and I stretch my arms over my head and press my hands to the headboard to gain traction.

"I'll never quit you, Iris," he grounds out before slamming into me harder. I can feel the head of his cock swell inside of me before he pulls out abruptly and shoots his cum all over my stomach. He continues to pump himself through his orgasm until every drop is released.

Propping myself up on my elbows, I lean forward. "Good, because I wouldn't let you, anyways." Once he drops my legs, I come forward even more and press my lips to his. "So, does this mean you're willing to try?"

"I don't wanna know what the fuck you do with those

two. Don't want to hear it and sure as hell don't wanna see it. You'll be sleeping in my bed at least two nights of the week. I get to pick the nights."

"Shut up, and come here." I grab his face and pull his body down on top of me. Devouring his mouth with a sticky mess between us. "Looks like we both need a shower."

Jumping off the bed in a swift motion, he scoops me up in his arms. "You're taking one with me." He carries me into the bathroom while I'm sporting the biggest smile ever.

Two down, one to go.

## Thirty—Three

IT'S BEEN a week since Baron was shot. He's finally getting released from the hospital today and I'm anxiously waiting to go back home. *Home.* It's so strange to call that house my home, but the people inside of it make it home to me.

Gabriel and I have been holed up in the hotel for the last week. I'm not complaining; it's been nice. We've gotten to know one another on a deeper level, but I've missed Silas so much. He's been wheeling and dealing, taking care of business as usual, like nothing ever happened. His main concern has been my safety, which surprises me, considering his son was shot and his family is on the brink of crumbling.

I plan to fix that, though. I'm pulling this family back together since I was the reason it fell apart in the first place.

There were a couple nights that I was able to get away to visit Baron in the hospital. Gabriel wasn't pleased at first, but the second time, he even arranged my ride. Once again, he was waiting in my room like I needed to be punished for seeing another man, but that's just Gabriel. I'm starting to think he just likes to play rough. Another thing I won't complain

"You ready?" Gabriel asks as he pokes his head into my room. I slide my shoes on and grab my bag of clothes. Silas had more clothes delivered to me. A bag full of a week's worth of brand-new apparel. He also had a note placed inside that said, 'Hurry Home.' It warmed my heart and brought a smile to my face.

Giving the room one more sweep to make sure I'm not forgetting anything, I meet him at the door. "Yep, let's get out of here."

Throwing an arm over my shoulder, Gabriel pulls me close as we walk down the hall. I can't help but notice he's quieter than normal. "What's wrong?" I ask him. Tipping my chin up to look at his face.

With his eyes fixated in front of us, his voice wavers, "I dunno. Just gonna be weird. That's all."

Stopping him in the middle of the hall about a foot before the elevators, I stand in front of him. Taking both of his hands in mine, I try to assure him that nothing has changed. "It's still us."

He huffs. "And them."

Warm hands cup my cheeks as he pulls my forehead to his. "Let's just go somewhere. Let me take you away. Just you and me. I'll give it all up for us."

I draw in a deep breath, knowing that it will hurt him just as bad as it hurts me. "As tempting as that sounds, I can't. Just like I told Baron. I can't choose."

His eyes close as if he was actually expecting me to agree to run away with him. Shaking his head back and forth, he mumbles the word, "Fine."

Smiling, I give his hand a tug. "Come on. Let's go home."

$\sim$

My eyes shoot open when the car comes to a stop. With a pounding heart that's anxious to see Silas, I jump out the back door before the driver even opens it. Bumping into his leg, I apologize, "Sorry."

"Calm down, girl. They're not going anywhere," Gabriel says as he gets out and joins me. The driver collects our bags while Gabriel and I walk up to the house hand in hand.

"I know. It's just been so long. When does Baron get home?"

Gabriel shrugs a shoulder. "Hell, if I know. That's a question for Silas."

Once we're at the top of the steps, Gabriel stops me. "Hey." He presses his lips to mine in a soft and gentle peck. His fingers rake through my jet-black hair. "I'll give you and him the evening, but you're in my bed tonight. Got kind of used to sleeping next to you and I'm not ready to give it up just yet."

Smiling, I kiss him again. "Deal." I'll give Gabriel tonight, as long as he's aware that some nights I want my privacy, and other nights, I'll be in someone else's bed.

We walk inside and the house is just like I remember it. The smell, the sounds—or lack thereof. I don't see Silas, but I assume he's in his study. "I'll see you later." I stretch up on my tiptoes and kiss him one last time before I'm kicking my shoes off and sliding across the hardwood floors to Silas's office.

Looking over my shoulder, I notice Gabriel still standing where I left him. My heart breaks a little when I catch the displeasure in his gaze. This isn't going to be easy at first, but with time, I hope he'll adjust.

Swinging back around, I don't even knock before pushing the door open to Silas's study. His brown eyes shoot to mine and in a matter of seconds, I'm on his lap. Cradling his body while he sits in his chair.

Scooping my ass in his hands, his expression never changes. So stern and impassive. "I've missed you," I tell him.

Tilting his head to the side as I kiss every inch of his neck, he finally speaks, "Any troubles on your way back today?"

"No. No trouble at all." Breaking the suction of my kiss on his skin, I search his face for something that tells me he missed me, too. "Did you miss me?" I ask, sounding all too needy.

"Baron is coming home. I'd like to have a family meeting when he gets here. I assume you'll join us."

Damn, he's always so serious. One of the many things I love about him. It's all the more satisfying to get him to crack and show an ounce of emotion.

"Of course I will. You're letting him stay, aren't you?"

Tucking a strand of hair behind my ear, he watches his movements. "He's my son. He will always have a place to stay in this house."

"Good." Pushing myself off of him, I get to my feet and grab his hands. "Now that we have that settled, I want to show you just how much I missed you."

For a moment, I think he's going to resist me when his eyes search mine, but then he joins me on his feet. Titling his head down, he scopes out my breasts that peek from the top of my V-neck shirt. His index finger trails lightly over my cleavage before he sticks his hand down my shirt. With his free hand, he jerks my body against his and I can already feel his want for me digging into my upper thigh. "I did miss you." He hums into the crease of my neck before popping my breast out of my shirt and sucking my nipple between his teeth.

His scent—Bourbon swirled with cedarwood and sage—rolls off of him, filling my senses and igniting every cell in my body. "Prove it," I challenge him. "Show me how much you missed me.

Grabbing my leg, he lifts up, pressing my knee to his waist.

"Oh, I plan to." His cock grinds against me and my body seeks friction against my clit.

"I need you so bad," I whimper. Sliding my hand down between us, I stroke his cock through the fabric of his black trousers. He's so hard and it has me longing to feel him inside of me.

"Bend over." My leg drops and he tucks an arm under my waist and pushes my chest to his desk. I hear the clanking of his belt buckle before his pants drop to the floor. With one hand, he jerks my leggings down, taking my panties with them.

Looking over my shoulder, I watch him as he gapes at my bare ass, rubbing circles around the smooth skin. "You've got the tightest ass I've ever laid eyes on." He gives it a smack, but the sting only arouses me further. Rolling my hips, I push my ass up and he drives two fingers inside of me. "You're soaking wet for me, Iris. We need to do something about that." His words come out gruff and lust-filled. Circling his fingers, he pumps them inside of me, hitting just the right spot.

I release a muffled groan when all of a sudden, a banging noise rings through my ears. Like metal meeting metal along with the strumming of a guitar. The desk vibrates beneath me while Silas pushes deeper and faster. 'What is that?" I choke out between cries of intense pleasure.

"Gabriel and his damn music."

It gets louder. So loud that it echoes through my ears and drowns out the grunts and moans that escape me. I assume that's the point. That's why Gabriel is doing this. He's hurt, jealous, and angry.

Pushing those thoughts aside, I focus on this—on me and Silas and how good he's making me feel. His hand slides around me and he uses the pads of his fingers to do laps on my clit. I perch my ass up higher and my mouth drops open. "Oh fuck, Silas," I grumble. "Ugh, baby. I'm coming." I hold my breath and feel my muscles spasm as my arousal drips down his fingers. Before I can even let that breath out, his cock is filling me back up.

His pelvis thrusts against my ass in swift and rapid movements while his fingertips dig into my sides. My hip bone grinds against the ledge of the desk and I throw two hands over it to brace myself on the other side. Squeezing tightly, my nails graze the wood, likely leaving scratches in the finish.

Silas lets out a heady breath before pushing deep inside of me and releasing. One, two, three more pumps and his movements stop while he's still buried deep inside my pussy. A moment passes before he pulls out and I can feel both our arousals slide down my leg. Silas grabs a clean handkerchief from his drawer and hands it to me.

Once I'm wiped dry, I pull my pants up, still feeling the dampness pool in my panties. I adjust my shirt and lean back with two palms pressed to the desk behind me. Silas leans in and presses his mouth to mine. He goes to pull away, but I wrap my hands around his head and give him more than he asked for. Tasting the sweet bourbon on his tongue mixed with the saltiness of sweat on his lips. "Mmm," I mutter into his mouth, "I never want to be away from you that long again."

I finally release him, and he gives me one more peck before tucking his shirt back into his pants. "Even when the consolation is me greeting you like this."

I bite back a smile. "Well, when you put it that way."

His dark eyes bore into mine as he gets himself proper. "You should know, Iris, I love my sons very much. I might not show it, but I do. Please do not hurt them."

I'm a bit taken aback. "Why would I ever hurt them?" Does he think that I'm working with the enemy? Have I lost his trust somehow?

"I'm not a fool. I know what's going on. Just because I

don't talk about it, doesn't mean that I don't notice. I'd like you to stay with us, but you should also know that I will never give you the things girls your age want. There will be no marriage, no children, and I expect there will be no other men outside of this house."

"Of course not. Silas, I don't want any other men. You, Gabriel, and Baron give me all that I need. Are you…" I hesitate, wondering if I'm understanding this correctly, "are you saying that you're ok with my relationships with all three of you?" My heart pounds violently in my chest as I await his response. I planned to have this conversation with him, but I never could have imagined he'd be the one bringing it up.

"I'm willing to share whatever makes my boys happy. My home, my business, and you."

"Me? As in… sexually?" I have to ask. I have to be certain that we're on the same page.

Silas walks around his desk and sits back down in his chair. "And emotionally. I've raised Baron and Gabriel to shut off their emotions, but then you came along. I cannot be hypocritical and tell them not to feel when all you've done since you walked in that door is make me feel every emotion in existence. From loathing, to pity, to love."

Grinning from ear to ear, I lean over the desk, invading his personal space. "Did you just say love?"

"I said what I said." He speaks sternly. "No games and we'll all be fine."

I press my lips to his, loving every moment of being in his presence. Silas has the ability to make me feel more important than anything in the world. He's admirable and deep down, sweet. He's fierce and loyal. Strong and seductive. He's everything I want.

This life is everything I want.

*Thirty-Four*

IT'S BEEN two weeks since Baron was shot and things fell apart, but I feel like they are slowly being put back together. Baron was brought home by another one of the Black family drivers. I met him outside and helped him into his room. He's doing well, but still somewhat weak.

Silas has called for a family meeting today, and we've agreed to hold it in Baron's room so that he doesn't have to go back downstairs. He's been stubborn as hell and refusing much help, but that doesn't surprise me in the least.

"Are they coming up or what?" Baron huffs, as I adjust the pillow behind him.

"Should be." Silas has been busy with work these past couple days. He went on an overnight trip two days ago, returned yesterday, and he's been preoccupied ever since.

"Would you stop messing with stuff and just come here?" Baron smirks as he grabs me by the waist and pulls me down next to him.

Smiling in response, I curl my body around his, taking care not to hit the wound in his chest, even though the stitches have dissolved and it's pretty much healed up. "I just want you to be comfortable."

His lips press to my forehead and it's everything that I've missed about him. "I am. Now. I've told you, I'm fine. Barely any pain."

Ever since Baron was shot, it's like he's taken this new approach to life. He's still the same pompous asshole when he needs to be, but he's different toward me. He's been sweet and tentative and makes me feel important. It's a big change from feeling like gum on the bottom of his shoe when I first arrived.

The bedroom door opens and Gabriel walks in without even knocking. Unintentionally, I find myself squirming to sit up. Gabriel glares at Baron as he walks over to my side and puts his mouth on mine. Hands cupping my cheeks, in a full-blown make-out session, that's bittersweet with Baron only inches from me. I know what Gabriel is doing and it's certainly not copping a feel because of his feelings toward me. No. This is Gabriel leaving his mark on his girl.

I let Gabriel break the kiss on his own, because if I'm the one to do it, he'll start worrying again. He's been doing better, but he still struggles with the idea of sharing me. He's like a child who needs extra attention or he begins to feel left out and unloved. I've been patient with him, because I know that it's all part of the way Gabriel is. He's my possessive guy. Silas is my passive one, and Baron is a combination of both.

Gabriel straightens himself up and picks up a bottle of prescription pain meds on the nightstand beside the table. Twirling it around in his hand, he looks at Baron. I can feel my heart rising into my throat as the tension in the room becomes suffocating. "This shit any good?"

I breathe out a hefty sigh of relief. That was a normal question. No sly remarks about working for the enemy or bedding his girlfriend. This is progress. A baby step, but progress.

"Couple of those and I'm out cold," Baron replies with a placid tone.

They must be sleeping pills. Feeling like Gabriel's wheels are spinning, I snatch the bottle from his hand with a grin. "Let's just put those away." I pull open the drawer to the nightstand and drop them inside before closing it.

"What?" Gabriel sneers. "Not like I'm planning on taking any." He wraps an arm around my waist and scoops me into his arms, nuzzling his face in my neck. "I sleep just fine with you by my side."

Baron lets out an audible breath and suddenly, this isn't going the way I planned. Fortunately, footsteps come trudging down the hall and Silas makes an appearance in the room before things get too awkward.

"Welcome home, Baron. I see you've settled in," Silas says with his typical stern and serious tenor.

Baron's head drops to the side as he looks away. His eyes fixated on a beam of light shining through the parted blinds of the window. If I had to guess, I'd say he's ashamed of what he did and he sees himself as a disappointment to his father.

Gabriel's ruffling through the release papers that were sitting on the nightstand, and I'm sure it's just a distraction because we all feel an immense amount of unease.

Silas clears his throat before continuing, "Listen, I'm no good at this shit, but I called this meeting because, well, we needed it. I'm not going to rehash what Baron did. He knows he fucked up and he's willing to right his wrongs. Regardless, he is still my son." He turns to face Gabriel and slaps a hand to the back of his head. "As are you."

Baron's head twists, his eyes dancing from person to person to see if we all agree with what Silas has just said—namely Gabriel. I'm sure he's expecting some sly remark about how he doesn't belong here and how Baron broke everyone's trust.

No one else speaks, so Silas keeps on talking. "I raised you boys the way that I saw fit because I couldn't risk another loss in the family. I needed you both to have the courage and the strength to defend yourselves." His eyes hold tight to Baron's as he speaks directly to him. "The loss of your mother and David was a big one. It changed everything. Including me, and most importantly, you."

Baron's eyes widen as Gabriel steels his back. I'm not sure who David is, but the mention of his name shifted the air movement in the room, surrounding us with even more tension.

"Who is David?" I ask, all too curious who he's talking about before the conversation goes any further.

"My son," Silas quips.

"My brother," Baron adds, "my real brother." His gaze darts to Gabriel and an indignant look unfolds on Baron's face. "Gabriel just stepped in and tried to replace him."

"You son of a—" Gabriel lunges at Baron, but Silas throws an arm out and stops him.

Silas steps forward. "Stop it, you two. David was never replaced. He's gone, and he's never coming back. Gabriel needed us and we needed him."

"Yeah, as a depraved robot, not a son," Baron huffs.

Gabriel raises his voice. "You think I asked for this? Huh? I was six-fucking-years-old."

I interrupt again, needing the whole story. "Can someone please explain to me what happened to David and how it has anything to do with Gabriel."

Baron takes it upon himself to explain, though I'd prefer Silas do it because he's impartial to the anger Baron feels. "My mother and David were killed when I was thirteen years old. David was fifteen at the time. Life was normal then. We went to school, played sports, and actually fucking enjoyed life. When they died, they took our souls with them. We became empty shells because Silas was hell-bent that we live to survive and shut off all emotions because they only interfere."

"How'd they die?" I ask, looking from person to person.

Silas stuffs his hands in his pockets and takes a more serious tone, which says a lot for a man who is always serious. "They were shot. It was meant for me, but David and Rebecca were caught in the crossfire. There was a war between the Rossi family and the Blacks. I ended that war by killing the two Rossi brothers who ruled their empire—with the help of your father. That's why I owed him. That's why you were sent to me."

"Oh my God." I clap a hand over my mouth. "I'm so sorry."

"Remember me telling you about my first kill?" Baron asks from the bed.

I nod solemnly, still holding my hand over my mouth.

"It was then. I killed the man that shot my mother."

"Oh my god," I gasp.

"Not even six months later, he found this one washed up in a bathtub in the home of some low-life scums." Baron tips his head toward Gabriel. "Silas thought that by saving him, he could make up for the loss of David."

Silas snaps, "That is not why I took Gabriel in. No one can replace David. Just like no one can replace Rebecca." He looks at me and there's a pang in my chest.

I would never try to take the place of his late wife. I just hope that there is enough room in his heart for me, too.

Silas begins pacing in small strides. "It's understandable that this hasn't been easy on you, son." His gaze wavers to Baron briefly. "You and David were very close, but blaming Gabriel does you no good. It's time to let go and accept that this is our family now. We might not have it all together, but we have each other. I know you're upset about the change in my will, but Gabriel is my son, too. Blood or not, he is a Black."

It all makes sense now. Why Baron has been so bitter toward Gabriel. Why he carries this anger toward Silas. He blames Silas for the loss of his mom and brother. He blames Gabriel for trying to replace David, though that's not what Gabriel was trying to do at all. He was a small child and had no idea what kind of life he was stepping into. Silas built these guys to be ruthless and powerful, because David was not and he loves them so much that he didn't want a replay of events that took his son's life. If anything, it makes me love them all so much more.

Baron scoots himself off the bed and I join his side to try and stop him from getting up, but he waves me off. "I feel fine. I need to do this," he whispers into the small space between us. He gets to his feet and walks over to Silas. When he steps up, nose to nose, I think the worst, but then he slaps a hand on his shoulder. "I'm done trying so hard. For years I have tried to be the better son. The one you'd be proud of. I wanted your praise and sought out your attention. When I felt like I wasn't getting the majority of it, I reacted childishly. In the end, it all backfired. I never wanted to work for Maretti, I just wanted to piss you off because...I don't know why. I was angry. But I'm done."

"I.am.proud.of.you," Silas says, looking back into Baron's eyes. "Just because I'm proud of Gabriel, too, doesn't diminish the amount of respect and admiration I have for you. If I'm being honest, I gave the boy more attention because he needed it. You were always strong and independent. Gabriel was careless and messy."

Gabriel shrugs a shoulder. "It's true."

Baron lets out a throaty laugh. "Yeah, you do fuck up a lot

of shit. One of our dining chairs is all scratched up from your last knife-induced torture in the kitchen."

I watch the smile grow on Gabriel's face and suddenly, my heart is so full of happiness that it could explode at any given second if they don't stop all this mushy talk.

Silas follows suit and smiles in response to their remarks to one another. "I'm glad we had this talk. Now, we have business to attend to." His focus shifts to me. "You ready to get that revenge?"

My eyes widen. "Umm, yeah, but how?"

"Gabriel and I have a little surprise for you. Baron, you're welcome to come along, but I'd prefer if you refrain from doing anything strenuous. You're still healing."

Baron huffs. "There is no way I'm *not* coming along."

My thoughts begin running rampant as my heart rate increases with each passing second. Is this really happening—now? "Where do we find him? What do I wear? I need a gun to protect myself." I start spewing the nonsense that's flooded my mind.

"First of all," Silas says, as he pulls me to my feet. He doesn't let go as he holds firmly onto my hand. "Deep breath." I draw in a long inhale, but it doesn't calm me at all when I release it immediately. "Second, wear what you have on. You do not need protection because I'll never let that son of a bitch hurt you. We," he looks from Baron to Gabriel, then back to me, "will never let anyone hurt you."

"You got that right." Baron places an arm around my waist.

"We've got you, babe." Gabriel takes my other hand. My head falls on Baron's shoulder and happy tears well in my eyes.

This is my home. This is my new family. These men are all mine, and I'm theirs.

## Thirty-Five

IT'S BEEN ALMOST two months since I've been to this house. A place I once called home is now just six-thousand square feet of bricks, boards, and luxurious belongings. There is only one thing inside my family home that has significance to me, and I've come to collect it.

"Wait here. I'll be right back," I tell the guys in the back seat of the stretch Hummer. Gabriel gives me a snide look and I know that none of them like the idea of me going inside alone, but I have to do it, for myself.

The driver opens the door and I stand up, duck my head and climb out. My knees knock as I put my feet onto solid ground. Drawing in a deep breath, I walk toward the house, passing the spot where my father was shot and reliving that memory. So much fear, hostility, and anguish. The greatest loss of my life. My revenge on that bastard Maretti will easily be my greatest victory.

Curling my lip, I hold my head high. The weight of the world slowly being lifted off my shoulders and a fire igniting inside of me.

I tap in the code on the front door, wait for the beep, and

turn the handle, throwing the door wide open. The familiar scent of this place swirls in my senses.

Ignoring the mess around me that still lies unsettled from the ambush, I tear down some yellow caution tape in front of the staircase and walk up one step, then another, until I'm at the top. There are blood stains and trash thrown about. At least the bodies are gone, that's a plus. I'm sure this entire thing was brushed under the table by Maretti's people. I'm not even sure where Dad's body was taken, but once this is over, I plan to find out and give him the funeral he deserves.

This entire estate, all of dad's finances and belongings, are now mine. It was just never safe for me to come home, until now. Even still, I'm planning on selling the place and extinguishing the bad memories that live here. I only want the good ones, and those aren't found in materialistic things. I keep those safely inside of me.

Pushing open the door to my bedroom, I go straight for the closet. Grabbing the old wooden box, I tuck it under my arm and without giving the room a second look, I leave. Jogging downstairs and straight out the front door.

I stop in front of the house, turn around and smile at what was once my happy place—my comfort zone, my fortress. "Goodbye," I whisper before turning back around and walking to the car that holds my heart inside of it. In three of the most perfectly imperfect men lies my future.

"Whatcha got there?" Gabriel asks as soon as my ass hits the leather seat. The door closes and I click the clasp on the box.

Pushing the lid open and looking at the contents inside, I press my lips together. "Just some things from my past."

It's quiet for a few minutes, but as I rifle through some of the old memories inside, I find a picture of my mom and pull it out. She died in a car accident when I was just a child. I often wonder how different life would have been had she lived longer. My mind is still racing with random thoughts and questions that have yet to be answered.

Looking up from the picture in my hand, I ask, "Where are we going?"

Silas retorts, "Not far."

Nodding my head, I continue to think. He says I'm getting my revenge against Maretti, but that would mean Maretti is *not far*. "Do you have him in custody?"

"I do," Silas deadpans.

"Hmm." If it only took Silas a matter of days to get Maretti, why didn't he just do this from the start? "And you took him in? Or your guys did?"

His head twists and he cocks a brow. "Why all the questions?"

"I'm just curious why we didn't do this sooner if it was that easy? Could have saved a lot of worry on my part."

Gabriel, Baron, and I all watch Silas as he explains, "Because this wasn't my job. I could have done this sooner, but it wasn't my revenge to seek. You told me that you wanted this. I told you to prove it. And you did. It became personal when my son was shot, but I'm giving you the satisfaction of carrying out *your* plan, because you've shown me that you really do want it." He pauses for a beat. 'I believe now that you have it in you."

I should be angry that I've lived in fear these last couple months when Silas had the capabilities to bring this all to a head much sooner. But I'm a firm believer that things happen the way they are meant to. If he'd delivered me Maretti when I first walked in that door, I would have cowered. Let him go free and I probably would have never had the opportunity to get close to these guys. I understand why Silas was so passive in the beginning. He treated this all as if it was not his business, because it wasn't—until now.

Minutes later, the car comes to a stop. My heart climbs into my throat and I swallow hard, knowing that it's time.

We all wait for the driver to open the door, even though I want to just push it open myself and run inside and get this over with. I don't even know where we are, but when the door finally opens, I see that it's the same place Gabriel brought me when he was searching for Mickey Barton. It feels like an eternity ago that I was inside that building torturing my first victim, a woman, nonetheless. Then Gabriel and I had wild sex on the cold floor outside the room. It was that day that my feelings for him grew in my heart from miniscule to overflowing. I'm still not even sure who Mickey Barton is, or why my father put a hit on him, but I intend to get all my answers in a few short minutes.

Stepping out of the car, I'm followed by all three guys. We walk up to the building together, in complete silence. Me in my thoughts, them in theirs.

Silas pulls open the door, holding it for us. I walk in after Gabriel and Baron, followed by Silas. He places a hand on the small of my back as we shadow the others. The smell of wet cement mixed with a musty aroma draws the memories of the last time I was here to the forefront of my mind.

Walking down the same path, I gather that we'll be in the same room, but Baron stops in front of a different door this time. With his back pressed to it, he looks at me. "You ready for this?"

Patting the front pocket of my hoodie, I nod. "I'm ready." And it's true. I'm ready for this nightmare to be over. It's time to take my life back and it all begins and ends here.

Baron pulls the U-shaped handle of the wooden door, and I take a step forward before he puts an arm out and stops me. "If you need anything at all, just holler." He presses his lips to my forehead, and I return the gesture with a smile.

Once I'm inside, my pulse begins racing. Feeling the throb

in the side of my neck. There's a chair, much like the one that Mickey's wife was in. Only this time, a man sits quietly in it. His back is to me, and when I take another step toward him, I suddenly second-guess myself.

I've killed once and it has had little effect on me, but can I do it again?

This man in front of me killed dozens of men, including my father, do I want to be like him? Gabriel told me that Maretti doesn't have a family, but in taking his life, I'm also taking away his chance of ever having one. Then again, what would he do with it if he did, in fact, have one? He'd treat them as prisoners. Me—I'd be his prisoner.

No. This is the only way and I have to do this. I will do this.

Rounding the corner of the chair, I come face to face with the man who has stolen my identity, my freedom, my family, and my life. "So we meet again," I say with a shaky voice.

His mouth is gagged and his arms are bound to the arms of the chair. He doesn't even attempt to speak, but I'm sure he's sporting a menacing smirk behind the towel that's stuffed in his mouth. I can see it in his eyes. He's not scared of me. He's gloating.

We need to do something about that.

Looking around, I notice all the same tools, only this time, there's a gun. I'm not in the mood for games and I prefer this to be quick and less gruesome on my end, so I snatch up the nine-millimeter. WIth my free hand, I pull the towel out of his mouth and drop it to the floor.

"My pearl," he grins, "Oh, how I've waited for the day I'd see you again."

He's actually a very attractive man and it's such a shame that his hideous soul was put inside a body this delicious.

"I am a pearl, Mr. Marretti," I sneer, "but not yours." Raising my hand, I aim the gun at his forehead. The tremble in my arms is obvious to both of us, but I don't even care. He can see that I'm nervous, it will only give him doubt about my abilities. His last thought can be, *she'll never go through with it*. And then I will.

"That's where you're wrong. You are mine and have been mine for many years."

"That's ridiculous. You're only what, six years older than me?"

"Eight, to be exact. I was twenty-one years old when you were promised to me. You, only thirteen. I watched you run in the yard with your new puppy. Oscar, am I right?"

"How'd you know that?" I got Oscar for my thirteenth birthday. He died a couple years ago, but he was my best friend. My only friend, really.

The corner of his lips curl upward. "Because I bought him for you. You're welcome."

Why would he buy me a puppy for my birthday? My dad told me that he bought him for me. Why would he lie?

I laugh. "You expect me to thank you?"

"I see you're much like your father. An ungrateful little thing." His eyes skim up and down my body, making me feel naked while I'm fully clothed. "Our families have never been kind to one another, Iris. But I expect that will change once you become my wife."

"I don't have a family!" I shout. "In case you've forgotten, you killed the only member I had left."

"An eye for an eye," he quips.

"What's that supposed to mean?"

"That's how we work. The Marettis and the Pavettas. You see, my father had an affair with your mother shortly after you were born. The affair lasted many years. That was the start of the war."

Lowering the gun to my side, I shake my head. "You're lying. My mom was a good person and she loved my dad."

"Love has no boundaries. In fact, she was so in love with my father that she killed herself right in our living room. I remember the sound of the gunshot as I sat in my room. Your father blamed my father, killed him and the rest is history. You see, an eye for an eye."

He's lying. He has to be. But, why would he? He has no reason to lie to me. His story certainly doesn't save him. My mom killed herself because she couldn't be with another man. She left me behind because of her own selfish desires. "What does this have to do with me?"

"To this day, I have not forgiven your father for taking the life of my own. I was born into a powerful family and when I became the last one standing, I ruled the empire. I had every means possible to take you and your daddy out at any time, and he knew it." He smirks devilishly. "He was scared. So, I made him a deal. I'd spare your life for your hand in marriage. He was hesitant, but eventually agreed that he'd rather you live and be well-cared-for, than die and leave him to face the world as a lonely, grieving man."

"And you came for me? But he tried to protect me. That's why we moved right after my fourteenth birthday, he tried to hide me away. That's why he was so strict and didn't allow me to attend school or have friends."

"Likely so. But one of his men turned on him and gave up your whereabouts. In a matter of hours, I found you. He had no time to run. No place to hide. With only a short time to prepare, he put a hit out on my guy who betrayed him and rounded up all his security. Though, it was not enough."

"Mickey Barton," I mutter. "That's why my dad put the hit on him."

"Foolish man he was. Never cared much for him anyways. So, now that you have the story and you're aware that you are owed to me, let's make this easy. Untie me and walk away with me, and I'll let your newfound family live."

"And if I don't. You'll kill them? You're not exactly in any position to be making threats."

"You won't kill me. You don't have it in you. But, mark my words, you will be mine."

Raising my hand slowly, I point the gun back at his head. I'll never be free if he lives. He will find me and he will keep me. He will likely kill Silas, Gabriel, and Baron and this cycle will continue with him standing tall as the king. I'll bear his children who will live a destructive lifestyle and eventually behave the same way he does. *You don't have it in you.* The words replay in my mind.

"Your father was a dishonorable man who didn't back his end of the deal. He deserved to die."

*Pop.*

Pinching my eyes shut, I gasp for a breath and let the gun slide out of my hand. The door flies open and all I focus on are the guys rushing to my side. Trying to avoid looking at a dead Vincent Maretti, I walk around the chair and leave him behind.

Baron grabs the gun off the floor with a towel and begins wiping it off. "Holy shit, she really did it!"

Silas and Gabriel both look at me like I'm a stranger. Like they didn't expect me to actually go through with it. Walking past them all, I exit the room without a word.

It's bittersweet, really. On one hand, I'm free to live the life I want now. On the other, I just took a life, again. I should feel guilt, pain, sadness—but all I feel is relief. Does that make me a bad person? Maybe. It also makes me a fighter. No longer being told how I'm going to live and where I'm allowed to go. I'm free. Free from my dad. Free from my past. Free from Maretti.

I'm finally free.

## Thirty-Six

"How are you doing?" Silas asks as he sits on the edge of my bed, watching me dry my hair with a towel while I stand here with another one wrapped around me.

"I feel great. The shower felt nice."

His expression is comforting. "That's not what I mean. How are you really doing?"

"I really am doing great." I chuckle. "Is that not ok?"

"I just want to be sure. We've all been there so we're here if you need us. You know that, right?"

Smiling at his response, I nod. "I guess I probably shouldn't be feeling this good after murdering someone, but this was always the plan, wasn't it?

"It was." He stands up, and meets me in the center of the room. His fingers sweep down my arm, to my waist and he pushes the towel down until I'm standing in front of him completely naked.

My bedroom door swings open and Baron comes in. No one ever knocks on my door, and I'm beginning to be ok with that. "Shit, sorry," he says before ducking his head back out. "Dinner's ready," he calls from the hallway, looking anywhere but at me standing in his dad's arms completely naked.

He goes to leave, but I stop him. A wicked idea crosses my mind—or rather, an unspoken desire I've had since I came home. I know it's a risk to even imply it, but I just killed my worst enemy, ended a decade-long deadly feud between two families, and I'm feeling pretty fucking invincible right now. "Baron, wait." Silas gives me a crooked grin and I look at Baron. "Stay."

Silas opens his mouth to speak. "What are you—"

I cut him off by pressing my lips to his. With our mouths still connected, I stretch a hand out to Baron in hopes that he'll take it. He hesitates, but to my surprise, he does. Giving him a gentle tug, I lead him over to my side.

There's a moment of hesitation as soon as Baron touches me, as if they can't decide if they're comfortable continuing down this forbidden path we're on, so I ease their worries. Putting my body between them, I turn back to kiss Baron as I pull Silas closer to me by the back of his neck. Sandwiched between them, it only takes a moment of hesitant kisses before they both lose themselves to the desire.

Baron's tongue invades my mouth possessively as Silas's rough kisses on my neck dance their way down to my exposed breasts. I let out a high-pitched moan as he kneads one in his hand and pulls the other into his mouth, pinching my nipple between his teeth.

"What the fuck?" a dark voice snarls from the doorway.

The three of us freeze as our heads snap in unison toward the sound. Gabriel is glaring at us, his jaw clenched and the anger in his gaze penetrating the perfect moment we were just enjoying.

"Come here, baby," I call to him in a sweet tone. As I reach toward him, he glares in disgust at my outstretched hand.

"I made dinner," he snaps before turning and rushing

down the hall. "You're all out of your fucking minds." His voice carries from the stairway as Silas and I look at each other.

"Did he just say he made dinner?" I ask.

From behind me, Baron adds, "Yeah. He sent the staff home and made pasta. I think he wanted to make it special for you..."

"All this talk of making this a home," Silas adds, and I wince. "He thought you'd like it."

"I just ruined it, didn't I?"

They're still both positioned in front and behind me, Baron kissing my shoulder and Silas staring down at me with his signature solemn expression. "We should go eat," he says.

After throwing on a quick dress, sans bra and panties, we head down to the dining room to find Gabriel sitting alone at the giant table, four bowls of red pasta placed at four empty seats.

He doesn't look at me as I take the seat next to him. His brother and father sit across from us, but I can't take my eyes off the hard, scary as shit boy I met when I first got here. He's changed so much in the past two months, and it brings tears to my eyes to think he changed for me.

"You did this for me?" I ask, reaching out and touching the back of his neck. I can tell he wants to flinch, but he melts under the contact, aiming those crystal blues at me.

"It was nothing."

I pull his face toward me, planting a kiss on his lips. "It's so much more than nothing."

Without another word, I dig into the red pasta covered in parmesan, and surprisingly, it's not bad. In fact, it's actually really good. Maybe food made with love really is better, because the four of us demolish our dinners in minutes.

"We need something to drink," Baron says as he stands. "And I think today calls for a celebration." After leaving the dining room, he returns a moment later with a bottle of wine and four glasses.

Neither Gabriel nor I are old enough to drink, but Silas doesn't look like he's going to protest this one. Considering I literally murdered someone today, underage drinking is nothing. After Baron finishes pouring our glasses, we raise them and look at each other, and I watch as their eyes all dance back and forth from me to each other.

Is everything mended in this family? No. There are probably so many hard roads ahead of us, but for now, we're on the right track.

"To family," Silas says.

"To family," the rest of us echo before we clink our glasses together.

The first glass goes down easy as the four of us sit around the table, talking and laughing, and I can't help the way Baron's wide smile warms me from the inside out.

Glancing over at Gabriel, I feel my cheeks flush just thinking about what he almost walked in on. Would he have joined in if he wasn't announcing dinner? If I invited him to touch me too, would he? My thighs clench together just thinking about it, all three of them—all mine.

Baron empties the bottle, refilling our glasses. I don't know if the guys are feeling the effects from the wine the way I am, but it's giving me the courage to let my legs hang open while they talk, to run my hands along Gabriel's leg, and bite my lip while I watch Silas tell us a story about his early days in the business, letting his guard down enough to actually crack a smile.

When the table grows quiet and the wine in my glass is emptied, I finally have the nerve to lean toward Gabriel and pull his lips to mine. He kisses me back, letting out a sweet hum as I tug his lower lip between my teeth.

I know Silas and Baron are watching, and I can sense the

way Gabriel devours me as a show of possession, something that only turns me on more, using his aggression to my advantage. Climbing from my seat to his, I straddle his hips, rubbing myself against the thick bulge in his pants.

"I'm taking you to my room tonight," he mumbles against my lips.

"Why go to bed when we have a perfectly good table right here?"

He responds in a growl, grabbing my ass tight in his hands and grinding me even harder against him. When his fingers lift my dress, I remember that I'm not wearing anything underneath, and Gabriel discovers this instantly.

There's a growl coming from across the table, my ass on display in Gabriel's lap.

"You never were good at sharing," a voice says that I register as Baron's.

Turning my head, I smile at him. He looks like he could explode out of his seat at any moment. His hungry eyes are trained on my body, his jaw clenched as he leans forward. It only takes one signal from me, reaching my hand toward him, before he's out of his chair, rounding the table in a rush. As soon as he reaches me in his brother's lap, he steals my lips for himself.

Gabriel reacts by jerking me closer and grabbing my face roughly by the jaw and pulling him back toward him.

"Boys," Silas barks as a warning from across the table.

The grip on my face loosens, but neither of them can take their hands off my body. "I want you," I whisper against Gabriel's lips. "All of you." My gazes finds Baron's, that intensity between us burning even brighter because I know deep down he wants this as much as I do. He needs to know he's one of us again.

Then, I turn the opposite way and steal a glance at Silas

who is sitting back in his chair, ever the serious father figure, content to watch and keep us all in line.

Suddenly, my dress is lifted easily over my head and I'm sitting naked on Gabriel's lap. I stare at him with wide eyes as I see the acceptance in his expression. He's not fighting this anymore, and I let out a sweet smile, kissing the tiny heart tattoo next to his eye as his lips latch on to the skin of my neck.

Then Baron is there, his mouth on mine. My fingers fumble with the belt of his pants as he tears his shirt off. My eyes catch on the still healing wound on his chest, the bullet he took for me, and I graze my lips there, staring up at him. With his hand in my hair, he holds me closer, and my heart pounds for him.

In a rush, Gabriel shoves aside our plates and glasses from dinner and lifts me off of his lap, depositing me on the table. Our movements are frantic, infused with lust and need. As I work to shed Gabriel of his pants, Baron is already stripped down to nothing, and I reach for him, kissing him in a rush while my hand finds his rock-hard length, stroking him and pulling deep growls of pleasure from his chest.

Gabriel's kisses work their way down my body until his mouth is buried between my legs, and he's devouring me. Letting out a high-pitched moan, my thighs squeeze around his head, pulling him in closer. His tongue darts in and out of me, and I cling to Baron, whose lust-filled gaze is penetrating me as Gabriel sends pleasure through my body.

My strokes on Baron's cock match the cadence of Gabriel's tongue, but he pulls my hand away in a rush, which I assume is to stop himself from coming too quickly. There is no stopping the mouth between my legs though, and just as he pierces me with two fingers, hooking them to hit the right spot, I explode with an orgasm that spreads like fire from head to toe.

I barely have a moment to come down before I'm ripped from Gabriel's arms and clutched hard to Baron's body, straddling him on the table as he sets me on his cock, sliding himself home in a slow, torturous movement. Completely seated on his shaft, my knees resting on the table, he kisses me and whispers against my mouth, "ride my cock, Iris."

Looking into his eyes, I latch onto his neck and do as he asked, rocking my hips hard against his body, pulling him as deep as I can take him, grinding myself closer to another climax. As soon as I see him wince on a particularly rough thrust, I freeze.

"I don't want to hurt you."

"You can't hurt me," he whispers, kissing me again.

"Lie down," I say, pushing him back. Carefully moving through the pain, he reclines completely on the table, turning sideways so he's stretched out like a beautiful, muscled buffet. As I begin to ride him hard again, he puts his hands on my hips, our bodies moving to the same rhythm.

Just then, a weight settles on the table behind me. Gabriel's warm body embraces mine, his hand roaming my back while the other travels around to my breasts. He steals my attention, forcing my face to his and taking possession of my mouth with his.

His heavy erection rubs against my back, so I reach back and hold it tightly. His crystal blue eyes bore into mine as I pull him closer. "Fuck me, Gabriel."

My hips are still moving in a steady cadence on Baron as Gabriel's eyes go wide. "Are you sure?"

Leaning down over Baron, I pull his cock to where I want it. He begins to press himself into the tight entrance, and I'm hit with a burning pain.

"Wait," I gasp. "Get it wet."

He spits on the head of his dick and then on my ass. Rubbing against my entrance, I let out a guttural moan when it slides in a little at a time. Slowly, he works himself in, spitting again to lube himself up, and it's so damn dirty, a wave of arousal pulses through my veins.

I'm overwhelmed by the sudden feeling of fullness as they both fill me. My body is engulfed in pleasure and need. I'm consuming them as they consume me, and as we move in unison, the moment is absolutely perfect.

Pressed flat over Baron's body, I lift my head to see Silas, sitting in his large chair at the head of the table, watching me intently like I'm the only thing in the universe that matters. I don't pull my eyes away from his, giving him every sound of pleasure from my lips. He doesn't move, and I know he won't. It would be crossing a line for him to get involved now, but the eye contact between us is just as intense as any touch could be. There's real affection in his eyes, and I want to stay like this forever, the four of us as one.

Baron's hands run up my thighs to my hips, squeezing my flesh as he thrusts upward, hitting a spot inside me that lights a fire, pure ecstasy flooding my veins while Gabriel keeps up the exquisite movement behind me.

This thing between us is beautiful. We are so perfectly in sync, moving in harmony, as each of us chase our climaxes together, and I keep my eyes locked on Silas as the room is bathed in our moans and cries. At once, they fill me up, pumping their releases into me. A raspy scream vibrates through me as my orgasm shreds my insides until I'm left shaking and trembling in their arms.

Collapsing on top of Baron, I don't know whose hands are whose or whose lips are on my back, my shoulders, my face. But I let them worship me, loving the unfiltered attention they're giving me. Because it's not just me and Gabriel, me and Baron, or me and Silas—it's all of us. We don't live in an ordinary world, so we made our own. It might not be the perfect family home Baron remembers from his childhood, but it's a hell of a lot better than Gabriel's.

Suddenly, I'm being lifted, cradled in a pair of strong arms, and I gaze up into Silas's eyes. He presses his lips to my forehead, and I know he's carrying me to his room.

"Good girl," he says with a hum as we reach the large bathroom attached to his room. Setting me on the counter, he turns to start the shower and sheds his clothes, and my eyes catch on the rock-hard erection that springs out of his boxers. When he comes to me, he pulls my gaze up to his face. He doesn't have to say a word because I can read the stern expression on his face, his furrowed brow and his tight lips. He's not going to fuck me, and I'm probably crazy for being a little disappointed by that.

Instead, he pulls me into the shower, lathering up a washcloth and taking his time with my body. And I was right—he's not going to fuck me, but as he pulls my body against his, tucking me under his chin, he lets me wrap my soap-covered hand around him, stroking him until he's panting. He squeezes me impossibly tight as I feel his release in my hand.

When I look up at him, Silas gives me something he doesn't offer very often—a smile. Pressing up to my tiptoes, I kiss him, tasting the happiness on his lips.

After our shower, he carries me to bed, tucking me under the covers before climbing in next to me and pulling me to his chest. Rubbing my hand along his chest and drifting off to sleep to the cadence of his heartbeat, I try to absorb the contentment I feel at this moment.

I'd give anything to have my father back, but he made this sacrifice for me, and I understand that now. He sent me here, and while I'm sure he never would have thought it'd end like this, what I have here is far more than I would have ever had on my own. This home, this family, is my world now. I am theirs, and they are mine—all of us, together.

*Epilogue*

STRIDING across the office in my red heels, I drop into the chair next to Silas. The client, a balding man, with sweat beading across his combover, follows me in, sitting hesitantly in the seat across from us. He's glaring at us like *we're* going to kill him. Well, Silas, really. He probably thinks I'm harmless, but of course, he'd be wrong.

He's a liaison—a middle man—most likely for some big politician who doesn't want to get caught using us to clean up his messes, and we don't need the details. We don't care about that. All we need is a name and a deposit.

With a tremble in his hands, the man passes the manilla envelope to Silas. "My client is willing to offer fifty-thousand."

I scoff, and the man's eyes dart in my direction, his brow furrowed as he glares at me. In my slick black dress, my jet-black hair draped over my shoulders, he probably thinks I'm nothing more than Silas's arm candy. Word on the streets is that Silas Black has adopted another stray, this time a daughter, but as far as I know, no one has connected this rumor to my identity. Iris Pavetta was killed in a shootout with her father.

Iris Black is a new protege in the Black family business. That's all they need to know. No one needs to know what goes on behind closed doors, and the fact that it's our dirty little secret makes it all that much better.

"You're not giving us very much here, Mr. Ward." Silas passes the envelope to me. "What do you think?"

While I browse through the files, mostly grainy photos and some phone records, Silas's arm loops around my chair, running his fingers down the strands of my hair. "Do you know how much work it's going to take to find this guy? Probably a whole week? We're going to need at least seventy-five."

Dropping the folder on the desk, I stare back at the man, crossing my arms. His eyes dance between Silas and me as if he's waiting for Silas to say something or correct me. The corner of my mouth lifts because I know he won't. I know what I'm doing. I was taught by the best.

"Don't look at him, Mr. Ward. I know what I'm talking about," I say, and he looks genuinely appalled.

"I'm sorry, sweetheart, but this is between your dad and me."

As soon as the words come out of his mouth, I wince. That was a big mistake. Silas is out of his seat in a heartbeat, grabbing the man by the back of the neck and smacking his face hard against the cool wood of the desk. "Call her sweetheart again, and I'll cut out your tongue," he snaps as the man squeals.

Sitting back in my seat, I just smile. Mr. Calm, Cool, and Collected only has a few triggers that really get him going, and men disrespecting his baby is at the top of the list.

"I'm sorry, I'm sorry!" the man wheezes.

Silas looks back at me with a question on his face. I give

him a shrug, rubbing my thighs together, just seeing him want to kill a man for me. He won't kill him because that would be messy and unnecessary, but it's nice knowing he would.

Instead, he drags him to the floor by his neck and makes him crawl toward me. The man is blubbering and quivering in fear.

"Apologize," Silas snaps, letting the guy go and standing behind him, arms crossed and scowling.

"I'm sorry. I didn't mean any offense, I promise."

"Kiss her shoe."

His shaky lips hover close to the red soles of my black heels, and I'm biting back the laughter that wants to bubble out of me.

Silas picks up the folder and tosses it toward the door. "Tell your client we'll take the job for seventy-five thousand, but I want that deposit wired to my account by the end of the day, and at least one week to do the job."

"Two weeks," I say, interrupting him.

"You heard the girl."

Mr. Ward fumbles across the floor, grabbing his papers and scrambling out of the room, leaving me alone with Silas Black.

"Thanks, Daddy," I say with a laugh as Silas stalks toward me. Leaning down, he plants his hands on either side of the chair I'm in and presses his lips to mine.

"You're getting the hang of it," he mumbles against my mouth.

As I reach for his belt buckle, my lips curl back in a smile. "We have almost an hour until our next meeting."

"Aren't you supposed to be helping Gabriel in the garage?" he asks, snatching my hands away from his pants.

"This won't take long," I reply, biting my bottom lip. "Come on, it's my birthday..."

"Exactly,' he says, and suddenly I'm out of my chair. He

sets me on his desk, dropping into his chair between my legs.

He lifts my dress up around my waist and hooks his fingers around the hem of my panties, tearing them off in a quick swipe. When his mouth hits the spot between my legs, I let out a moan, my fingers digging into the hardwood of the desk. Leaning back, my legs drape over his shoulders as he pierces me with his tongue, sending me flying with pleasure.

Even if I could resist this man and all the raw power he exudes, I wouldn't want to. To be in Silas Black's life is one thing, but to be the center of his universe is more than I could have ever asked for.

And after I come hard, my screams echoing against the walls, I pull his face up to mine, kissing him hard.

"Happy birthday," he mumbles against my lips.

"Thank you."

After I catch my breath, I kiss him again. "I better get to the garage before he starts throwing a fit."

He pulls up my panties, and leans back in his office chair and watches me leave. Before I pass through the door to the living room, I sneak a glance back at the man behind the desk, remembering the first day I came here, almost six months ago. He was so intimidating to me then, and I was so unsure of what my future held at that time. I'll never forget the day I asked him to give me a chance and let me prove myself. How much I've changed since then because he didn't just take me in to teach me to be an assassin. He made me a stronger, more independent version of myself.

Pausing in the doorway, I don't say the words on my mind, not because they're not true, or that I've told him already how I feel about him, but because Silas doesn't do words, not the way his sons do. So when he glances up at me, and our eyes hold their gaze for three seconds, it's our little way of saying those three little words.

I can hear the screaming from the basement as I pass

through the house. Gabriel is interrogating a man we were hired to extract some valuable information from. I don't normally help Gabriel out with this stuff—I had my fill of the torture stuff with Donny Wright, but every once in a while, Gabriel likes to include me, so I indulge him. He's still the most possessive, more prone to jealousy, but all-in-all, he's handling this situation better than I expected. He gets his two nights a week and doesn't complain *much* when he sees me with his dad or brother.

I have a soft spot for Gabriel. He was the most tortured one when I arrived, so quick to anger and so incredibly deprived of affection that I absorbed it all, willingly. Sometimes I wonder what Gabriel would be like if he lived a normal life, had access to other women and the opportunity to be a regular eighteen-year-old boy, instead of an assassin. Would he want someone else? Would I still be enough for him?

"There's my birthday girl," he says as he drops the bloody pliers he's holding. A wide smile stretches across his face as he walks toward me.

I finally made Silas give Gabriel the proper work space he needed to do his job. No more kitchen interrogations. And seeing Gabriel in all black, working like an artist in a studio, I realize that this was always where he was meant to be. Maybe Silas saw that in him when he took him from that house in the slums.

"Sorry I'm late," I say as he scoops me up by the waist, kissing me hard and humming against my lips.

"Well, you showed up at the right time. I think he was just about to talk. Want to give it a go? You know I love to watch you work."

A wicked smile spreads across his face, as I take in the man strapped to the chair. There is blood dripping from his hands to the floor.

"Just stay away from the blowtorch, Princess" he jokes, and I give him a playful scowl over my shoulder.

Leaning against the wall, he watches as I work, starting with some playful flirting and making the guy in the chair think I'm not going to hurt him as badly as Gabriel did, but when he makes a crude remark about my tits, I break his wrists.

"Oh my god, that's hot," Gabriel growls behind me. One look at the stiffness in his pants, and I can see just how much he's enjoying this.

Keeping up my work on the man who's finally starting to crack, when I eventually bust out the plastic bag, holding it over his head the way Baron did to Donny, he blubbers out the information Gabriel was looking for. But I don't even care. All that matters to me at this moment is the way Gabriel's looking at me from across the room, like he can barely resist the urge to reach into his pants and relieve himself while he watches me work. I almost wish he would. I could totally be down for that.

Tossing the bag to the floor, I saunter over to Gabriel, and he gathers me in his arms hungrily, kissing my neck and grinding his rock-hard bulge against my stomach. Growling into our kiss, he quickly unbuttons his pants, and I take a hold of him, stroking as his mouth moves its way down my neck. After pulling my breasts out of the top of my dress, he bites one nipple greedily between his teeth as I keep my hand around his cock.

Suddenly, there's a knock on the door and someone clearing their throat.

"Sorry to interrupt, but if we're going to do this, we need to go now."

Pulling away from Gabriel's kiss, I turn and stare at Baron with confusion on my face. "What are you talking about?"

Gabriel barely hears his brother at all, his mouth keeping up the assault on my tits.

"We have a birthday present for you," he says with a mischievous smile.

"A present for me?" My heart starts to pick up its pace in my chest as I consider what the guys could have gotten for me.

"Fuck off, Baron," Gabriel mutters against my chest. "We'll be ready in ten minutes."

Baron holds up his hands in surrender as he disappears through the door. Dropping to my knees in front of Gabriel, I quickly take his cock into my mouth. A low moan vibrates through his body as his hands dig into my hair and he thrusts deeper into my throat.

Gabriel has come so far since we started having sex six months ago, but he still can't seem to last long once I get my lips around him.

"The things you do to me," he mumbles in a low growl. "Princess, you make me crazy."

Tightening my grip against the base of him, I feel him swell before warm jets of cum shoot down the back of my throat. I keep my eyes on him as I swallow him down.

He lifts me to my feet, kissing me hard, and penetrating me with his icy blue stare. "I'm so crazy about you."

"I'm crazy about you too," I reply, before capturing those perfect full lips of his.

"We should get going so we're not late," he says in a cool tone.

"Where are we going?"

"It's a surprise."

We leave the man passed out in the chair as we walk together in a hurry toward the front door. Silas and Baron are both waiting there, but I don't take my hand out of Gabriel's as we reach them.

"What's the surprise?" I ask, biting back a smile.

"You'll see," Silas answers flatly, looking down at his watch.

Following them out the door to the black stretch limo waiting there for us, I climb in excitedly. I didn't see anything special on the schedule today. And I really have no clue what these guys could be giving me that I don't already have. My life is literally perfect now. I have a purpose, a family, and freedom. It was everything my life was missing before. When my dad was alive, we were happy and we loved each other, but it wasn't a family. It was a prison, love in the form of iron bars that kept me from living my own life.

The conversation on the ride over is small, mostly Gabriel debriefing his dad on the information the man in the basement spilled. And I notice the way Baron smiles when he hears how I used his trick to make the man talk.

The ride is short, and when we pull to a stop, I hear what sounds like a construction site, heavy machinery running and men yelling. Silas gets out first, holding a hand out for me. Immediately, I recognize the street corner. I stood just across the street from here at that bus stop where I met Donny Wright and let him bring me back to this motel. Looking back at that day, I feel like a complete idiot for what I tried to do alone but also a little proud of myself for what I had the guts to do. I found myself that day, and I shed the role of doormat, mafia princess and became what I am now. Which even I can admit, I don't always know what that is, because I'm still finding myself. I love being a part of this family and I love being in the business, but I'm still searching for what I truly want out of my life, but the fact that I have a choice now is everything.

The sounds of machines are coming from the motel where caution tape surrounds it, the street blocked and construction workers walking around.

"What is going on?" I ask, looking at the guys.

"It's being demolished," Silas says.

"Why?" I ask, my eyes trailing from him to Baron, who finally steps up next to me and puts an arm around my shoulders.

"Because we told them to."

"I don't understand."

"We bought this motel because we know you hated it, and we're having it torn down. Now the property belongs to you. So you can build whatever you want here. You still have all of the money from your father's estate, and I know you'd like something of your own. Maybe you can build a women's shelter or I don't know, rebuild a nicer motel. Whatever you decide, it's up to you. It's yours."

My mouth goes dry. How does Baron do this? How does he always know exactly what is in my heart and in my head? He sees right through me, sometimes giving me the things even I didn't know I needed.

"I don't know what to say..." Tears fill my eyes as I watch the machines roll up to the dilapidated building. Just as it tears into the roof, shattering the windows and bringing the place that harbored such pain and misery to nothing but rubble, my tears finally fall.

I have no clue what I'll do with the space, but just having the choice excites me more than anything ever has before. It's mine, truly mine. Not my father's. Not Silas's or Baron's or Gabriel's. Just mine.

A smile spreads across my face. We stand there and watch them for about thirty minutes, each of them touching me, taking my hand or planting a kiss on my cheek.

"Thank you," I say to them as we get into the car. Each of them respond in their own way. Silas with a stoic nod. Gabriel with a sarcastic shrug and eye roll. And Baron with a kiss to my hand.

When we get back, the guys scatter to do what they need to, but I am too distracted by all of my new ideas. For some reason, I find myself in Baron's bed, waiting for him to finish up whatever he's doing in the armory. Sitting on his bed, I flip open my notebook, scanning through the pages of notes and lists I made. This is really the first time I've had a chance to look at it since everything ended, so when I reach the list, I freeze.

*Kill Vincent Maretti*

Grabbing a pen out of Baron's side table, I draw a line through those words. It feels so final now. Everyone on this list is dead. Gabriel killed Mickey Barton in Italy. I killed Donny Wright. Baron killed Victor Marazzi, something he admitted to me later on—although I had my suspicions. On that late night I caught him sneaking in, he was really out killing the last guy on my list. He did it to cover his tracks, so I wouldn't find out he was working for Maretti, but I've forgiven him for that. He's done more than enough to prove that he can be trusted.

When he finally passes through the door, his eyes find me immediately and he smiles. Jumping into bed, he crawls up to my lap, placing his face against my chest and hugging me tightly.

It still surprises me sometimes by how affectionate and warm Baron is, considering he was the coldest to me when I first arrived. It's almost like he's allowing himself to be happy again. After they lost his brother and mom, he and Silas have been punishing themselves. Baron seemed to forget he was even capable of being loved. Now he loves the hardest and gives the most.

"I know you thought of that," I whisper against the top of his head.

He looks up at me with those warm copper eyes trained on my lips. "Do you like it?"

"Baron, I love it."

"Good. I want you to have everything you love."

Holding his face in my hands, I kiss his soft, pink lips. "I do have everything I love."

His mouth presses to mine again as his body blankets mine on the bed. Putting himself between my legs, our kiss becomes heated quickly. I can't get enough of him, ever. There is no such thing as enough when it comes to Baron Black. I want everything, all the time.

He pulls my dress to my waist as I tear open his pants, shoving them down his legs. When his cock presses against me, I lift my hips for him, practically pulling him home. We groan in unison as he fills me, and what started as hurried fucking, slows to a sensual rhythm, our eyes not leaving each other's for one second. His thrusts are hard, but slow, and the power behind them reminds me so much of our first time.

"I love you, Iris Black," he moans against my lips as he shudders out his release inside me.

And I try to return the sentiment, but my body is tangled in pleasure, and I can hardly breathe. I clutch him on the back of the neck, pulling him as close to me as I can bring him, and all I can manage is to breathlessly whisper his name before he kisses me.

We stay in that embrace for a while, him still buried between my legs while I stroke his back with my nails. Carol knocks hesitantly on the door, announcing dinner. Baron and I laugh as we see her cheeks turn red when she sees his bare ass on the bed and my dress pulled up with my legs wrapped around him.

Poor Carol. The staff and security all clearly know that I belong to all of the Blacks, but some of them still aren't quite used to there being so much sex with the doors open around the house—or any sex at all, I guess. Before I came along, there weren't any women here.

"Thank you," I call before she scurries out the door. After Baron and I clean up for dinner, we walk downstairs together. I pause once we reach the dining room. There on the center of the table is a birthday cake with four candles on the top of it. The cake is pink, which is about the only pretty thing about it. It's caving in on one side and looks like it was iced by a three-year-old.

Immediately, I know Gabriel must have made this for me. Ever since we killed Maretti and solidified my place here in the family, he's been trying to turn this house into a home. He's a far cry from the scary looking boy who was breaking fingers in this very kitchen. Now he's baking birthday cakes.

Baron bites back a laugh when he sees the cake, but I can't seem to hold back my smile.

When Gabriel walks into the dining room with plates and forks, he makes a grand gesture toward the cake. A laugh bubbles out of my chest.

"I only had four candles," he says. "But then I thought that was perfect. There being four of us and all."

"It is perfect," I agree. "But is this what we're having for dinner?"

"No, Carol made dinner, but I couldn't wait to give this to you."

Silas steps into the dining room behind me, putting his hands on my shoulders and kissing my cheek. Then he puts on his best poker face and holds back a laugh when he sees the cake.

The four of us gather around the table as Gabriel flicks his lighter and Baron turns off the overhead lights. The four single candles on the cake illuminate the room, and I actually gasp when they start singing.

Surrounded by the house staff and the three men I love, I shut my eyes and make a wish as I blow out the candles. Of course my only wish is for things to stay exactly like this forever. I don't want our unconventional relationship to be a temporary thing. These men have my heart, equally. They are mine, and I am theirs.

Forever.

**The Black Family returns in Five**

*Acknowledgments*

We had so much fun writing this book together and we hope everyone enjoys it. The idea came to us on a whim when we saw the cover in a premade group. Ideas starting flowing and the next thing we knew we were writing our first reverse harem romance. These characters have stolen our hearts, and maybe wounded them just a little. Four is a book about redemption, revenge, and finding love in the unlikeliest of places.

A big thanks goes out to...

Editor: Rebecca's Fairest Reviews
Amanda Anderson with Wildfire Marketing Solutions
Our PAs, Lori Alexander and Carolina Leon
Amanda Kay Anderson, our beautiful beta reader
Our graphics designer, Claudia Lymari
Cover Designer: Tempi Lark
The readers and members of Rachel's Ramblers and Sara's Sweets
Our amazing ARC and Street teams
All the wonderful bloggers who have supported and shared for us. We couldn't do this without you.

Love,
Sara & Rachel

*Also by Rachel Leigh*

Guarded

Devil Heir


Claim your FREE copy of Whiskey Lies

Find me on Facebook

@rachelleighauthor

Reader's Group: Rachel's Ramblers

Or visit

www.rachelleighauthor.com

# Also by Sara Cate

# About Rachel Leigh

Rachel Leigh writes Contemporary and New Adult Romance with twists and turns, suspense and steam. She resides in West Michigan with her husband, three kids, and a couple fur babies.

Rachel lives in leggings, overuses emojis, and survives on books and coffee. Writing is her passion. Her goal is to take readers on an adventure with her words, while showing them that even on the darkest days, love conquers all.

Bookbub bookbub.com/profile/rachel-leigh
Readers Group http://bit.ly/rl_ramblers
Goodreads goodreads.com/rachelleigh
Instagram instagram.com/rachelleighauthor
Facebook facebook.com/rachelleighauthor
Amazon amazon.com/author/rachelleighauthor
Newsletter https://bit.ly/rl_news
TikTok http://bit.ly/rl_tiktok

# About Sara Cate

Sara Cate writes forbidden romance with lots of angst, a little age gap, and heaps of steam. Living in Arizona with her husband and kids, Sara spends most of her time reading, writing, or baking.

You can find more information about her at
www.saracatebooks.com

Printed in Great Britain
by Amazon